The Accidental Terrorist

By

S. P. Harris

Copyright 2013 S. P. Harris

Table of Contents

6 - The Dark Corner

13 - The Pain in the Ass

20 - Brothers

27 - Oh Shit

36 - At the Bottom

47 - Amalek

61 - Hey Jealousy

73 - Just Far Enough

81 - Boom

92 - Shit Zeke

103 - Tenderized Pork

111 - Goodbye

118 - Good Riddance

124 - Pardon Me Sailor

132 - Last Man Standing

145 - Stay Cool Hunny Bunny

155 - What's Cooler Than Being Cool?

167 - The Old Shit

180 - Who Do You Pull For?

187 - And You Will Know That I am the Lord, When I Lay My Vengeance Upon Thee

196 - Prepare Your Anus

206 - Electric Boogaloo

218 - It's a Hit!

231 - Keep That Bitch Cool!

243 - Whale Belly

252 - The Finder of Lost Children

262 - Tell Your Children Not to Walk My Way

278 - A Wee Little Man Was He

289 - Pilgrim's Progress

295 - Brother's (Reprise)

308 - Where Does My Help Come From?

321 - About The Author

Part I: Run as fast as you can.

They're shooting to kill.

The Dark Corner

Jerry bobbed his head to the rhythm of Judge getting the shit beat out of him like it was his favorite song. "Do you boys know where we are?" he asked from his preaching rock. *Yeah, and I know a million places I'd rather be*, thought Judge. *Or is this a trick question? Maybe not...we're here every day, aren't we?*

Judge lowered his meaty hands from his bloody face to look around. Zeke moved too fast for him to react. The rat-faced young man smiled. His hips turned. His feet planted. His right fist flew straight into Judge's jaw. Zeke was shorter than Judge by half a foot and had to punch upwards to hit his target. The tall pines overhead swayed in the wind like a bored crowd pointing downed thumbs at the losing gladiator.

It took a moment for Judge to feel the pain. "Ow!" he screamed. He reeled back, his useless hands clutching the spot where Zeke hit him.

"Did I tell you to stop?" Jerry was yards away on his rock, but his tone, dripping with venom, made Judge put his hands back up. Zeke continued to dance in a wide circle, looking for openings to fill with his fists. "Sometimes I just don't get you, Judge. You've got 50 pounds and five inches on Zeke. You're faster than him, smarter. I don't get how he always gets the best of you, know what I mean?" In silent reply, Zeke took a wild swing at Judge's head. It was easy to sidestep. *Don't get angry at me, Zeke. You should just be glad he didn't mention how ugly you are.* "Keep dancing while I talk, okay? You know none of us are good at setting bones."

Judge recalled Jimmy Two's worthless right hand, broken as punishment for swearing. He tightened up his arms in defense. "Now, and this is a rhetorical question so Zeke doesn't ruin that pretty face, but do you boys know where we are?" Jerry picked a stick up from the ground and started scraping a hole in the ground. "Bout...150 some odd years ago, this blasphemous nation of ours was at war. I don't approve much of them public schools, but the ones around here probably at least get them facts right. The war over states' rights raged all over. Men were dying, most going straight to Hell. A few of them soldiers wisened up, said 'We're dying for this sinful state's rights, let's make our own state, die for what we want to die for.'

"So those soldiers left, started running, marched back up over the Sandhills, up into the Piedmont, where we are now." The wind whipped around the trees as if the ghosts of those men knew they were being spoken of. "They had a vision, probably saw what we had now. Other men joined them. Instead of being conscripted to get cholera and die in some muddy field, they ran up here to carve out their own name. Thought South Carolina would sympathize, with them seceding and all, know what I mean?"

Jerry kept scraping his hole in the ground and the brown soil started to turn into red clay. Judge danced as Zeke landed glancing blows and opened a red slit over his lip. None of Judge's punches connected. "They ran away from the world. Up here they thought the world would just leave them alone. But we all know you can't run far enough, right? The state would send their troops up here. Some weak men would hide, but the smart ones stood their ground. They knew that they were done running, that in the end, they'd have to slow down. And the state gave up. Started calling this area the 'Dark Corner'. Those men learned that if they stood up tall enough, they'd never have to run again." Jerry filled the hole back in and cracked the stick.

The sound distracted Judge. Zeke saw an opening, spun around and landed the back of his fist on Judge's neck. The hit made Judge collapse on the ground. He looked down at the spot of blood and spittle on the cold dirt. *If this were a Rorschach test, I'd say that looks like a clown raping a dog.* "That's enough, Zeke," Jerry said. "I don't want you to kill him." Zeke backed up, checking his scabby knuckles. "Get up, son. I'm not done talking yet." Judge heard the wind howling in the air, but couldn't feel any breeze on the ground. *It sure would feel good right now, too.* He had to fight gravity just to get to all fours. "Over time those men forgot to stand, started running again from the way God wanted them to live. They built cities, got telephones, radios,

TVs, computers. Joined the rest of the world. Look at me when I'm talking to you, son."

Judge couldn't get off his hands and knees. He craned his neck up at Jerry as if he were a dog about to get mounted. *Zeke hit too hard this time.* Jerry seemed to grow more annoyed than angry. "Help him up." Zeke snickered and brought the bottom of his boot hard on Judge's butt, pushing him down onto the ground. "Funny, Zeke. But really, help him up." *This dirt tastes awful.*

Zeke gently reached under Judge's arms and pulled him to his feet. *How can someone so small be so strong?* "I need you to hear this." *Jerry, we have heard this. Probably hundreds of times. It's been bullshit from the start.* "If the soldiers had stayed who they were supposed to be, who the Lord was calling them to be, didn't start running when things got hard, maybe our nation wouldn't be in such disarray. And that is why we're here. We've already turned this dark corner into a beacon of the Lord's light." *Is that what you call eating old MREs and pooping in an outhouse?* "We might be the mustard seed now…" Jerry looked off in the distance. "…but the Lord will raise us to be a mighty tree, with roots deep enough to stand up to any storm. We will not run."

Jerry shook his head and looked at the boys as if he was just remembering they were there. "All right, Judge - your turn. Zeke, all that dancing was nice, but you know full well that it's just as much about taking suffering and pain as it is about destroying others." Zeke stood in front of Judge and smiled an ugly, angular smile, as if his mouth was just a scar on his face. *He's just smiling cause his mouth isn't full of blood.* The trees danced in the wind, but Zeke stood perfectly still. "Whenever you're ready." Judge was having a hard enough time standing up. Swinging his arms would likely topple him. *This is going to be embarrassing.* He grabbed Zeke's left shoulder to steady himself and punched Zeke in the stomach as hard as he could. Zeke's only response was a small breath that could have been a bit of indigestion.

"Come on, son! You can do better than that!" Jerry goaded. Judge tried again and connected a meaty fist on the side of Zeke's neck. Judge swayed and almost fell. Zeke rubbed his neck like a mosquito had bit him. "This is getting pitiful. Take this." Jerry handed Judge a stick the size of a baseball bat. *I don't want to do this.* Zeke widened his stance to take the blow, and his smile grew hungry as if a large meal was set before him.

Judge tightened his grip, but couldn't make himself swing. *This might actually hurt him. I don't want both of us to be useless tomorrow.* Jerry put his hands on his hips and said "We're waiting, son. Or I could rebuke you both. I know it's been a while, but we got those crosses somewhere." *Damnit. I better make this look good.* Judge reared the stick back and swung. It hit Zeke hard on the back, and the crack sounded like thunder on helium. Zeke couldn't help but stumble. Judge stumbled with him. Stifling any sign of pain, Zeke was first on his feet. "Pretty weak, Judge." *Or else Zeke is proving himself to be superhuman. I hit him hard. I hope he's ok.* "You two get on home, and then it's lights out after your devotion."

Zeke pulled Judge to his feet and they walked back in the dark towards their cabin. Judge's slow waddle from the kick slowed him down enough so that he truly noticed how different everything looked at night. *This corner does get pretty dark.* A shadowy figure approached, carrying something shiny and silver that caught the glare off the moon-lit clouds. *Who is this?* Judge stopped, but Zeke kept on walking and said "I'm going to go on. See you in a minute." *Braver than I am...I hope I don't need his protection.* As the shadowy figure became a person and Zeke became a shadowy figure, Judge heard Zeke say "Evening, Am."

"Hey, Zeke." Amittai walked closer to Judge. His hands and coveralls were black with grease, and he was cradling a complicated looking metal piece the size of a sheet of notebook paper. All protruding wires and sheet metal, it was easily the most complicated piece of technology in the whole camp. *What's dad been working on?* "Is Jerry up at his rock?"

Nice of him to ask why my face is covered with blood. Judge looked at his father and the machine in his hands. His vision started to blur. *Damnit Zeke. I'm not going to be able to read my Bible like this.* "Yeah. I think he should still be there," Judge said. "I think I'm going to go right to sleep. I'll do an extra Bible reading tomorrow morning."

Amittai pushed his glasses up. The clouds broke, and the blurry moon reflected in the lenses. His eyelid twitched wildly underneath. "That's fine," the father said. "But you know what happens if Jerry tests you on it and you fail." *Yeah. I know. But I can't get much bloodier, can I?* Amittai walked off into darkness as Judge stumbled towards the warmth of his bed. *Wonder what he's meeting with Jerry about.* He brought a trembling hand over the back of his neck, and the pain nearly stopped his breath. *Shit, Zeke. If I'm not better by tomorrow, I might just have to figure out how to kick your ass.*

The Pain in the Ass

Through his one good eye, Amittai watched Judge lower himself in the creaky chair. The other eye twitched like a screen door in a storm. When Judge's butt hit the seat he winced and popped up an inch, then sat down slowly, as if he were wading into a scalding hot bath. He tried to use the rickety table for support, but it groaned a threat to collapse. *Do I sound like that?*

Judge's breath was rhythmic and heavy by the time he was finally flat in his chair. He reached for the pile of bacon in the middle of the table. "What's wrong with you?" his father asked.

"Nothing. I just…" He trailed off and put a black piece of bacon in his mouth. When he bit down it sounded like twigs snapping. *Bleh.* He made a sour face and reached for a glass of water to wash the burnt flakes out of his mouth. "I just had a weird dream is all."

Zeke had been eating so quietly that his gentle laughter reminded everyone that he was still there. "A dream, huh?" Zeke said. "That made your rear hurt. That's…." His mouth opened in a wide smile. Little black specks of burnt bacon dotted the front of his teeth.

"Yeah, yeah. Laugh it up."

"Eggs are ready." Jerry had to reach around Judge to lower the pan on the table. When Judge leaned to get out of the way, the scraping pain burned deep inside his bottom and he yelped. Zeke's toothy smile opened up again, but Amittai frowned, worrying about what his son had gotten himself into. When Judge finally got comfortable again, he went to scoop some eggs for himself, but was only left with the watery dregs. *Might as well have been eating egg-powder soup.* Jerry shoveled a spoonful of eggs in his mouth and said "You know, I'd like to hear about your dream if it's all the same."

Mumbling nothings with a full mouth, Judge tried to skirt the subject, but Jerry wouldn't have it. He said "Jacob and Daniel had a gift of interpreting dreams. It was a gift from the Lord." He set his fork down and stared at Judge with his big blue eyes, far too pretty for a man that hard. He poked his pointer finger down on the table as if pointing to an invisible Bible. "From the Lord, son. God's gifts are not something to be trifled with."

Judge glanced at his father. He was rooting around in his eggs as if there would be something better underneath. He hated how his dad let Jerry have the run of things, but Judge knew better than to defy Jerry.

He took a deep breath and said "Well, it started out and I was back in my old house. Dad, you weren't there. I was watching the TV and saw this story about these guys had taken this motel hostage. They were keeping all the people there, and no one really know why, or what was going on in there. At least I didn't know.

"I get this feeling, and I don't know how to explain it other than it was a feeling. It was like one of those dreams where it's so real and you can smell whatever's around, but I don't know how I got this feeling. Just felt it, you know?" Jerry nodded intently. Amittai's good eye squinted like his son was a book too far away to read, and Zeke snuck his sixth piece of bacon. "And this feeling tells me I can help these people. The news showed all these SWAT teams and I think the army was there camped around this hotel, and had been for a few days.

"But I'm looking at the hotel on the news, and I know that hotel. I don't think I've ever seen it before in real life, but suddenly in this dream, I knew about a kind of secret way in from the back through some woods. It actually wasn't that hidden, and I don't know how the Army didn't figure it out, but I got this feeling, and it tells me that I can go free these people. So I went and…" Judge stopped, remembering the rest of the dream and deciding he didn't want to relive it.

If he had been any smarter he would have taken the conversation down a different path and distracted them like he always did. But his backside was burning and it felt like the fire inside was flaying his colon. He couldn't think as fast as he normally did. Jerry flopped his hand in the air and said "You went and what? I know that's not the end of it."

"I'd really rather not talk about it, if it's all the same."

Jerry looked at Amittai, who sat up straight and looked at his son. "Now Judge, don't disrespect Mr. Jerry that way. Keep going with your story. Like he said, it could be a message from the Lord." Jerry nodded his approval and Amittai went back to dissecting his scrambled eggs. Judge hated his father for taking Jerry's side again.

He thought about just ignoring the command, but Judge remembered an afternoon's rebuking for getting the Sadducees mixed up with the Pharisees, and that got his mouth moving fast enough. "...I snuck by this military battalion. It wasn't hard. I got in the hotel, and they were keeping everyone crammed into this one room. They all looked terrified when I walked in, and then they panicked. It didn't seem like they were trying to escape. It was more like they were telling me to leave. They were speaking gibberish, but I understood that they didn't want me to become another hostage. I told them I could get them out, but they still just wanted me to leave. They all looked beat up, and sick. It was like they hated being there, but they still wanted to stay. But I knew I had to save them.

"I grabbed this fat guy's arm, but I couldn't pull him because he was so fat." Judge glanced at Zeke, not mentioning that the fat man in his dream was Zeke's late father. By now

Zeke was paying attention. *Are you picturing your father too?* "I made too much noise, and these guys with guns bust in wearing masks." The soreness in Judge's rear started up again, and he leaned to the side, hoping to take some of the pressure off.

"These guys are shouting at me and the other people are crying and I'm scared cause now I'm a hostage too. Suddenly I realize that all the other hostages are in their underwear. I don't know how I didn't notice that before, and…" He paused and sighed. "…their underwear is all bloody." Zeke started snickering again, but Jerry put a huge hand out. Zeke stopped like a well-trained dog. By now, the soreness was so strong that Judge was squatting, hovering over the chair like women in a gas-station toilet. "They grab my neck and rip my pants off and I can't stop it and…" Judge trailed off, but Jerry's relentless 'and?' face was too leering for his liking. "dad, I really don't want to finish this."

Jerry interrupted. "No, keep going. This could be a message from the Lord and…" He saw Judge roll his eyes. "Don't trifle with the Lord, son!" He looked at Amittai, seemingly too entranced by his breakfast to discipline his son. "You'll finish telling this, or we'll get your dad to rebuke you. It might have been a while since I…we've had to do that, but the Lord's discipline never sleeps."

Still hovering over his seat, Judge knew better than to ignore Jerry's threat. *He prides himself on making good on those, and I don't want to be reminded of how creative he can be.* "The guy raped me, ok? It hurt. And the guy who did it kept talking about how he had no demands. He only wanted to ruin some people. He knew they would all die, but he didn't care as long as they could rape as many people as often as they wanted. And it hurt...like I could feel it. I *could* feel it. Tearing and burning and his punching my back..."

"Then what happened?" Zeke said in a suddenly sincere voice.

"Then that was it. I woke up." He didn't tell them he woke up sore from the dream raping and that there were spots of blood on his underwear, but he suspected that they could tell by the way he winced anytime his backside touched the chair.

He expected Zeke to laugh or for Jerry to reprimand him for having a sexual dream, no matter how unwanted it was. Instead, Jerry turned to Judge's father and said "You remember what I was talking to you about last night?" Amittai looked up at the larger man, his face as blank as it always was. Judge knew this was just Jerry's way of continuing his lop-sided conversation. Judge wanted to say something, but couldn't find the strength to. "I think this is a sign from the Lord. Judge might be the man."

"But he got raped in the end." Amittai's complaint had as much feeling as someone eating a TV dinner.

Jerry leaned forward to intimidate his meek friend. "I don't think you get it." He looked at the two boys at the table. "Judge, Zeke, I need to talk to Am alone. Go out and start splitting that wood." Zeke ran out, eager to outshine Judge with an ax. Judge waddled out, trying to reason what Jerry was talking about. As he left the room, he overheard Jerry's forceful whisper. "He loses in the dream, and that's the point. We need that..." Walls came between Judge and the two men, and he couldn't hear the rest of what they were saying about him.

Brothers

Judge could feel the cold air outside even before he opened the door. *The weather moved in quick.* It provided a minor distraction from the pain in his bottom, and he was glad to have some time outside away from Jerry, his runny eggs and his signs from the Lord. He looked at the chopping block, didn't see Zeke, and knew something bad was coming. Before he could turn around to spy Zeke from his normal hiding spot under a bench, Judge heard a rustle and felt a pointy fist hit him square in the middle of his butt. It reignited all the pain from his dream and the day before and he yelped loudly. It rang through the abandoned summer camp that *The Hand* called home. Jimmy Two and Ezra looked up from their work at the chicken shack. Beard poked his head out the window, his clean-shaven, eternally surprised looking face finally fitting the situation.

Judge didn't mind so much that those losers heard his cry – he'd heard them all howl at the rebukings and trials Jerry had set for them. What really bothered him is that Zeke heard him, and now Judge would hear nothing but Zeke teasing for the next few hours they'd be splitting wood.

"Aw, come on. I didn't hit you that hard." Zeke ran on up ahead of Judge and walked backwards so he could look him in the face as they walked, but Judge just stared at the dirt. "It's just… I know that dream was probably scary, but it's also pretty funny." Zeke smiled and chuckled, trying to get Judge to look up. "I mean, how would you feel if I told a story like that?"

As much as he'd been trying to hide it, Judge did look up, and Zeke saw the tears welling in his eyes. "Aw, man I'm sorry. I didn't mean to…I'm just…here…ummm…" He ran up to Nehemiah's porch, grabbed a ratty cushion, and set it down on the stump of a stubborn oak tree they'd felled yesterday. "Here. Sit down. I really shouldn't have hit you so hard. Let me do the splitting until you feel better."

"No, that's not fair. Let me…" Judge tried to wrench the axe out of another tree stump, and pain welled out from inside his anus to the tips of his fingers and toes. Zeke saw it, pulled the axe out himself, and gently nudged Judge down to the cushion. Judge complied, but said "What's Jerry going to think when he sees me sitting down and you working?"

Zeke shrugged and brought the axe down hard on a log, splitting it in two. Judge watched him and occasionally failed at getting up, half in an effort to not get in trouble if Jerry were to show up and half in desire to warm up on that cold morning.

Judge had zoned out staring at the steaming lake when he heard Jerry's passive-aggressive voice shout from the porch of their cabin. "Boy, why are you sitting down? I just finished talking to your Daddy about how you was something special, and I come out here to see you being lazy? Don't tell me it's because you're hurt from some dream. We all know what happens to lazy boys, don't we?" He wagged his finger. Judge just about wet his pants

With a loud grunt, Zeke buried his axe into the chopping block. "I know, Jerry! I'm sore about it too! He thinks he's hot stuff. He comes up to me and says 'I'll stump you in Bible. You lose, you chop my wood.'" He pointed a veiny, calloused hand at Judge on the stump. "And wouldn't you know it, he did beat me, and now I got to chop twice as much."

"And study twice as hard. Good thing he stumped you and not me," Jerry said. Judge was grateful. He and Zeke both knew that if anything could deter Jerry's wrath, it was his belief that Bible knowledge was the most important thing in the world. Still, Jerry had been played before and found that he enjoyed meting out punishments. "What was the losing question?"

Despite the pain, Judge didn't skip a beat. He knew Zeke had played his part, and now he had to play his. "Who joined forces with the Ammonites and the Moabites to wage war against Jehosophat in second Chronicles?"

"And I said it was the Seirites. Genius Judge here reminded me that Seir was just a mountain, and that it was the Meunites who joined the war." Zeke picked up the axe, set a block of wood on the stump and swung hard. "And now, I'm chopping his share. I oughtta know better than to play Bible games with Mr. Scripture Scholar."

Jerry smiled at Judge. "Well, I can't find a fault with that now, can I? He's a regular Jacob. And Zeke?" His smile dropped. "Esau is not a man to be emulated. But Judge, you can't just sit there doing nothing. 'If any would not work, neither should he eat.'" His eyes shifted between the two of them. "Splitting wood is good, but the word of God is quick, and powerful, and...finish it up boys."

He walked away as the two of them finished his scripture out loud "...sharper than any two-edged sword, piercing even to the dividing asunder of soul and spirit, and of the joints and marrow, and is a discerner of the thoughts and intents of the heart."

Once he was out of earshot, Judge watched Zeke split the wood and said "You know you didn't have to do that."

"I shouldn't have hit you so hard."

"But you didn't hit me that hard. I just...I can take care of myself and Jerry isn't..."

Zeke buried the axe again and looked at Judge on the stump. "You can take care of yourself? Not with me you can't. Look, I shouldn't have hit you so hard, and that's that. Besides, isn't that what brothers are for?" He laughed as he got back to work.

"You know you're not my brother." Judge snickered. No one would have mistaken them for relatives just by looking at them. Zeke was short with an angular face, two eyes that were far too close together, sandy blond hair, and a frame that was all bone and no meat. In the real world, people would have made fun of him for looking like a rat, but almost everyone was ugly in *The Hand*, and Zeke could have been their king. Judge, on the other hand, had the size and looks to excel in anything. Thick shoulders, a slim torso, and strong legs always made Zeke jealous, and if there were girls around *The Hand's* camp, Judge's jet black hair, strong chin and inviting blue eyes would have left Zeke to play the perpetual second fiddle.

But they could have been brothers with the way they acted. Zeke bought into and fully believed everything Jerry taught. Judge just went along with it to avoid punishment, but they were still closer than best friends. It could have been because they were the only two people under 35 at the camp, but somehow they got along despite their differences. Zeke was too often the antagonist, and Judge too often the victim, but Zeke was always quick to apologize and Judge always quick to forgive. The two loved each other even though they had few reasons to.

"I could be your brother," Zeke said, smiling. Judge smiled back and shook his head, sad that Zeke felt so disconnected that he could never let it go. *Yes*, he thought, *it is remotely possible that you are my brother, but the probability must be in the trillions.* Judge did have an unknown brother floating around in the world somewhere, an accident from before

Amittai and Judge's mother were married. He wanted to keep the baby and she didn't. As was the case most of the time, Amittai lost.

Judge didn't even know about it until they arrived at *The Hand's* camp a few days after his 11th birthday. Am and Judge had met Jerry before, but to gain entry into the camp, Jerry made them stand in front of everyone and confess their sins out loud so they could be pure soldiers in the Lord's army. They called it mutual criticism. Jerry took the command to 'confess with thy mouth' literally, and some of the deeds Judge heard confessed over the years were both disgusting and titillating.

Amittai said some of the usual things that embarrassed his son, but they were small iniquities that every man was guilty of. The only thing that stuck with Judge was the fact that he had some long-lost brother somewhere out there, probably living the life that Judge dreamed about, away from this *The Hand*, its crazy cavalry, and Jerry the Grand Inquisitor.

"Zeke, I really don't think you're my brother."

"But I don't know who my mother is. Maybe before she had you she met your Dad…"

"Yeah, but I do remember my mother. My Dad might have taken me away from her a while ago, but I do remember that she was beautiful." Judge stood up slowly and the pain receded from his body. Towering over his would-be brother, he grabbed the axe out of Zeke's hand. "And there was no way a woman like her could have given birth to a little pipsqueak like you."

Zeke gave a mocking laugh and gathered the split wood as Judge pushed the pain out and brought the axe down. It always amazed him that it took him multiple swings to split a log where it usually took Zeke only one. *He might not be my real brother, but I guess it wouldn't be so bad if he was.*

Oh Shit

The wet cold front that came through was unseasonably cold enough to make everyone miserable, but it was too early in the season to snow. This was a bad thing - even terrorists hate a cold rain. It turns them into the stereotypical, I-hate-everything-and-everyone terrorist. If you were watching from a distance during their everyday events (minus the extensive combat and demolition training) you would see that the men of *The Hand* were generally happy people, or at least people who could tolerate the harshness of life without giving up. But this rain made them smell and look like shivering wet Chihuahuas. They had to run everywhere they went to keep from catching pneumonia, and the consequent shortness of breath made them all sound like they were constantly trying to start and lose fights. While they might have looked relatively normal most of the time, the cold rain made them look in turn both pathetic and terrifying.

Judge might not have been exactly like the rest of them in most ways, but the cold rain that only teased snow made him every bit as malignant as everyone else. The lingering pain in his ass wasn't helping things either. He assumed his body would be fine dashing from his porch to their meeting space, but as his legs started pumping, pain spread again from his sphincter to the tips of his body. Worrying that he had internal bleeding, he had to resort to a painful, soggy trot to the meeting space.

There was always the scant hope that Jerry would prove to be human and be affected by the rain or cold, that he would let them have their meeting inside, but that hope was never fulfilled. In August when you couldn't stand under the harsh sun for more than ten minutes without surrendering to heatstroke, in February when the snows were ankle-deep and the air was frozen so that every breath turned your nose into a snotsicle, in late October when the cold turned the autumn rains into a cruel cosmic joke – Jerry never once took a meeting inside in the seven years Judge had been there. He wouldn't even take them under the covered picnic areas that were mere yards away. Judge had suspected that he was constantly testing the men's mettle, but it had been at least two years since anyone old had left or anyone new had come in, and now Judge decided that Jerry was just being cruel.

The other men had to have been suspecting the same thing – Judge could see it on their shivering, soaked faces. Jerry, however, seemed to only see eager foot soldiers in the Lord's oncoming war. Either ignoring the cold and damp, or lacking the ability to be discouraged by anything, Jerry stood on top of what he called his 'preaching rock'. It had two foot-shaped grooves worn into it from years of his daily preaching. Once, when he first arrived at the camp, Judge stood in the grooves and realized how small his feet were compared to Jerry's. As the years went by, he never got up there again, even when his feet would have fit in those grooves. Those were shoes he never wanted to fill.

"Brothers, let us pray." *Oh great. Another of Jerry's half-hour long prayers.* Most of the time these daily meetings were just some quick announcements and a small devotion, Jerry's way of keeping tabs on his men. But when he started with a prayer, they all knew this meeting was going to be a marathon. They always started with those four words, and three hours later, Jerry would still be babbling on about something. His head bowed, Jerry loudly said "God, thank you for your gifts, and the judges you send to hasten your return. Amen." *Too short. Weird. Maybe the cold is finally getting to him.* After the 'amen' a few of the men kept their eyes closed, having not even fully set themselves into their praying rhythm. The rest looked at Jerry, wondering what made him break the meeting routine he'd been using for years.

The man on the rock reached into his jacket and pulled a metal contraption out of his pocket. "Anyone know what this is?" It was no larger than a slice of bread, but it was silver, shiny, and hopelessly complicated. The multi-colored wires bunched inside of it and the compact, clean construction told Judge that only one person in the whole camp was capable of making something so intricate – his father, Amittai. "I don't suppose you fellows would know, so I'll tell you. It's an answer to our prayers, a gift from the Lord, a beacon to shine the light of God's truth from our dark corner, illuminating a darker world."

A chill creeped up the back of Judge's head like someone was dusting their fingers on his neck. *I don't want to know what that is.* But he did know what it was, because he knew what his Dad did before they came to *The Hand* and became the Lord's men. He made bombs. Specifically, he was the head of one of the seven facilities in America that still made nuclear bombs after the Cold War petered out. Amittai could rebuild an engine block, fix a toaster and reinforce farming tools, but Judge knew that the machine in Jerry's hand was nothing like that. It looked too complicated and too innocuous to be anything but dangerous, and Jerry's words confirmed his suspicions.

The rain lightened up, but the cold didn't as the group leaned in, wanting to know what Jerry was holding. If the seven years Judge had been living in Jerry's cabin in that abandoned Summer Camp had taught him anything, the leader would just ramble random bible verses and make vague references to late 18th-century Millerite splinter group literature.

We'll never get a straight answer out of him. He'll forget about it in a few weeks, like when he banned forks because he said they were symbols of the excesses of modern life. They had to scoop stew out of a communal bowl with their hands for a few weeks until the day Jerry pulled a fork out of his pocket and started eating like a real person. No one questioned him on the ban or his dismissal of it, afraid he would rescind another luxury.

This'll probably be the same thing. I just need to wait it out. The other idiots in the group would call whatever he said prophetic, and understand none of it. Judge would try his hardest to stifle laughter. Jerry would keep going on and on about the Lord. The other guys would cry because they would think they should feel moved. Judge would cry because he really wanted to be moved far away from all of them.

He watched the last of Jerry's silent survey of the group, so familiar with Jerry's mannerisms that he could count down the seconds until the leader launched into the next ridiculous phase of his speech. *He's looking at Beard, then Nick. No one is to the left of Nick, so 5, 4, 3, 2,1,...0. 0. Oh shit. He's looking at me. This is new.*

"Brothers" he said from his rock with his eyes firmly locked on Judge, "this is an activator to a 25 megaton nuclear bomb. Amittai, a man anointed by the Lord with skills in nuclear physics, prayerfully made it for us, and his son, Judge is going to set it off in Brice stadium during the biggest football game of the year. It's going to immediately annihilate at least one hundred five thousand sinners in the stadium, and the blast radius will envelop the whole city in the Lord's consuming fire. If we're lucky, the toll could reach the millions. Judge will be lucky enough to meet the Lord before all of us do. The blast will set him in the Lord's bosom. He'll be a martyr, all to the glory of our Lord."

Jerry's heavy words didn't register with Judge at first. He was too busy getting over the fact that the leader had actually said something straightforward. *I wonder if the other guys will still be crying and speaking in tongues now that they might comprehend what he actually means.* Judge looked around at the group. No one was crying or mumbling in the language of the angels. Instead, they were staring at him and he couldn't figure out why. He looked closer at them and noticed that Zeke was glaring at Jerry. His Dad was as blank-faced as ever, but tears were rolling out of his emotionless face. *I know I've watched the other guys bawl in the spirit hundreds of times, but I've never seen Dad cry. And it's like the rest of his body doesn't know his tear ducts are working – it's embarrassing. He can't even cry like everyone else. But why is he the only one crying, and why am I getting so much attention?*

What Jerry actually said finally hit him like a nuclear bomb activator smacking him in the chest when Jerry threw the nuclear bomb activator at him. It bounced off his chest, and he tried to catch it, but it fumbled through his hands and plopped in the mud. Judge bent over to pick it, and as he stood up he saw Jerry mere feet in front of him. "I'd be more careful with that if I were you. It's your opportunity to bring the Kingdom of Heaven down to Earth. Wipe that mud off, son."

With Jerry in his face and all eyes on him, Judge knew to do what he was told. The leader put his arm around the would-be martyr and turned to look at the rest of the group. "And brothers, when Judge here, like the Judges of old, like Ehud and Gideon and Abimalech and Deborah..." *Why did he pick Deborah instead of Samson?* "brings this sinful world to reckoning with the wrath of God, and when the Lord himself returns because Judge has brought about the end of things, I shall hand deliver us to Christ himself..." *This is when the other guys are going to start crying along. Thank God – I thought Dad's twitching eyelid was going to unhinge and fly away.*

"Imagine it brothers! We'll hear the explosion that dear Judge will set off – an explosion in the hearts of all men. Yes, most will burn, but a few will turn back to God. And we'll see the Lord come down from the sky. He'll conscript us in his army, and the great war and the final battle will commence. We shall be the vanguard, marching to the destruction of this filthy, degenerate world, bringing sinners to justice with the Lord at our side. All thanks to our mighty Judge, so willing and eager to sacrifice himself for our salvation!"

It stopped raining, and the sun had even started to shine, drying the camp out, but all the men's faces were soaked. Amittai had started silently crying again and Pentecostal Jake was shouting in an odd *patois* of Mandarin and Spanish. Judge kept his head down and pretended to be intently interested in cleaning the mud off the nuclear piece. In actuality, a nuclear bomb might as well have been going off in his mind.

Oh shit oh shit oh shit. What do I do? I don't want to die. But If I don't act like I'm into it, I'm going to end up like Zeke's real Dad. He looked over at Zeke. He seemed to be prayer fighting an invisible demon, his fists swinging wildly and his face looking like he was trying to bite its tiny demon head off. He didn't want to, but he glanced at his Dad. He was bent over in the mud, silently making a new puddle with his tears. *And do they really believe that this'll start the Apocalypse? And is my Dad going to let this happen? Ah, who am I kidding – he lets everything else happen. What am I going to do? Oh shit oh shit oh shit...*

"I think you got all the mud off the activator." Jerry's arms squeezed around him and he felt warm whisper breath in his ear. In the cold it felt strangely comforting, but it did little to calm Judge's brain down. "Let's go where we can talk and pray in private about this."

Jerry turned him around and cradled the Lord's chosen one towards his cabin. Judge tried miserably to find a way out of whatever conversation they were about to have. "But...umm....I don't...I think my Dad

…mmmhmmm….uhhhh…guh…" Judge babbled, trying to find the right word to change Jerry's plan.

"Oh praise the Lord!" Jerry stopped and lifted his right hand in the air, his face pointed upward towards the sun. "Praise the Lord! We thank you Lord! Your gift of tongues on Judge right now is a most welcome sign that we're following the narrow path! Gaoiuer ldifjeifsdi lasdoiu…."

Jerry kept on babbling and resumed dragging Judge towards their cabin, being the sort of religious multitasker who can speak in tongues and march a young man towards his martyrdom at the same time.

At The Bottom

Judge sat at the same chair where he'd sheepishly explained his rape dream earlier that morning. Then, it had taken every bit of his willpower to put his butt on the seat, but now, he didn't notice the throbbing in his sphincter because the world was spinning in delirious circles around his head. *Oh shit oh shit oh shit I'm going to die I'm going to kill millions of people there's no way out of this oh shit oh shit oh shit...*

Jerry's heavy hand slapped him on the back and snapped him out of it. The leader set a dirty cup of water down on the table in front of him. Jerry took a loud sip out of his own cup and sighed. "Ahhh....Nothing better than a nice cup of water after getting baptized by the Holy Spirit, know what I mean?"

Judge picked his cup up and drank. He hoped it would help calm him down, but instead it just accentuated the bile that had been rising in his throat. He downed the rest of the cup in the hopes it would wash the taste out, but it just made it worse. By the time he set the cup down, Jerry was sitting on the other side of the table in his normal seat, but instead of a greasy meal between them, there were just two empty cups and too much silence. The leader's adoring smile gave Judge chills, and he had to break the silence. "Jerry, I....uh, I...don't know where to begin..."

"Speechless in awe of the Lord?" The corners of his mouth raised up even higher towards his eyes as his smile widened.

He looked like a lizard about to flick his tongue at a fly. "I was speechless too when the Lord first revealed his plan to me. You're probably thinking the same thing I did. I looked up to the Lord..." he raised his head and looked at the drooping ceiling tiles. *What is he looking at?* "And I said 'Lord, I've been thinking the same thing. I've been desolate over how the world can live in such filth, how they always return to their own vomit, no better than dogs. And Lord, you and I both know your wrath is long overdue, and you've been merciful long enough. But how do you want me to do it? I don't know the first thing about bombs, and you know I'm a man of faith, not science.'"

If only he'd stopped there and shunned science altogether, he'd of died of that pneumonia he got last year, like I prayed for and I wouldn't have to be dealing with this. Oh shit oh shit...

The sound of work resumed outside – Amittai's hammer, Beard's chainsaw, Jimmy Two's glossolaliac turn at their constant 24 hour prayer vigil interlocking strangely with the rhythmic thunking of Zeke's axe. Jerry looked back down at his martyr. "You probably don't think you remember that day, but I know you do. The morning of the day you and your Dad arrived was the day the Lord chose me to hand-deliver *The Hand* to him for the final battle. I had the 4am shift at the prayer vigil, and God told me what to do, and I was in anguish cause I couldn't figure out how to do it. The rest of the day I was in despair - and I know that isn't what the Lord wants us to do, but I was weak and worried anyway."

He normally tells the same six or seven stories, but this one is new. I wonder why I've never heard this? I mean, the rest of the group didn't seem too surprised a few minutes ago when he said his plans for me – why am I the last person to hear about this?

"And I knew your Daddy from my recruiting at the gun club, and I knew he worked at the SRS, but I didn't put two and two together." He did the wide lizard-grin and shrugged. "But that's what so great about the Lord – he puts two and two together for us. We do the heavy lifting, the grunt work. He does the planning. Kinda like how we do here, know what I mean?"

Judge's mind calmed down listening to Jerry's ramblings, and that gave the pain in his butt time to flare up again. He leaned forward to take some of the pressure off, cursing how he was getting it coming and going. *Jerry's got it right - that is how it works here. Everyone else works their asses off while Jerry just sits there, studies the Bible and tells us what to do. I wonder how he'd react if I asked him about his God complex? Probably put me in the box or something...*

"And you were a little pill. Can you remember?" Judge forced out a genial nod to keep Jerry going, even though the memory still made him feel like he'd been punched in the stomach. *I remember too well.*

"You hated being here, always asking for your Mom. And when you found out you had a bastard brother somewhere? That's all we heard for months." *My brother? Oh shit. What if he's in the blast radius? Did Jerry think about that? Does he know he might turn me into Cain? I think I might can out-Bible him on that.* "But we rebuked that right out of you, didn't we? Your Dad might have spared the rod, but we got that demon out of you, yessir."

The voluminous punishments Judge had received – lying locked for hours in a dark coffin to "come before the Lord in fear and trembling", driving nails into wood with his knees while kneeling in prayer to teach him contrition, being tied to a tree outside overnight to make him understand Jesus' sacrifice – these rebukings did nothing to change how Judge saw *The Hand* or Jerry's ideas about the Lord. They only taught him how to hide how he was feeling and pretend like he was a true believer. Sometimes Judge secretly wondered if he was the only one who acted this way. *Can't be, can it?*

Judge's Dad walked into the kitchen where they were sitting. *Is he just an actor, like me?* He kept his head down, scared of Jerry. *I can't tell. Why haven't I ever figured this out? Is he ok with me being sent to my death? If he isn't, he deserves to be on Broadway.* Amittai grabbed a cup, filled it with water and downed it quickly, doing his best to get away from Judge and Jerry as fast as possible. Judge was sickened by the whole ordeal and decided to ignore that his father was there, but Jerry wasn't as courteous. "Getting that post-tongues glass of water, eh? Nothing better than drinking water after drinking the water of life, that's what I always say."

I've never heard him say that. I wonder if I can find a way to convince Jerry to tie himself to the bomb so no one has to hear him say stupid shit like that ever again. He watched his Dad's awkward expression as he shuffled back outside to fix things that weren't near as broken as his relationship with his son. The thought of bringing his Dad along on his suicide mission crossed his mind, but that made him feel sad. *I wish he'd say something, try to help me out, but I don't want him to get hurt. With someone as scary as Jerry, I can kind of understand why he's so silent all the time, although now would be a great time for him to finally assert himself.* The screen door slammed shut. *Another time, I guess. Probably not, though.*

"Now where was I?" Normally Judge would answer this question with a non-sequitur to get Jerry off topic or to draw out one of his few stories that were actually interesting. But now, Judge just wanted to get away from that table. He said nothing. "Well, can't be that important, right? Let's get down to brass tacks."

Crap. I should have said that he was telling me about his time in Vietnam. At least that story has a prostitute in it, even though it just ends with his confusion in attempting to convert someone who spoke a different language. Whatever he tells me now is just going to end with a mushroom cloud, and me at the center.

Jerry pulled a neatly folded sheet of yellowed notebook paper out of his back pocket. This was obviously a plan he'd been working on for quite some time. It crackled like dead leaves as he unfolded it. "I know you're a good boy…a pious young man, but I'm surprised you're taking this so well. I was worried I'd have to…convince you."

Good thing he can't read my mind. I haven't had to hear him 'convince' since I said The Hand was kind of like Al Quada. He made me roll in the dirt for hours until he decided that I'd learned my lesson. I'm going to do whatever it takes to not hear him 'convince' ever again. Does that mean I have to go along with this? I mean, pretending I think Hollywood has joined forces with the secret circle of Muslim senators to undermine true Christianity is one thing, but letting them think that I'm fine with slaughtering hundreds of thousands of people?

The smack of Jerry's hand on the table straightened the paper out and shocked Judge back to attention. There was no way he could ignore it now. Jerry's lanky pointer finger went down a numbered list. "Well, we got Amittai to make the Bomb. Prayed over the bomb, received sign from God that you should do it…that dream of yours truly was a blessing…I prophesied to the group about it, and here we are." Judge looked at the sheet and saw his name on item number four, written in blue ink. The rest of the sheet had been written in pencil a long time ago, like he was the answer to Jerry's fill-in-the-blank God test.

"Your Daddy is going to teach you to put the activator in, then we're going to send you off to do the Lord's work. We're going to send you alone, and you're going to have to hitchhike to Brookland and maintain radio silence so no one can trace it back to us, understand?"

The cold, too-cruel-to-turn-to-snow rain started up again outside. They could hear it pounding on the cabin's roof. *Sounds like the world is applauding Jerry's decision. Or else we're getting pissed on.* The men outside whooped in shock as if God was playing the bucket-of-water-over-the-door prank on them, and it made him smile. But it wasn't just that that lifted his spirits.

Alone and radio silence? I must be a better actor than I thought. He really thinks I'll just do as he says with no one to keep tabs on me? What makes him think I won't just run away? That's it. That's what I'll do. I'll hitchhike to California, then maybe Australia. China? Alaska? Anywhere but here. I'll toss the activator in the ocean. It'll be hard to leave Dad and Zeke, but maybe once enough time has passed, whenever someone finally smarts up and kills Jerry, I can try to get in touch with them and we can be a messed-up family again.

Doubts started to creep in as Jerry's bony finger moved down the rest of the list. *Even if he thinks I'm some holy child, he has to have some sort of back-up plan, doesn't he? Even Jerry isn't that stupid. Although isn't faith just confidence in stupidity?*

Judge's voice worked the way he'd wanted it to for the first time since he'd heard the news. "How will you know when I get there?" For some reason, it felt strange to hear himself speak.

"I have faith in the Lord, son. And besides, that bomb's big enough, we'll hear it all the way out here. Now, once you get to Brookland, you'll need to – do you remember Lawrence?" Judge nodded even though he could only recall a vague picture of a man who was at the camp for a few brief weeks a couple of years ago.

"Was he the short guy?"

The leader's eyes squinted in disapproval. "Well, I would say that he wasn't as tall as some of the other guys in the camp, but that's not a nice way to label somebody, especially someone so dedicated to the Lord, son."

I'm not your son.

"Remember, Zacheus, was a wee little man…" *and a wee little man was he.* "…but he taught us one of the most important stories in the whole Bible. Lawrence wasn't just…not tall. He was also a computer network specialist, whatever that means. He was the only man who was able to get a job at the nuclear plant to get the rods for your daddy's bomb." Jerry tapped on the sheet. "You'll meet up with him. He'll let you know where the bomb is hidden, and then...you'll bring the Kingdom of Heaven to Earth." Judge saw Jerry get that far away look in his eyes he got when he was speaking in tongues, and he mused about what Jerry was always looking when he did that. *Wouldn't it be funny if at the end of all this we find out that Jerry sees little clowns or something when he does that?* "The Lord will return, and we'll be there to meet him. We'll cleanse the filth from this sinful, broken world."

THWAP! The screen door slammed shut, cracking like a whip and Zeke walked in shivering and dripping. Both the leader and the martyr jumped at the noise and looked at Zeke. Drenched like that, he didn't look like just a rat, but a rat skeleton, and the glare he shot at the two of them didn't make him look any more humane. His heavy breathing revealed how hard of a time he was having staying calm. "Jerry, can I talk to you? In private?" He glared at Judge, and his faux-brother wondered what he had done. *I haven't seen him this fired up since that one time we went protesting and a girl flashed her breasts at him. That was a good day.*

"In a minute, son. Go wait outside before you turn our kitchen into a lake." Zeke stormed out, leaving a small stream in his wake. Jerry sighed. "We just keep getting interrupted, don't we? Well, I don't think I had much else to say anyways.

The big game between the Jackets and the Eagles has apparently been sold out for months. At least that's what Lawrence says. That's when you're going to deliver the Lord's justice. Until then, I suggest we just do what we've been doing, and that you spend as much time in prayer as you can."

Jerry stood up, patted Judge on the shoulder and stepped outside to talk with Zeke. *Do what we've been doing? How can...I just don't understand Jerry. Maybe the coming wrath of God is normal for him, but I have to pretend I'm excited about nuking a city, and keep it up 24 hours a day. Maybe if I just don't say anything at all they'll take that as being too committed to speak.*

He stood up slowly, doing his best to not awaken the pain demon living in his rectum. He hobbled out of the kitchen. He hadn't done anything to be so exhausted but his body felt like it couldn't stay awake any longer. *I wonder if I can get away with going to bed early and skipping vespers now that I'm Jerry's golden boy. Might as well give it a shot.* He limped up the stairs to his room and pretended that he didn't see the blood stain on his sheets. *Could a dream really have made me bleed? I guess so. And now Jerry's dream is going to make others bleed and explode and burn and disintegrate.*

Judge set the activator on his nightstand, turned over and closed his eyes, but sleep didn't come. He rolled over and stared at the activator. The moon came through the window and gave it a pale glow. *How can something so little cause so much destruction?* The sound of Jerry's sermon played over and over in his head and kept him awake. *Calm down. Radio silence is my only hope.* The thought cleared his mind, and he faded into sleep.

Amalek

The air inside the cabin was freezing when Amittai woke Judge up. It was warm under the pile of ratty blankets, and there were no bad dreams, so he moaned at his father and begged to stay in bed. But even before he saw the activator and remembered that he was meant to commit the largest mass murder in recorded history, the routine that Judge had been living in for the past seven years popped into his mind. *This is a protest day, and we're going to a college. If I pretend yesterday didn't happen and that Jerry isn't 10 pounds of crazy in a five-pound sack, this could be a good day.*

He took a deep breath to brace for the cold outside of his covers, and sprang out of bed in a quick motion to get the shock of the temperature change over with. The clothes came on quickly despite his shivering.

Breakfast was strangely silent over bowls of oatmeal thick as drywall putty. Normally Jerry would be repeating some ridiculous story they'd heard thousands of times before. Amittai and his son would just stare at their bowls as they ate, but Zeke would devour all of Jerry's words. Judge always got the impression that Zeke was sucking up to Jerry, but he couldn't ever figure out why. This morning, it was almost as if enmity was excreting from Zeke like the steam coming off the oatmeal.

Zeke tried his best not to glare at Jerry and Judge, his squinty eyes darting back to his bowl of oatmeal as soon as he thought someone noticed his angry eyes. Judge spied his hand trembling out of the corner of his eye and saw that his knuckles were ghastly white from squeezing his spoon too hard. *I wonder what's wrong with him. Why hasn't Jerry tried to 'encourage' him with some bible verse yet? I would ask him about it, but I'm enjoying this silence too much. Maybe my Dad's awful oatmeal has finally pushed Zeke over the edge...*

Judge ignored it, just like he'd been ignoring his mission since he'd woken up. *If I ignore it, hide the piece under my mattress, maybe they'll all just forget about it.* And for a while, it looked like his strategy was working. They all managed to get down the concrete oatmeal before it completely solidified in their bowls. They went to their morning prayers. Jerry did his normal rambling and made no mention of bombs or destruction or Judge's death, and then it was to the van to make the trip to Brookland Technical University to protest against, as Jerry put it, "the heathenry and total collapse of the American Education system."

They made the hour and a half-drive in silence, as Jerry commanded. They were supposed to be praying for strength and courage for a successful protest, but Judge just dozed and stared out the window at the outside world flying by on the side of the highway. He heard Zeke sniffing back some tears in silent prayer and worried about him, but nothing could bring Judge down – protest day was always the best day of the month. He got to see the world he'd been denied since his father brought him to the camp at age 11.

As much as Judge loved any chance to leave the camp, protesting at colleges and universities were always his absolute favorite protest days. They made the rounds of the area schools once a year, and it was his only chance to see girls his own age. It wasn't as if he ever actually spoke with any of them. Most of the time, he would just stare awkwardly as they yelled at him, but he was just glad to be in their presence. Fortunately, a common form of counter protest was for the girls to flash their breasts at them. The other men acted like they were being attacked when this happened, but Judge lived for it. *I'd protest every day and get as vile as possible if it caused that to happen more often.*

I miss women. There hadn't been any women at the camp in years, and the ones that were there while Judge was there were either too young or too old to be attractive. He could only recall three or four, and they arrived around the same time Judge and Amittai did, back when Y2K fever was sweeping the nation.

There were rumors of a coming apocalypse, and Jerry took advantage of people's fear, peddling his theories at gun shows and right-wing protests. He promised that he'd been stockpiling food and supplies to ensure a paradise in the coming wasteland. The future martyr and his father were two of 10 people who joined *The Hand* in the months before the clocks flipped from 1999 to 2000. Zeke and his father arrived at the same time as Judge and Amittai, as did the Newtons and the Cains, with four females among them. Mrs. Newton was a good cook, but didn't take well to the lack of central heating and air at the camp. Fat Mrs. Cain and her four-year old twin daughters prayed and spoke in tongues with the rest of the men, but disparaged the rationing of the food, especially after the millennium came and went without incident.

    The Cains were gone by January 12th, 2000, and Mr. and Mrs. Newton left soon after Jerry had a revelation that led him to completely ban sexual intercourse on the pretext that with the world ending soon, any procreative acts were futile, and therefore, sinful. Judge wondered if Jerry had done it on purpose to get them to leave. He kept on preaching the ban after they left, even when the camp was only peopled with ugly, heterosexual men. Judge thought that rule should have gone without saying. *I certainly wouldn't have sex with any of the guys even if I was gay.* The whole ordeal taught him that Jerry wasn't just a paranoid swindler – he was deathly afraid of women.

    Since then, any time Judge saw a pretty girl at a protest, he tried to find subtle ways to tell her he wasn't a fundamentalist, while still trying to sound fundamentalist enough to keep Jerry off his back. He liked the way he'd notice a girl looking at him at first, the way she'd give a little sly smile, maybe flutter her eyelids. But as soon as Jerry told them to hold up their signs, whoever-she-was' smile would always turn to a frown. One time when he was feeling bold, he walked up to a pretty redhead and asked her name. He'd forgotten that he was holding a sign displaying a bloody aborted fetus and she spit on him. The only women he ever had contact with left in disgust or hurled epithets at him. Either way, it resulted in him having no idea how he was supposed to talk to a woman if he ever got the opportunity.

For now, he'd have to settle for just looking at them. *Being yelled at by a pretty lady is still better than nothing.* He stared out the window of the van as they got closer. *At least we aren't protesting at a middle school this month. Seeing pretty girls there just leaves me feeling confused and dirty.*

When the van finally parked at the university, Jerry shouted out an "amen" to let everyone know they could finally stop praying. Judge peeked outside at the busy quad in the distance. Taking advantage of the few moments before they invaded the campus and drove all the students into a frenzy, he tried to notice how normal people lived – how guys dressed, how women walked, the way everyone's hands moved when they talked. He had hoped for tips to help him blend in when he took the activator and hid from *The Hand*, but it just made him feel inadequate. His shabby coveralls looked nothing like what the normal people were wearing, and the graceful way the girls walked was something he thought he'd never get used too.

The beautiful extended quiet disappeared in an instant when Jerry stepped outside of the van, hoisting a sign that read "9/11 WAS GOD'S WRATH". Almost automatically, there were students shouting at Jerry and the rest of the guys as they held up their signs up like an acolyte baring a crucifix. Judge wanted to sit in the van for as long as he could, but Ezra, who had been sitting next to him so quietly, was now pushing him out the door in an effort to get outside and lambast a particularly effeminately dressed young man.

Hoisting a giant picture of an aborted fetus as low as possible while still high enough so he could convince Jerry that he was doing his part, Judge followed the troupe of angry men to the quad. A group of college kids followed them, half of them texting friends to come down and yell at the protesters . *Don't they get it? By yelling back and inviting friends they're just vindicating The Hand. Jerry probably thinks that their opposition is a sign that he's doing the right thing. If they ignored us, we wouldn't come back and... then I wouldn't ever see normal people. I guess I'm glad they're not ignoring us.*

The protest quickly grew to full fury. The signs *The Hand* held up were as offensive as possible. Most of the men were quickly on the way to going hoarse from blasting sinners. They were surrounded by indignant college students, many of them beautiful, young women. Judge tried to memorize a few of their faces so he could remember what a woman looked like in the long month between coming home from protest and leaving for the next one.

With all the noise and vitriol going on around him, he zoned out, glaring at one girl in particular that looked familiar. *She kind of looks like how I remember my Mom, or at least what Mom might have looked like at 20 years old. Is it wrong that I think she's kind of hot? I wonder if that's what my older brother looks like. I wonder what the odds are that he's here right now. Probably not too good, but what if? Would I recognize him? Would he want to recognize me?*

He remembered that Zeke always wanted to be that long-lost brother, and that he had seemed to have been having a rough morning. *I hope he's doing all right.* Glancing over, he saw that Zeke was in the middle of a shouting match with a professor, a man in his late 50s with a snow-white beard and a corduroy blazer. The old man kept pointing at the sign. He said, "'Feminists created AIDs' doesn't even make sense! I don't mind you having a differing viewpoint from mine, but at least keep your internal logic consistent!"

As always, Zeke ignored whoever was arguing with him and started in on his doomsday prophecy. "A hard rain is going to fall, sinner! It's going to cleanse this world, scrub it down to the bone! Your blasphemous soul is just angry you're on the wrong side!"

The professor put his hands on his hips. "But it's a logical fallacy that-"

Zeke shouted over him. "You'll be in a sorry state when the Lord returns! Soon, the winnowing fork will be in his hands and your blood will flood the threshing floor!"

He might be brainwashed, but man is he committed! I wish I believed in something as passionately as he believes in all this Armageddon crap. How did we turn out so different when we've lived the exact same life for the past 7 years? It could be that I have my Dad and he doesn't, but Dad seems as dedicated to Jerry as he can be. Do real brothers turn out to be so different?

He tried to look back at the woman who looked like his Mom, but the view was blocked by a young bearded man who could have been Zeke's professor's son. His mother's look-alike was standing next to him. "Hey, man. I saw you staring at my girl. You got a problem?" Judge didn't know what to do. "I asked you a question. You some kind of pervert, looking at someone else's girl? I knew all you Jesus freaks were pervs, but I thought you only like little boys."

Judge saw that everyone else in *The Hand* was busy getting yelled at or busy yelling at somebody. "Little boys? No, you don't understand...I..." He looked at the girl. She gave him a shameful stiffy and he almost forgot how to talk. "I think she's my mother...I mean..."

The guy's eyes widened and he brought his face inches away from Judge's. His breath smelled heavily of coffee and cigarettes. "What did you just say?" Judge said nothing and backed up a little bit. The guy stepped forward to stay close. "Did you just say my girl looked like some old lady? Some old lady retarded and ugly enough to give birth to an ugly fuck like you?"

"No...I...ummm..guh....therewer...."

The guy kept inching closer, and Judge was surprised by how his beard seemed to change from brown to red as he got closer. Judge felt a whispering in his ear that said "Now is not the time to speak in tongues. Do something." He turned his head and saw Zeke mere inches from his left ear. With two guys' heads severely encroaching on his personal space, Judge took a step back.

"What?" Judge said.

"Are you gonna let him talk like that to you? I know Jerry says we can't do anything that would get us in real trouble. But you are the chosen one, right?"

The boner his would-be mother gave him mixed with being close enough to smell the two guy's breath confused him. The guy looked at his girlfriend and said "Did you hear that?" He turned back to Judge. "The chosen one? Chosen for what?

To get his face caved in so that he looks like this fucked up baby on your sign?"

Zeke leaned in between their faces. *I didn't like having this guy close enough to kiss me, but a three-way kiss with him and Zeke would ruin my day, especially with my hot young mom watching.* "Just you wait. All this will be purified when the Lord comes back in his wrath." The guy stepped back and stared at Zeke as if he was speaking in another language. "You, this heathen university, all of this sinful, rotting city..." He looked at the girl, and his voice dropped to a sinister whisper, like the snake sneaking in the garden grass. "They'll all be turned to ash, even your ugly whore."

An ugly whore? You'd have to be blind to call this woman ugly. Wait - is Zeke trying to provoke – Judge lost all control of his mind and body when the top of the guy's forehead crashed into the bridge of his nose. First he saw sparks, then a pale yellow covered his vision, like he was drowning in urine, and then there was only a dull blackness as he fell to the sidewalk. It was hard, but he maintained consciousness enough to hear shouting from ten different directions. "Hey!" "Calm Down!" "Zeke, stop it, you know we can't have this!" A woman's high pitch scream sounded off like the horror movies Judge remembered from before he was brought to *The Hand*.

Judge's vision went briefly black and he was back in the house where he grew up. *I think that's where I am. At least it feels familiar, if it doesn't look familiar. Have I really been gone that long?* He smelled something warm and sweet. *I know what that is.* Judge walked down an unfamiliar dark hallway into a messy kitchen.

His mother was standing next to the oven. Cinnamon buns were sitting on top of the stove, beautiful golden brown swirls, with white icing oozing over the top and down the side onto the pan. He saw his mother's dark brown eyes and long brown hair. *She does look just like the girl at the protest.* He reached a tiny hand up to grab one. *Mmm....*It had no taste when he bit into it. He looked at his mother again, and the world went black.

His vision brightened again and the real world, where Jerry ruled and Amittai cowered, returned to view. It was drastically different from where he left it. To his left, Jerry and Beard were doing their best to keep five or six guys at bay, swinging their signs like poleaxes. Nick and Jimmy Two were lying on the ground under them, and Nick was bleeding from a giant gash on his cheek. Judge didn't see his father, and was worried he was buried under the feet of the group of students trying to make Nick bleed some more.

Oh shit. They're going to kill me, like they killed my Dad. Fighting to get to his feet, he had to fight waves of nausea that tried to release his breakfast from the confines of his stomach. *I wonder if it would taste like cinnamon rolls.* Standing up was taking longer than he thought it would, and he wondered how he hadn't been trampled yet. He heard Zeke's rough voice shouting, and saw him laying waste to people.

His faux-brother brought his fist down onto the ribs of a skinny young man lying on the ground, his face already puffing up from Zeke's blows. "Now go and smite Amalek, and utterly destroy all that they have!" Two linebacker-sized men tried to grab him, but he punched one in the dick and the other in the neck, leaving him gasping for air.

"And spare them not; but slay both man and woman!" After he dropped those two giants, the crowd backed up, but Zeke rushed at them hungrily, bringing his heel straight into the front of an old Asian man's knee. It bent backwards like a satyr's. A young lady standing next to the man cried something in another language that sounded like Jimmy One's Glossolalia. She swung a book at Zeke. He sidestepped it, grabbed her hair, and brought an elbow down on her forehead like he was driving a nail in her face.

As she collapsed, Zeke turned around to see Judge rising. The smile on his face was uncontrollable and hungry. *Why is he so excited about this?* "Glad to see you're finally awake, brother." He leapt over to Judge and helped him finish the long journey to his feet. "I thought you might like a taste of that bomb you'll be dropping." *Even he doesn't know me that well.*

Incensed by Zeke's vicious attack on the Asian woman and having finally figured out that they needed to approach cautiously, a group of five young men inched towards Zeke and encircled him as if he were a circus lion escaped from his cage. "Zeke, how do we get out of this?"

He shifted from foot to foot, looking at each lion tamer in turn, smiling that hungry smile. Ignoring his would-be brother's question, Zeke said "the assembly of the wicked has inclosed me" and leapt at the biggest of the five, his open hands shooting for the man's chest.

What do I do? Zeke can't possibly fight them all off. The two of us probably could with all the training Jerry makes us do, but I don't want to hurt anyone. But he's the only brother I have...

"Hey! Hey, I'm talking to you, man!" Judge turned around to see the same bearded heckler from earlier, storming towards him and bleeding from his right ear. His mother's young look-alike kept grabbing at the young man's arm, trying to pull him back, but she was too small to make any real difference. *Thanks for trying, Mom.*

Judge looked at her for a brief second and could feel Zeke staring at him, his fake family together for just one too-brief second. *I wish I could freeze this moment, and make it real. Zeke might have gone crazy today, but he's not that bad. He is fighting for me, isn't he? It would be me, my brother Zeke, my hot young mom, and this guy's fist barreling straight for my face...shit...*

Judge could have easily sidestepped it, but he didn't, and then everything went black.

Hey Jealousy

The whip-crack of the screen door slamming shut startled Judge to wakefulness. His whole body tensed, and he was racked in pain. But instead of it just being in his ass, the pain throbbed in the middle of his head, like a parasite's egg hatching inside the host, only to pour out and devour the entire body from within. Trying to sit up wasn't even an option. He brought his hand up to his face, and the brow over his right eye met his hand two inches before it should have. It shot snakes of pain through his whole body, their serpentine bodies carrying venom to every inch.

Turning over, he tried to open his eyes to see if his Dad was in the bed across from his, but only his left eye would open, and even that writhed in pain. He wanted to yell for help, to call his Dad and ask him what was going on, to cry and have his fake young mom from the university come cuddle him back to sleep, but he only emitted a lonely bleating, as if he was the one sheep lost from the 99. *Blargh...* Thinking actual thoughts was proving to be difficult. Unable to do anything else, he tried to fall back asleep, but was kept awake by sudden shouting coming from downstairs.

"Why am I not the one doing this?!" It was Zeke, irate and shouting at someone. His voice was raised in a rare form that normally only came out in *The Hand's* most intense worship moments.

"I told you, Zeke." It was Jerry, his voice at normal volume, but stern. "This isn't something we're going to talk about anymore – it's been preordained." Normally that voice and statement from him would end any and every conversation.

"No! We're going to talk about this. Right now!" Zeke was shouting loud enough for the whole camp to hear. *They're probably sneaking up under the windows right now to catch a glimpse of Jerry's fury.* He tried to picture the scene going on downstairs, but he couldn't imagine how Zeke would look yelling at Jerry. He did, however, have a brief memory of how Jerry looked the last time someone worked up the nerve to yell at him.

It had only happened once in the whole time Judge had been there, at least in his recollection. The blood downstairs must have been boiling much the same way it had back then – it had been Zeke's real father, about a year after they arrived at the camp. Zeke and Hank had arrived at the same time Judge and Amittai did, and they were the only ones that stayed after the Y2K furor died out. They were the last leaves on the tree, and Zeke and Hank took pride in that.

Zeke's fathe quickly became Jerry's second in command because of his fierce loyalty and short temper. He was Jerry's enforcer, at least until what Jerry dubbed 'The Big Disagreement'. It was so big, Judge decided, because it was the only time someone had stood up to Jerry. It certainly wasn't big because of what the disagreement was over - they both agreed that the Old Testament laws were a good guide to living, but Jerry thought that men should keep their faces clean shaven and Hank thought that shaving your beard was an affront to God. "If the Lord wanted us to shave, why does it keep on growing?" was Hank's constant refrain.

Judge always had to stifle laughter whenever they argued over it, partially because the issue seemed so inconsequential, but mainly because of how profusely Hank sweated while he was worked up. It finally boiled over during the coldest March they'd had in a long time, and the two of them argued alone by the rock in the snow, the other men afraid to step in and face either's wrath. Sweat was dripping off Hank's face and quickly freezing in the brutal weather. His beard was a solid chunk of ice by the time the arguing subsided. Jerry said that was the final sign from the Lord that beards were sinful. Everyone but Hank's facial hair was shaved off within a matter of hours. Beard faced a moral dilemma. "Just saying the word isn't a sin," Jerry said to a crying and clean-shaven Beard who suddenly demanded to be called Mike.

The situation got more serious when Jerry threatened to punish Zeke for Hank's insolence. He commanded the boy to shave with sandpaper and gasoline. Judge wanted to point out that the Bible said that sons would not be punished for their father's sins, but wanting to keep his own face from being carved up and burnt, he kept from wagging his tongue. Jerry's threat worked, and Hank claimed to concede to Jerry's point of view. He shaved his beard off, and looked as baby faced as his teenaged son. Everything seemed to be back to normal, albeit slightly less manly. Things went back to normal until Hank tried to leave with Zeke in tow one midnight in late April.

Strangely enough, Zeke was the one who ratted to Jerry that Hank was trying to take him away. The rebukings Zeke had been forced to endure, the hours of rolling naked in the dirt for not closing his eyes during prayer, the standing still while people stood inches from his ears and yelled for hours on end – these had all worked on Zeke where they hadn't on Judge. Zeke took to brainwashing like a cheap t-shirt takes to fading.

Zeke snitched to Jerry the day before Hank was planning to make their escape. He spilled which path through the woods they would take, what supplies they would steal, what hotel they would end up staying at, what they were going to tell the police. Jerry and the rest of *The Hand* were ready for him. Hiding in the woods along the path they knew he'd be taking, the men climbed up in the trees and dropped a net on him as soon as they passed Jerry's rock. Hank didn't resist out of fear for Zeke, and soon enough, he was tied up to a cross Jerry had rigged up earlier that day.

They left him up there for two days with only the trees for company. When they finally took him down, he was so sick that only a herculean medical effort would have saved him. At the meeting the next day, Jerry preached that he'd had a revelation disavowing modern medical care in favor of a strict diet of prayer. Hank died the next morning in his lumpy bed sobbing like a baby.

Jerry kept Zeke away so he wouldn't have to hear it, but Judge could recall the sounds of Hank's death pitch-perfectly, and it made him shudder. "I'll shave my beard and be a good boy!" He must have said it a thousand times and it had degraded to sounding like a drowning man's shouts when he finally passed. Zeke made sure his father was clean-shaven before they buried him, his face as smooth as glass. They rolled Jerry's rock away and buried Hank beneath it. At the funeral, Jerry stood on Hank's grave and claimed it must have been God's will, and then rescinded his ban on medical care. Zeke believed every word and became Jerry's de facto son. Judge didn't believe it, and learned to never attempt escape.

Since then, Judge had remembered the lesson Hank taught him and did his best to avoid any need for medical attention. Zeke, however, was downstairs proving that his memory of his father's inglorious death had disappeared far too quickly. "Aren't I good enough? Why are you having Judge set off the bomb?" Judge hadn't been listening too intently, but now that he'd heard his name, he was paying close attention. *Are Zeke and I on the same secret side? I never thought that he was just a pretender too. And he's risking punishment to protect me? I couldn't ask for a better brother.* Even though it hurt, Judge let out a sly, ugly smile. *I wonder what he'll say next.* Zeke let out a little growl and said "Why didn't you pick me?!"

Oh.

"I told you already, son. It isn't that I didn't pick you. It's that the voice of the Lord told me to pick Judge, know what I mean?" *What do the voices Jerry hears sound like?* "And we know we shouldn't question, the Lord, right?"

There was a loud smack on the table, different from the crack of the screen door slam – it was heavier, more like pushing instead of falling. Judge couldn't picture Jerry betraying any emotions like that. *That sounded painful. I hope Zeke's hand is ok.* "You know I'm not questioning the Lord. I'm questioning you." The house was silent. Zeke must have been remembering the punishments – his voice dropped almost out of the range of Judge's hearing. "I mean, I'm not questioning you, I'm questioning...I guess, why the Lord would pick Judge and not me. What haven't I done right?"

More like what has he ever done wrong? Yes, neither of us have been rebuked since Zeke got King Jehoash and King Amaziah mixed up and Jerry made him sleep on the floor for a week, but I'm just an actor, and I don't even do that particularly well. You'd think God or Jerry or whoever makes the decisions would give Zeke points for enthusiasm.

"Well son, I thought about that too. I see Judge as a real man of God, but even I have to admit that sometimes he isn't as…zealous as you are, but…well, I don't like to speak for the Lord, but I can think of a few things he has that you don't."

He heard them pulling chairs out from around the table, and his stomach growled out of habit. *I wonder if they're eating anything. When's the last time I ate? What day is it?* Judge realized he couldn't hear them speaking, and he had to force himself to get out of bed to find a better spot to listen. The room spun. He had to fight back the urge to vomit, and he thought he peed his pants a little bit, but he made it to the floor by the door. He sat with his back against the wall and cracked the door enough to hear the conversation.

Jerry's voice was slightly raised, and Judge inferred that Zeke said something quiet that might have bruised him. "If you'll let me talk, I'll tell you. Or would we be better served having this conversation outside? I'm sure I can find somewhere up high where you'll be much less comfortable." *His father's cross.* Judge had heard Jerry use this threat before, and it always worked. "You do look more and more like your Daddy every day."

Zeke didn't reply, and Judge could picture him staring at the floor like a dog who had learned to fear the mere sight of his master's fists. "That's more like it." Jerry's voice was back to normal. "For starters, he had that dream. It might have been an obscene dream, and we might have to watch him to make sure he doesn't get light in his loafers..." *Really?!* "...but I know not to take dreams lightly, especially one where someone like Judge saves people by taking their place of pain."

The pain from the dream still lingered whenever Judge moved too fast or used the bathroom too powerfully. Zeke's laughter from the breakfast table lingered as well. It wasn't that Zeke didn't laugh often, but his laugh that morning had a hint of cruelty, which Zeke normally reserved for the nonbelievers who challenged him at protests. Sure, Zeke made up for it later, but it didn't burn the memory from Judge's mind. *I wonder if he's laughing now.*

"And, he's got that name. And his dad's got his name...with something like that, it would almost be a surprise if God didn't use them for something amazing." *Our names. Another decision of my Dad's that is trying to put me in the ground.* Amittai and Judge's names had been a topic of conversation from their arrival at the camp. People always asked Am why he didn't name his son Jonah, after the son of the biblical Amittai. He always said it's because he wanted his son to be a man of God without having to go through all the waffling that Jonah went through. He never told anyone that it was actually chosen at random during a drunken viewing of *Fast Times at Ridgemont*

High. Judge had only heard the truth for himself a year ago when his father came to him crying, claiming he had one more confession to make. Judge was just glad he hadn't ended up as a Spicoli.

Surprised that being out of bed and on a hard floor was actually helping clear his head, Judge kept listening. "And this was all Am's baby, even from the start. He built the activator, and gave instructions on how to build the bomb. I thought he should have the honor of being the father of the boy who fires the first shot of Armageddon."

Zeke is probably cursing his Dad all over again, wishing that he and I could have switched fathers – that's one of the few things we can agree on, and I wouldn't have snitched on the escape. I wonder what my Dad really thinks about all this. I could ask him, but he probably wouldn't give me any answer other than a repeat of whatever Jerry said to make him think it was a blessed idea.

"Do you think I could go with him?" pleaded Zeke. *No. No no no. It'll ruin my plans. Please Jerry please. He'll kill me when I try to run. I know you make us do everything together already, but please...*

"Thought about that too, but the Lord didn't tell me anything about two people. I think we need you for the battle. You're the best sniper we have and you've always been...hungrier than him." He could hear the smile creeping into Jerry's voice and got chills. *That's true. As much as Zeke has tried to help me with the gun training, I've never been able to hit a picture of President Obama from more than 40 yards. Zeke could do it from 200. When Jerry would threaten to punish me if I didn't get better, Zeke would do his chores quickly so he could get time away to help me learn. And as patient as he was with me, I never picked up his bloodlust.* The chills stayed as Judge thought he had a revelation. *Is that why he's sending me? Am I some sort of weak link?* "But you know, I don't blame you Zeke. I can't think of a bigger honor than the one Judge is getting, to get to see Jesus sooner, and to descend with him from the clouds? I can't think of anything better, know what I mean?" *I wish I could see his face to see whether he's being sincere or just wants me out of the way.*

"But what if Judge doesn't do it right? I know he's got a smart Dad, but he hasn't always taken to the training." An owl hooting outside was the only sound. Everyone knew that the rare moment of quiet from Jerry meant that something had peaked his interest. *Should I be worried?* "Yes, he might know the Bible a little better than I do, but" Zeke paused to think. "...take yesterday for example. With all the training you make us do, there's no way that little guy should have been able to lay him out twice." *I've been unconscious a whole day? Where's my Dad?!* "And even after I bought him enough time to wake up and man up, he didn't do anything to help me in the fight against those people. If Am hadn't driven up in the van, he might have ended up in jail with the rest of the guys."

Jail? That would make things easier. If we get found out, I could get out of here without having to pretend to want to nuke a city, and I wouldn't have to think about the Lord or Jerry ever again. Maybe they'd even let Zeke come with me in witness protection after he gets some therapy...but they'd probably put Dad in prison, and I don't like to picture how the other prisoners would treat him. If Jerry can push him with just a few religious words, how little soap will the other inmates have to use to get him to do what they want? Crap. There goes that plan.

"You make a good point, son, but then again, the Lord's ways are not our ways. I-"

Zeke interrupted. "So there's no way I can change this?"

There was a rumbling outside like a retarded thunderstorm, all deep growls that sputtered into nothing. Judge turned around slowly to keep the room from spinning and saw the van pulling up the dirt road. His Dad was in the driver's seat and the rest of the men piled in the back. Jerry shouted to be heard over the noise. "Well there they are now and looks like Am got them all out, praise the Lord. That man can fix everything." *Not everything.*

The slamming car doors meant Judge wouldn't be alone for much longer. He crawled back to his bed and practiced his moans so he could milk his injury for as long as possible.

Jerry's voice was muffled, but he heard him say something to Zeke, quickly so the other men wouldn't hear it. "Son, I don't know if you can do anything to convince God otherwise, but I think if you wanted to catch God's eye, you'd need a pretty big sign. And even if it doesn't work, it can't hurt to try, know what I mean?" Judge heard that treacherous smile sneak into Jerry's voice at the word *hurt*. He could only think of a few things that made Jerry smile like that. None of them were good.

Just Far Enough

God, is this prayer ever going to end? Jerry was coming near to the end of the second hour of praying and prophesying from the rock. *I wish he'd at least pretend to tire to make the rest of us feel better.* Judge opened his eyes to look around every few minutes, and he could see the men shifting between their feet, their bodies sore from the riot and a night spent in jail. Still, they kept their eyes closes and looked to be moved.

The only thing Judge had paid attention to during the entire prayer came at the very beginning, when Jerry thanked God that Judge would be learning to activate the bomb later in the day. *Shit. Another thing I'll have to pretend to care about. And this time, I'll actually have to learn something. Better not be too complicated.* Jerry went off on a tangent about Enoch and Judge quickly zoned out. Two hours later, Judge had mapped out possible occupations he could take once he'd ditched the bomb and ran away. *Police Officer, so I would know whether or not Jerry was coming after me. Banana farmer, cause I miss bananas. Laser gun inventor, cause that would be badass.*

Jerry sounded the 'amen' just when Judge had decided on a design for his laser bazooka. *I'd come back and make Jerry shit his pants.* Jerry clapped his hands and said "Well, men, as you know, we are sending Judge out later this week to bring the wrath of God to Brookland. He needs to be ready. Yes, brother Amittai will be showing him how to activate the bomb later, but he'll need to be ready for more than that. So, Judge, I'm going to give you 3 minutes to run. I want you to pretend we are soldiers or police or catholic priests trying to stop you." *No. Please no. Not chase training, especially not today. My body still hasn't recovered from seeing my pseudo-mom.*

"Men, remember the rules. Judge, I don't want you killing anyone." He looked around at *The Hand*. The men who ended up in jail looked just as disappointed and tired as Judge did. *I know how you feel. I don't feel like running either.* "He has to stay alive for an hour. Judge hits you good once, you're down. But, we're almost ready for the end. It might not be how we used to do it, but we're done with rehearsals. We aren't using live ammo, but you don't have to stop until Judge hits you, know what I mean?"

Shit. That woke the sore men up. Normally, it was one hit and you stop, but the promise of being able to beat someone to a pulp brought an ugly smile to many faces that rarely had a chance to relieve their tension. But Zeke wasn't smiling. *He knows he might have to beat me half to death. Even when he wants to take my spot, he still loves me. Not enough to not beat the shit out of me, but just enough to feel sorry about it. Damnit.*

Jerry turned to Judge and said "I don't know why you're still standing there, son. You're down to two minutes 15 seconds." Judge hobbled away until the stiffness in his legs subsided and then broke into a wide-strided run. Every time a foot pounded the soil, a pulse of pain shot through his head, but he didn't have time to worry about that. *These are angry men who never get the chance to let any of their anger out. If Jerry didn't make us sit naked on a block of ice when we get caught masturbating, things probably wouldn't be so bad. But now... I don't think any of them will kill me, but I don't exactly think they were smiling because they were looking forward to giving me a soft pat on the rear.*

Judge made it a third of a mile out when he heard the gunshot. *They're coming.* He found a tall branchy pine and started scrambling up it. *It'll take most of them a while to get out here. And it's only an hour. I could probably just run the whole time.* Climbing down the tree, he remembered back to previous chases where the rules were a little safer. It was more like hide-and-go-seek and he didn't have to worry about almost dying. *Then, I could just stand my ground and hit whoever I needed to and they'd stop. Can't do that now.*

I have to run just far enough. When Judge thought he had reached that point, he cut left and hid behind an old gnarled oak tree. Its leaves were constantly bare. In the summer it looked pitiful. All the other blooming, green leaves seemed to be laughing, but when the lean times came, the old tree always looked prepared. *I'm going to have to be just like this tree. Being sad half the time isn't so bad, is it?*

He heard a rustling growing behind him, and the noise was soon accompanied by a man huffing and moaning. *Easy.* Judge peered around the tree and saw Beard bent over. *Please don't throw up.* Judge knew that if Beard vomited he would end up retching himself, and it would give him away. Instead, he snuck up slowly behind Beard, careful not to snap any twigs.

When he got behind him, Judge pushed his foot hard into the back of Beard's knee. It brought him to the ground, and Judge slipped a hand over Beard's mouth. *Really, PLEASE don't throw up.* Beard struggled, but Judge squeezed his hands harder around where the man's beard used to be. "I don't have to hit you, do I?"

Beard looked up and shook his head. "Ok. I'm going to let go. You're down. If you make *any* noise, I will find you later and hit you. More than once." Judge pulled his hand away and pushed Beard on the ground. He whispered "Stay down" and sprinted hard towards the highway. He had no way to keep track of the time, but as he ran, he guessed that the hour exercise was at least half over. *I've never been this far on my own before. Yeah, I was out here when we all had to go catch Hank, but...could I just keep going? If no one sees me now, they wouldn't see me then, would they? I could just skip this whole mess of learning the bomb and pretending to care and then...and then Jerry would just let Zeke do it. Hundreds of thousands would still die. My faux-brother would be one of them. Shit.*

So I can't go all the way, but I still don't want to get the tar beaten out of me. Judge cut to the right this time, and didn't hear a sound for 20 minutes. Eventually, he slowed to a walk and heard nothing. *The guys must really be hurting to be so slow.* It was peaceful out here. Judge looked up at the trees, just starting to yellow and brown from the autumn. The breeze stirred them slowly, and Judge could smell the earth reaching for the sky. *As terrible as it is to live with these guys, I am going to miss living here. Do forests get this magnificent anywhere else? I'll be surprised if they do.*

The breeze picked up and raised little chill bumps on Judge's arms. *Can't be long now. I've never been able to tell time by looking at the sun like Jimmy Two can, but I could probably start walking back. I'll hear that ending gunshot any minute now. And, the sooner I get back, the sooner I can get my Dad's bomb lesson out of the way.*

He turned around and started a slow, peaceful walk back towards the camp. *If I do meet anyone, I can just run until the bullet sounds. Can't be that long, can it?* Judge felt so alone that he didn't pay attention to where he stepped, and twigs and old pine straw snapped and creaked underneath his feet. When twigs and old pine straw started creaking and snapping behind him, he didn't notice it was out of rhythm with his footfalls.

"You just can't run far enough." *Shit. How did he...*

"Didn't you hear the gunshot? The chase is over."

Judge turned around. Zeke was alone and looked like he hadn't taken one step any faster than a trot. *I had to run for almost an hour to get out here How did he...*Zeke stepped forward. Judge stepped back. "I didn't hear any gunshot. Not yet, at least." Zeke kept encroaching, Judge kept retreating. *The end can't be more than a few minutes away.* "I'll hand it to you though - you did get pretty far, but you know it can't ever be far away enough."

Almost faster than he could comprehend, Zeke leapt at Judge. It took every bit of energy Judge had to sidestep it, but it was no good. Zeke's boot connected with the side of Judge's face. A clanging, like the sound of a hammer on metal, briefly exploded in his head, and Judge saw lights. *Shit. I don't want to do this.* His vision cleared quickly enough to see Zeke regaining his balance. He leapt again, leading with a fist this time. Judge was somehow able to get a hand up and shoved Zeke down into the muddy ground. *He's impossibly good at hiding how tired he is. Wish I could do that.* Judge said "That was one good hit, all right? We're done."

"I tripped."

"Whatever. We don't have to fight anymore. Time's almost up anyways."

Zeke crawled to his feet. He wiped his muddy hands off on his shirt. "Them aren't the rules, Judge. You know this is for your own good. What if you get chased in Brookland? Those cops are going to shoot first, ask questions later." *And that's why I'm never going to Brookland.* "If anything, I should hit you harder so its not such a shock when it happens later on."

Shit. I don't want to be his signpost to God. He seemed angry enough yesterday when he yelled at Jerry. Would he sacrifice me to become the chosen bomber? Judge looked at Zeke and saw the way his lips pulled back over his gums when he smiled, leaving his teeth to reflect the yellow sunlight. *He would.*

Judge turned around and ran as fast he could. His head pounded with every step. *Thanks to you, Zeke, I'm going to look like a leper for my grand entrance into the real world.* Zeke pursued, and his heavy strides were beating a faster rhythm than Judge's. "You can't run far enough, Judge!" His voice was somehow even despite his speed. *He's getting closer.* Judge craned his neck and saw Zeke gaining. *Shit. If he does this, I might be stuck here, and that bomb might actually go off. What do I do? Oh shit-.*

A gunshot went off in the distance. Judge stopped and bent over, his hands on his knees. "Good try, Zeke." He had to let out a word between each huge breath. "But I think I won this one."

"Yeah, but I think you learned your lesson." Judge didn't see Zeke's face as he sped back up and ran towards the camp, but he could hear the disappointment in his pseudo-brother's voice. *I still love you Zeke. You're the closest to a brother I'll probably ever have, and I hate that the only lesson I've learned is to stay away from you. I don't want to be the bloody pelt you use to curry God's favor.* Judge regained his wind and started the long walk back to the camp.

Boom

Why is Zeke here? The light from outside poured into Am's workshop as Judge opened the door. Instead of just illuminating the rusty tools and random machines that Judge now knew were probably pieces of a nuclear warhead, the light hit Zeke. His smile widened until he saw the giant mass of lumps and bruises that his boot had left on Judge's face.

"Oh man, Judge. I didn't realize that I hit you that hard." *How does he never realize how hard he hits me? And why can't I help but believe him every time he says that?* Zeke reached his hand up gingerly, slow enough to give Judge time to back away or beg not to be touched. He saw the worry on Zeke's face, his already tiny eyes squinting with empathy. Judge realized that Zeke wasn't mad at him. He was just fighting anger at a God who would pick someone else to start the apocalypse. *Damnit, Zeke. I just want to be angry at you, make you my enemy, hate you for trying to ruin my plan, but I can't. Why do you have to be so goddamn earnest about everything? Would my real brother have loved me this much, even when he's trying to steal my fake destiny? I'd have to guess no.*

He let Zeke touch the goose-egg that used to be his right eyebrow. "Careful. It's going down, but it still smarts."

Zeke snickered and said "Going down? It looks like your face is trying to escape being attached to that scrawny neck." He laughed again, but only after he got a smile out of Judge.

"Ha. Real funny. It doesn't really hurt unless it touches something or I think too hard about it."

"Well, not thinking oughtta be easy for you."

Judge laughed at that one. He wanted to be tough, to prove himself more serious about his 'destiny' that Zeke was, but he couldn't help it. "The hits just keep on coming, don't they?"

His father coughed, too shy, even around his own son, to initiate conversation. "Well, boys, I'm glad you're here." His twitching eye blinked up and down like a cow's jaw chewing the cud, and Judge wondered how he could build something as complex as the machine behind him when his vision was only half-good half the time. "I'm going to teach you how to set off a nuclear warhead." Amittai said such a heavy statement with such little gravity that a little grin floated off of Judge's face. He looked at Zeke to share in the joke. But instead of smiling back, Zeke was rapt in attention. He pulled a yellowed notepad and a knife-carved pencil out of the front of his coveralls.

Judge stopped smiling when he saw Zeke scribble 'How to turn sinners into a pile of dust' at the top of his paper. *Shit. This is serious. He really is trying to take this from me. Time to out-Zeke him.* "Great, Dad," he said. "Let's get going." He snatched the notepad and pencil out of Zeke's hand, tearing Zeke's note out and snapping the pencil in two. He kept the rest of the notepad and the sharpened end of the pencil for himself. *What to say...hmmm...*"You know, I had a dream about this last night."

Amittai crossed his matchstick-thin arms over his chest, not in disapproval, but merely to keep his meager frame warm. "Oh, yeah? About me teaching you how to activate it?"

Zeke's face mirrored this question, but his furrowed brow suggested a more sinister intention as he whittled the bottom half of the broken pencil to a sharp point. *I've got to make this sound right.* "Well, the dream wasn't about right now. It was about when I set it off. It was like Jesus was standing next to me, in a suit of white armor. We were on this hilltop overlooking Brookland and he said to me 'When thou shalt activate they father's bomb, thou shalt not die but join me in paradise.' And he shook my hand real hard, and there weren't any holes in his hands. And I pressed the button -"

"It's not really a button. Oh. Sorry. Didn't mean to interrupt." He looked at his shoes and blinked erratically. *At least I have his attention, but Zeke looks as suspicious as ever. I've got to step it up.*

"Well, prophecy was never my strong suit. Either way, the bomb went off and I didn't die. I was wearing a suit of armor like the Lord's, and we just watched the shock wave resonate off the bomb. I saw buildings crumble, and I heard throngs of people crying, and it was beautiful, like a chorus of angels singing the shepherd's song." Zeke started to lean back like the dream shock wave was pushing him. *It's working. If I knew they put so much stock into my dreams, I could have been king of this place years ago.* "And I had super vision and I could see people's bodies being ripped apart, their blood feeding the soil. Men, women, children, dogs, babies. You couldn't see the ground on account of all the severed limbs."

I wonder if I can work up some tears. It was easier than he thought it would be. The tears made his eyes glisten and gave instant gravitas to whatever he was saying. "And the Lord and I walked around, and we stepped on pieces of nuked out flesh and blood like they were the streets of gold." His voice rose slowly as he reached a crescendo. *Time to bring it home.* "Hallelujah! And then I saw you Dad, and Zeke, and Jerry and Beard and everyone else leading the vanguard in the final battle! Hallelujah! Taco poblano manana relleno burrito verde..." The 'tongues' bubbled out of his enraptured face. He finally stopped when he ran out of Mexican foods to mumble.

Amittai mumbled along in gibberish for a few seconds, then sighed and let out a monotone "Praise the Lord." He never put any emphasis into what he said, and sometimes Judge suspected his father was just being sarcastic. The constant winking only made things worse. "The Lord must have reached you in this dream, Judge, especially to give you the gift of tongues." Zeke didn't look convinced. He pulled out his knife and whittled the shard of pencil down to an even deadlier point.

Wiping the tears from his cheek, Judge forced himself to sniffle. "Thanks Dad. You probably have to teach me-" *I hate having to pretend like Zeke isn't here* "-a lot of stuff to set it off."

"Not really." Amittai turned around to a giant metal ball on the workbench behind him. It was pieced together with random scraps of metal that met at jagged angles. It looked like the serial killer from a movie Judge remembered about a guy who made suits out of human skin. Am plucked the activator from Judge's hands and pushed it in a hole in the side of the contraption. "You just put it in..." With an arm motion that was surprisingly wide and animated, he flipped a switch next to the hole where the activator rested. "...and flip the switch."

Zeke and Judge both stopped writing and looked up at Am, confused. "That's it?" Zeke asked.

"That's it. Boom." If the actual explosion was going to be as exciting as Am's boom, Judge would probably cause more damage with a mild fart.

That had to be sarcastic, right? With the arm flourish and the tired 'boom'? Maybe that's why Dad always seems like he doesn't care about what he's saying - he actually doesn't believe it. Maybe this whole bomb plot was his long-con to get me out of here. Am I gaining a modicum of respect for my dad?

Judge tried to read his father's face, but he was halfway turned around, blankly pulling the activator out of its home. *Nothing there. Surely that's his way of trying to tell me that he doesn't mean it. Or is that just how he is?*

Amittai had always been that way, at least for as long as Judge could remember. Judge recalled that even his mother had a hard time getting a read on him. Even though he said everything plainly, she had to constantly ask him what he meant. Judge didn't remember his mother very well, but he at least recalled that she was normal enough to have body language and inflection. But Amittai never had, and anyone who thought they had a handle on unspoken signals always thought Amittai was just making fun of them.

That is what led to their separation. It was one of the few memories Judge actually had of his Mother. One day out of the blue, Amittai started talking about taking them to a church out in the boonies. It was the sort of place Judge's mother wouldn't have been caught dead in normally, but she misread Amittai and thought he was being sarcastic and just wanted to go to goof on it. Once she was there, she realized that Amittai had been deadly serious about this church, and this church was deadly serious about end times prophecy. Amittai kept attending this hard-line church, but his mother started sleeping in on Sunday mornings, storing her energy so she could ridicule him for attending. He never fought back against her complaints, and quietly kept on attending the church. Judge suspected that his Dad understood how his lack of passion drove Judge's mother crazy, and that being so deadpan all the time may have actually been Amittai's way of fighting back.

The final straw for Judge's mother was when Am started listening to Jerry. The father had met him at a gun show, and he quickly started attending one of Jerry's small groups. The mother went to one meeting with Am, followed by a long fight where she yelled and stomped and cursed and Amittai just breathed softly as if he was sleeping. She was gone the next morning before Judge woke up. *I wonder what he actually said to her to make her leave. Or didn't say.*

At the time, Judge was glad she hadn't taken him with her. He had seen her nagging at Amittai and thought it would be easier to live with his Dad, who never yelled or cursed. It didn't take long for him to curse his mother for not taking him - a month later they had moved into the Dark Corner, and Jerry, the tall, spindly, leader had replaced his soft, beautiful mother.

I've lived with this man for 19 years and have never figured out how to hear what he's really saying. This could be good or bad - I don't think there's going to be any in between.

Zeke, however, was as easy to read as a porn-obsessed teenage boy too dumb to delete his browser history. His smile grew hungrier after Am told them that it was as easy as placing the activator and flipping a switch. *It's disgusting how excited he is about being two steps away from starting the apocalypse.*

Judge had to reclaim his territory. If Zeke was telling with his smile, Judge would set off metaphorical bombs of obviousness. "Praise the Lord! Hallelujah to the Lord of hosts for making it so simple, and for giving me a Dad so knowledgeable in the ways of wrath!"

Zeke stared at Judge and just said "Thanks, Am." *I wish he wouldn't call Dad by his first name.* Zeke slapped Judge on the shoulder and walked out of the garage, folding his note up and putting it in the front chest pocket of his coveralls. The cold light from outside floated into the dim workspace.

Judge was starting to find it strangely fun to act like Zeke. His acting let him tap into a passion and honesty that he hadn't felt in a long time, even if it was just a sham. *At least, I hope it's just a sham. Sometimes even I have a hard time telling the difference.* But the time for play was over; he had to know if his Dad was being honest. *Is he actually physically incapable of sounding inspired or is he being a creative mastermind in playing Jerry and finding a way for me to escape?*

I have to approach it gently just in case Jerry's ears reach this far. "So, umm… Dad, are you sure this bomb is going to work?" His Dad looked at him blankly, save for the occasional hard blink. "Not because I don't want to murder tons of people.

I mean, are you sure Lawrence finished the other half all right?"

"Well, yeah. We went over it while he was here, and he would make a fine scientist." There was nothing in that voice other than those words. *Come on, old man. Give me something.*

Judge remembered seeing his Dad shed a few spare tears at Jerry's announcement. *He wasn't breathing heavy or sobbing, but there was some emotion coming out there. Exploit it.* "But I saw you crying when Jerry told us about the Lord's plan. Was everything all right or..."

His father sighed and his eye stopped twitching. *Does that mean something?* Am said everything quickly, in one breath, like he needed to get it out before it disappeared. "Sure, I was a little shocked at first, to lose my son like that, but I know we've got to have faith in the Lord." *There was a little bit of embarrassment in his voice just now, but I think that might just be from his usual worry of not having enough faith. That doesn't help me any. Maybe if I was sticking around I could use it as blackmail, but now...* "I would say that you'd understand when you have a son, but you get a privilege far, far greater, praise the Lord." *Was that a mixed message, like he wants me to have a son? To do that, I'd have to keep on living. I still can't tell. Give me something, Dad! Come on!*

"So there's no chance this bomb is going dud, is there?"

The twitching eyelid was resting, and Judge looked deep into his father's eyes for the first time in as long as he could remember. *They look a little sad, but that might just be because there isn't anything else going on.* "Nope. No chance. I can do all things through Christ who strengthens me. I have faith. You should too."

Not very likely. Judge kept his eyes on his father, hoping for anything. He saw his Dad's eye move, and it looked like a lone wink, disattached from the usual twitching. Afterwards, his eyes were still. *Did he just...was that a wink? Oh my God! It was...I think.* Judge couldn't help it. Against all reason, the pure biological love all humans have for their parents bubbled out. He read the lone twitch as a vindication of his father, as proof that he was a good man misled, that he was just using this whole bomb plot as a last-ditch, nonviolent way to help his son escape.

Oh, Dad. Now I know why you're so indifferent to everything. And all along, I thought you just didn't care about me. Judge winked back and Am's eye started twitching again. "Now go and see to your chores," he said to his son. *Playing as Zeke and getting away from here is going to be easier now that I know my Dad isn't trying to explode me and a million others. The machine he had Lawrence build is probably just a box filled with old pinball parts.*

Any doubts Judge may have had were edged out by a newfound love and trust in his father. He had always thought that Amittai was just being weak, that the separation from his mother had destroyed any gumption and personality his father might have had. Now he thought that his dad was a genius that had somehow conned Jerry into letting his son escape.

I know his eye has twitched at random ever since he was six and my grandmother sprayed Clorox in his eye for looking at the underwear section in a Sears catalog, but that twitch felt different. I could swear that there was love in that wink. I've never been one to step blindly into something, but I can't help but believe my Dad wants what is best for me. Is this what faith feels like? Judge smiled as his Dad turned around and started to reassemble an old, rusty gun.

Shit Zeke

With a moment of rare elation, Judge trotted out of the garage and left his Dad behind in the dark. *I've always loved my dad because he's family and I have to, but is this how it feels to actually like your dad?* His joy was short-lived, however, when he heard the familiar *swish-thunk* of an axe splitting wood. *Oh yeah. I forgot. What was Zeke doing in there?*

He found his faux-brother in the clearing next to the storage shed, bringing his axe down hard, his small pile of firewood growing larger. Zeke saw Judge walking over but ignored him and continued swinging the axe. He put a huge log on the block. Normally it would have taken three swings to break one that size, but with an unearthly grunt coming from deep inside him, he was able to crack it in one. Judge saw a shockwave go through Zeke's body after he hit it, and he looked exhausted when the wave was done passing through him. *Was he trying to say something with that?*

Breathing heavily, Zeke tried to talk, but could only get three or four words between each breath, as if he'd traded his powers of speech for log-splitting supremacy. "I though that...*huff*...that you...*huff*...got off your chores...*huff*...give me a second..." He plopped down on the chopping block, and despite the unspoken competition between them, Judge worried about his would-be brother.

"Are you all right? Can I get you some water?" Zeke shook his suddenly-sweaty head. *Why am I worried? I hit him in the face with a baseball bat once and his nose didn't even break. Zeke is as close to indestructible as you can get. A split like that would have broken my arms, but not his.* "You know, just because Jerry took me off my chores doesn't mean you have to rush through to get them done. And you could have asked for my help if you needed it."

Zeke picked up the axe and it steadied his hands. "It's not that," he said. "It's not like you were ever good at this anyways." Zeke tried to look up at Judge, a brother making sure that his insult burnt the intended ears, but the sun was beaming behind Judge's head like an interrogator's lamp. Zeke squinted and looked at the axe in his hands. "I was…" He stood up, smoothly, as if the unsteadiness had disappeared in an instant. "Can I be honest with you?"

As long as I don't have to be honest with you. "Sure. But let me help you out." Zeke handed the axe over and Judge set a log on the block. It was a twig compared to the tree Zeke had just destroyed, but it still took him two swings to get through it. *I'm the Lord's chosen man and he still makes me look like a pussy. Was Jesus a decent carpenter or did he just say that so people wouldn't question how soft his hands were?*

"No offense, but I can't figure out why the Lord picked you to set off the bomb." Judge stopped after Zeke said it. *I guess I should act surprised.* Judge tried to give his best shocked look, his eyes wide and mouth scrunched, but it looked more like he had just sniffed a poopy diaper. Zeke looked around, unable to figure out why Judge was making that face. "What? Did you smell something?"

Note to self: don't try to make up facial expressions anymore. "Oh, nothing. Thought there was a skunk." *I guess I have to be honest now, at least to a point.* "You know, I can't figure out why the Lord called me to do this either." *This oughtta get him off my case.* "I thought if it should be anyone it should be you." Judge swung the axe on another log so his face didn't betray him. He missed and Zeke snatched the axe out of his hands. "I mean, you might not be as handsome as I am, but you're better at most everything else."

Zeke brought the axe down and split a log like a child tearing apart an assembled jigsaw puzzle. "You sure I'm not as handsome as you?" The two smiled at each other, and anyone looking would have known that Judge wasn't lying about that.

"But you know," Judge said, "I was thinking and…" *Make it believable* "…praying and speaking in tongues and the Lord spoke to me…through me and I remembered Gideon and Moses and Paul. God always seems to pick the most unlikely people, Zeke. You should take that as a complement really. It means you're actually a worthwhile person. Me, I might should take it as an insult. I'm just…"

"That's true, but honestly, I think I'm the more unlikely person of the two of us. I mean, your Dad is a science genius. You might be terrible at splitting logs-" Zeke split another log beautifully, as if it was meant to be in multiple pieces. "-but you got your lineage going for you."

"No, I meant...you know it says that God hath chosen the weak things of the world to confound the things which are mighty. The weak thing he's talking about is obviously me. And the Lord says..." Judge trailed off, scrambling for more scripture references.

"But I'm clearly the weaker of the two of us...you know that."

Are we really arguing over who is the weaker of the two of us? "See? That's my point. I'm definitely the weakest cause I've lead this conversation down the stupidest path. My point was, I don't know why the Lord picked me, but he did." Zeke tried not to look sad, but his drooping head gave him away. "Don't worry. I know the Lord has something planned for you."

Zeke head was still low, and he whispered, almost out of Judge's earshot. "I can take it from you, you know." Judge had to strain to hear him. *Was that an offer or a threat*? Their eyes met and Zeke looked strangely hungry. *Threat*. He kept his voice low, but it was never angry. "I think...I think Jerry might have been wrong. Don't tell anyone I said that." *You know I wouldn't.* "And…I think the Lord might have other plans for you."

You're right about that. "Now Zeke, it isn't a sin to be sad and disappointed, but…" Judge whispered as if God couldn't hear low frequencies. "…you know it's wrong to question the Lord."

"But what if…what if the Lord just wants us to start Armageddon and doesn't care how we do it?" *He's doing a good job trying to make it sound like he isn't angry.* "I know you might want to do this…" Zeke looked at Judge and squinted. *Was that supposed to mean something, or is the sun just in his eyes? What does he really know?* "…but I think I can prove it to Jerry and Ezra and Beard and your Dad and everyone else that I'm the man for this. You'll get to live and see the Lord's return."

I have to act like this bothers me, as sweet/disturbing as I think it is. He said "What?! The Lord…I think-"

"I love you, Judge, but it doesn't matter what you think." Zeke picked the axe back up and it sung through the air, it's whirring soprano ending on the split end of a log. He set up another log and didn't take his eye off the chopping block. "I'm going to smash Babylon's face in." He grabbed the axe handle in the middle with a fist and punched it into Judge's chest. *Ow…* "The Lord has other plans for you, brother."

Judge held the axe across his torso like a baby and watched Zeke walk off. *Smash Babylon's face in? That's an oddly specific way to say 'drop a nuclear bomb and start Armageddon', but if he thinks he can just follow me as I hitchhike away from my past, I'll have to find some way to lose him. But I've never been able to run far away enough from him before.* He thought about slipping a sleeping pill in Zeke's drink at some roadside diner, about knocking him out and leaving him on the side of the road, about telling the cops what Zeke was up to, about slitting his throat while he slept – it hurt to think of doing something that painful to his would-be-brother, but Judge knew he might have to if it came to that. *He'd do the same thing if he had to. This is my only chance out, and it won't work if Zeke is with me. I can't squander all my Dad is doing for me. What am I willing to sacrifice to be free?*

Judge sunk the axe into the chopping block, and it was barely stuck enough to hold on. *That was close, though. What if this is Zeke's way of saying he knows about my plan? How long will it be before Jerry figures it out? And Zeke wants me for a brother – Jerry just wants me as a bomb casing. I don't think it will be very nice if our leader finds out what I really think, and I feel like my act is already fading. I need to gather more fuel for my fire in case Zeke lets my secret out.*

Tiny was the closest. He was sitting on the front porch of his cabin like he always did right after lunchtime. From the rocking chair he was sitting in, his feet didn't touch the ground. A small man cursed with friends who didn't understand wit, irony, or sarcasm, Tiny had been given that nickname at a young age. Not the brightest lightning bug himself, he always viewed the name as an insult instead of seeing it as proof that it was merely his friends being too stupid to understand why people are normally dubbed 'Tiny'. The chip it built on his shoulder drove him to *the Hand.* Judge didn't like calling a small man Tiny, so he made wide gestures and heavy eye contact to get Tiny's attention.

"Hey!" Judge waved both hands high up in the air. Tiny looked over. "How's it going?"

"Well if it isn't Judge, our saviour…I mean…our…Judge…" Tiny got flustered so easily. It was more sad than funny.

I'm going to hate myself for doing this. "Hey…I'm trying to pray with everyone before I leave the day after tomorrow." Tiny's eyes lit up. A terrible public speaker, he had seldom been asked to pray out loud. "Can you be sure to pray especially for why you think we should set the bomb off?" *Don't sound too suspicious.* "I'm nowhere near as wise as you, and I need to –"

Judge didn't have to finish explaining. "Dear Lord Jesus God…" Tiny was chomping at the bit, praying away before Judge had even finished asking him to start. He went on for 15 solid minutes, and said 'Lord' 46 times during the prayer, but Judge had long ago learned how to tune prayers out. He sat kindly and waited for Tiny to say why he was so excited for the bomb to go off. *Here it comes.* "...and Lord Jesus, thank you for the many martyrs, Lord God, them bloods are going to plant...water the dirt, and seeds grow...your land..." *That's all I need to hear. I wonder if I can fall asleep before he's done.*

Judge did fall asleep. His eyes stayed closed after Tiny mumbled the 'amen'. Tiny thought he was just deep in prayer and left him on the porch while he went inside to get a drink. The sound of a dish rattling startled Judge awake and out of habit, he shouted out an automatic 'amen'. "Thanks, Ti...Thanks!"

The rest of the men Judge 'prayed' with were easier to deal with than Tiny – religion had inflated their egos to the point where they viewed every conversation, even ones with believers, as an opportunity to sermonize and convert. Fortunately, it had given all of them a golden tongue while praying. Pentecostal Jake spoke in tongues for a bit and then thanked God that Judge was going to "Wake America up from its long heathen slumber." Nehemiah said the same thing, but added abortion and sodomy to the long list of American sins. Jimmy Two prayed that he was looking forward to the crusade that would come after the bomb went off, that "he would finally get to kill them sombitches that always spoke so ill of Christians, to kill the faggots that turned my son gay, the rugmunchers who make them porno movies that ensnared me and drove my wife away."

The prayer with Beard was where things got interesting. He started by praying that the death of millions would wake people up to the evils of abortion and its infant holocaust, but then he mimicked Zeke and prayed for the destruction of Babylon. *Yeah, that's a common idea in the Bible, but I've never heard either Beard or Zeke mention it before. How can I ask him about it without him reporting to Jerry that I'd forgotten the Bible drills he made us do?*

Beard ended his prayer. "Amen. Thanks for praying with me Judge, and if it gets tough, don't forget that the Lord'll make a way." He got up and walked to his kitchen. "Can I make you some coffee or something?" Remembering that the last coffee Beard had made was thick as Ketchup and twice as tangy, Judge involuntarily made the same face he'd made earlier that Zeke had mistaken for a stinkface. Beard put his calloused hands on Judge's shoulder and shook him. "You okay?!"

"Yeah, why?"

"You just looked really shocked all the sudden. Did the Lord speak to you or something?" He hobbled over to the kitchen and poured a bag of coffee into a rusty, ancient Mr. Coffee.

These people... "No, it's just that your prayer..." *This'll be a longshot, but maybe it'll work.* "I loved the part about Babylon. I can't wait to destroy it, either."

"Well, I'm glad to hear that. You must be angry about how he treated us, too," said Beard. Just be happy you weren't in that jail with us." *Jail?* The gears wouldn't click in Judge's mind and he felt a stale throbbing from where Zeke's boot had rattled his brain. "Yeah, I pray all the time that that heathen Officer Matt Babylon will be in Brookland when you set that bomb off."

"Officer Matt Babylon?!"

Judge's mouth hung half-open and his forehead wrinkled up. *This is the face I should have shown Zeke.* "Whatsa matter? Don't like the smell of my Coffee?" Beard walked in with two mugs. He handed one to Judge. It barely moved as his hands trembled. *I hope my body language isn't this out of wack out in the real world.*

He recovered, the revolting stench of the coffee waking him up. Judge pretended to take a sip and said "Yeah, weird that his name is just like the Babylon in the Bible." *If he works at the university, he's gotta live over there, right? Surely he's far away enough to be safe for now. Zeke was probably just fired up, thinking about the future.*

"Yeah, don't think we didn't notice that too. Lord works in mysterious ways, I guess. His name might spell different, but that demon just lives up the street, close enough for us to smell his filth. If he ain't at work, he probably won't be in that first blast, but I'm sure as Moses going to be gunning for him first during Armageddon."

Judge heard none of that last sentence. He was out the door quicker than his father's eye twitching. *Shit, Zeke. What are you going to do?*

Tenderized Pork

He remembered seeing a police car on the way to the protests, parked at one of the lonely houses out near the camp. As far as Judge knew, no one from the camp ever talked with their neighbors, but he did remember Pentecostal Jake oinking at the car on occasion as they drove by, the sounds not far off from the noises he made when speaking in tongues. *Why in the world does this cop live so far away from where he works?*

Jerry was at the kitchen table poring over his ratty Bible as Judge ran through. The instincts of fear almost stopped Judge in his tracks, but he spied the keys to the van hanging from a rack on the wall. *So Zeke went on foot? I never could run as fast he did.* Something inside Judge made him grab the keys and keep running. *Would Jerry really rebuke me for keeping The Hand hidden? I am the chosen one, aren't I?*

He heard Jerry shouting after him but couldn't spare the effort to listen to what was being said. Before Judge knew what he was doing, he was in the van. The engine roared and he stomped on the squeaky gas pedal. It tore down the driveway and he saw Jerry in the rearview mirror, standing exasperated with his hands on his hips. *Shit. Chosen one or not, he WILL rebuke me. I wonder what he'll pick to do to me when I get back. At least Zeke will have to go through it with me. Shit.*

A discordant scraping sound came from the engine block, and it was then that Judge remembered that he'd never learned to drive. He'd watched people drive plenty, but time behind the wheel wasn't something Jerry deemed necessary when the end of the world was imminent. Judge knew it had something to do with the gear shift and the three pedals at his feet, but hitting and jiggling them at random didn't do anything to stop the noise. *If Zeke isn't already there he's going to hear me coming from streets ahead. Maybe that's for the best. Maybe he'll think it's Jerry coming to get him and he'll turn around. Maybe-*

Zeke was already there. The boxy blue squad car sat in front of a trailer home Zeke and Judge had passed a hundred times. The front door was hanging at a loose angle, only connected to the house by its bottom hinges, as if a bear had ripped it out. *I knew Zeke was fired up, but damn. What am I going to do if hasn't killed Babylon yet? I've never been able to stop him by myself before, and if he's in door ripping mode, I'm in trouble.*

He cut the van off. Its roar echoed through the woods and quickly faded into silence. *Everyone would have heard that. Jerry will know where we are. Shit. Nothing I can do about it now.* He said "Or" out loud to nobody in particular. *Or, if it was this easy to get away, I could just cut the van back on and drive off. Leave this all behind. I'm sure I could figure the gears eventually, or I could just ditch the van and hitchhike away like I would have done anyways. I could just skip the day after tomorrow altogether and start my escape right now.*

Judge looked at Babylon's mobile home and saw a fist rise up through a window. It came down and out of view with a terrifying velocity. *Was that Officer Babylon's hand or Zeke's? Who is on the receiving end of it? What if Zeke needs help? And what would Jerry do with my Dad if I just ran away?* He couldn't help but remember the image of Hank starving and shivering on the cross. For a split second, Judge saw his father up there instead of Hank. *I can't leave.*

The door to the van stuck a bit as he opened it. Jerry would have said that it a sign from the Lord to get back in and drive home, but it did nothing to stop Judge. He bent down low and shuffled towards the mobile home like Jerry had taught him, ducking briefly behind the squad car and the front stairs as he went. There was shouting inside, most of it incomprehensible gurgling, but he knew what the meaty thud sounds meant. *Someone is getting destroyed, and someone is doing the destroying.*

The window where he saw the fist flying was the last place he could crouch before going inside and getting into the fray. He poked his head over the bottom of the window and saw a fallow bachelor pad in disarray. Papers were everywhere. Pizza boxes and beer cans littered the floor. A thin, flat black box sat on the floor next to a pile of VHS tapes. *Is that what TVs look like now?*

Judge could hear the sounds of struggle but couldn't find the source. Scoping out the rest of the room, he looked back towards what he guessed was the kitchen. A chair was sideways on the floor next to a few scattered pieces of silverware. Finally, Judge found the source of the noise: two sets of legs and feet sticking out from behind a half wall like they were lying on top of each other. The feet attached to the body lying on its back was pants-less, barefoot and bleeding from its left toes. The body on top had Zeke's boots. The four legs trembled together, the naked ones more violently, expending the little, frantic energy they had left. *This could be turning out drastically different from how I imagined.* The two horizontal bodies shook in unison. *Oh, God, please let them be having gay sex. Jerry might kill Zeke, but at least he wouldn't die a virgin like I probably will.*

But they weren't having gay sex as Judge had hoped. He saw the same hand from the window, curled up in a fist, this time with a chain wrapped around it. It came down hard, then yanked back up, a string of blood and gore flying in its trajectory.

"Shit." Judge hopped up from the window, ran through the trashed living room and saw Zeke lying on top of a bloody man on the kitchen floor. The once-beige carpet drank up the blood. *Why would you put carpet in a kitchen?* Zeke hammered his chained fist down again and again on the man's face with blinding speed. His right cheek opened up. Judge could see clear to smashed bone. The cop might have been middle-eastern under all that carnage. *That explains the name, and why Beard hated him so much.* The officer moaned something, but his voice faded as his eyes closed and he lost consciousness. Zeke's face was bloody too. His hair was matted down with blood and a goose-egg was building on his forehead near the same spot that Judge had his. *At least this Officer Babylon got a few hits in.*

The chained fist rose up again in the same motion Zeke made with the axe, his hand ready to split this man's head as easily as a rotten log. *I've got to stop this.* "Zeke!"

The faux-brother turned around and smiled hungrily at Judge. He was missing a few of the front teeth that had been there an hour ago. "Judge! Did you come here to watch me prove to the Lord that I can do it?" Judge was sickened, not by the gore, but by how happy Zeke was. "I - ahhhhhhh.......!"

Officer Babylon had either been faking unconsciousness or had just woken up. The pepper spray in his hand was firing, and Zeke's face was absorbing it like a sponge. Judge was amazed at how quickly his face turned the color of the red clay soil. Despite his eyes being swollen shut, Officer Babylon's aim was true and he unloaded the canister into Zeke's face until he stood up, clutching his rat face in his hands. He shrieked in a display of pain that Judge thought Zeke was incapable of. *He didn't even break a sweat when his father died. This pepper spray must be torture. I wonder how that feels. I hope I never find out.* The canister was spraying nothing but loud air when Zeke, blind and howling, ran out the open backdoor and into the woods. Judge could hear him long after he lost sight of him, and the way the sound faded slowly made him think that Zeke was probably still running and shrieking, somewhere miles away.

I don't know if I could catch him. Officer Babylon dropped the empty pepper spray and moaned out a miserable "hhhheeeeeelllllllllpppppp" that sounded like a coffin creaking open. *Shit. What do I do what do I do what do I do what do I do. Shit. If I take him back to the camp they'll let him die and my escape will be postponed until we can move elsewhere. If I go after Zeke, Babylon will die and Jerry will rebuke us whenever Zeke drags me back to the camp. Zeke might be family, but he's made of tougher stuff than I could ever be. He'll be fine.* The officer moaned out another help and coughed up blood. It spattered onto Judge's pant leg.

Jerry might have tried to destroy me, but he didn't ruin my humanity enough for me to just leave this man here to die. He picked Officer Babylon up in his arms and carried him out to the van. He had to walk slowly to avoid slipping on the puddles of blood and teeth littering the floor of the mobile home, but Officer Babylon was easy to carry. *Good thing Jerry made my dad and I carry each other up and down the mountain.* On the way out, Judge glanced at a spit-shined badge on a shelf by the front door. It read 'Matthew Babbalan'. *That's a stroke of bad luck, but I'd rather have an unfortunate name than this unfortunate life.*

The officer flopped across one of the seats of the van, still moaning. Judge was glad his eyes were swollen shut. *He won't know who I am. I'll just drop him off at the hospital, ditch the van and make a run for the border. My old man will just have to take whatever punishment Jerry gives him. Maybe he can escape in this confusion.*

The van roared to life. Judge knew where the nearest hospital was from when they drove past it to protest at the Lutheran pre-school. He would have to drive past the camp's front entrance, but he was hoping he'd have the van figured out well enough to speed past anyone looking for him.

That familiar scraping sound cursed the bottom of the vehicle and filled the woods with ugly noises. The van wouldn't get over 30 miles per hour no matter how Judge fiddled with the gearshift. *I hope that's fast enough to get to the hospital before Officer Babbalan dies.* Speeding as recklessly as the van would let him, Judge turned around when the officer let out a banshee-wail from the backseat. *Oh shit. He's dying.* "It's going to be fine Officer Babbalan. Just hold on, we'll-"

Judge heard a familiar voice shouting from outside. *What?!* He turned back to the steering wheel just in time to swerve the van and miss his father and Jerry standing in the middle of the road. The top-heavy van flipped and rolled and rolled and rolled until it finally came to a stop wedged against a tree. Officer Babbalan was on top of Judge in the floorboard. He could feel the beaten man's cheekbone, bare and bloody, touching his clean-shaven face. *Gross.* He heard voices outside getting closer before he passed out.

Goodbye

For the 3rd time that week, Judge woke up in his bed wracked with an extreme pain he had a hard time explaining. *I have got to stop making a habit of this.* There was the lingering soreness in his sphincter, lumpy pressure in his head, and for reasons he couldn't completely remember, the two pains met in his middle. Any movement sent ripples of pain through his abdomen. It took him a moment to remember to breathe. *Why does waking up like this seem so familiar?*

After he remembered how to breathe, he remembered what had happened and why he had to do so much remembering. *Oh God. What have they done with Officer Babbalan? Did Zeke ever show back up? How is Jerry going to rebuke us for this?* Moving eventually grew easier and as he slowly sat up, he heard a familiar monotone voice. "Get up slow. Pentecostal Jake claims to have healed you, but you might still have a few broken ribs." *These aren't broken ribs –Zeke's given me enough of those to know what it would feel like. I'm just bruised as Hell. Good job, Pentecostal Jake.*

"Dad?" He looked around the room and saw his Dad sitting on the bed across from his. The light from outside was pink turning purple, the colors he imagined were staining the skin on his bruised midsection. "What time is it? What day?"

"You haven't been out that long. It's still Thursday, about 7pm." His eye started twitching again, but Judge felt too dizzy to pull any meaning from it.

He stood up slowly and gingerly pulled a t-shirt over his torso. "Did Zeke come back yet?" He looked out the window saw the van, mangled but upright outside the garage. "How's Officer Babbalan?"

Amittai walked towards the door and motioned for his son to follow. "That's actually something Jerry and the guys wanted to talk to you about," he said.

Oh shit. Last time we all gathered like that was when someone found that Nick had been hand-drawing pornography in his cabin. It was hard to tell if the naked, blocky figure on the paper was a man or woman, but he cried during his rebuking all the same. Jerry made us tie him to the same cross that killed Hank. He lost control of his bowels after a while, but he was smart enough to get caught in June and he lived. What are they going to do to me? It's not cold enough to freeze over, but I'm already in pretty bad shape. If they put me on that cross, I don't know if I could last as long as I'd need to. I really don't want to poop my pants in front of everyone.

Judge had no choice but to follow his Dad down the hallway. There were brief visions of pulling a Zeke, of escaping through the window into the darkening woods, but breathing with those bruised ribs was already too much when he was just walking. *I'm just going to have to take whatever they give me, praise God for it, and hope they still send me out with the bomb.*

Everyone was gathered around the kitchen table, some standing, some sitting. Jerry was in the middle. They were all calm and quiet, waiting for Judge to enter, like some morose reinterpretation of a surprise party. *Keep your head down, stare at the ground, talk quietly, talk about the Lord a lot. This will hurt, but act repentant, maybe they'll be easier on me.*

But when Judge found the strength to lift his head and look around, he was surprised to find that the men were smiling. It wasn't a pretty sight, but he was glad to see a small grin light onto even his dad's face. It was Jerry who spoke first. "Well, son, you gave us a scare, but the Lord must've been speaking to you." His voice came out begrudgingly through yellowed teeth as if he was loathe to admit whatever he was pleased about. "Honestly, I was ready to have to rebuke you, but then you showed back up." His smile broke and he looked back at Beard.

"And it was an answer to my prayers," Beard said. Jerry might have been conflicted, but Beard was beaming, the happiest Judge had seen him since before he'd had to shave his precious beard off. Beard smacked Jimmy Two with the back of his hand. "Why, just a few minutes before he run off, we were praying that God would send his wrath to that damned Officer

Babbalan for treating men of God like dogs. And wouldn't you know it? Judge shows back up with a dead Officer Babbalan in the van. He is so full of zeal for the Lord! Now, you shouldn't have driven if you didn't know how, but we always knew them giant knuckles would come in handy sometime."

Dead? He was alive last I saw him, and I felt his chest fill with breath when he was laying on top of me in the wrecked van. What did they do? Judge was having difficulty piecing a sentence together. "What...did he..." *This is going to suck, but I've got to use it.* "Uh, yeah. Praise the Lord that he lived in the Dark Corner, right?" He looked down at those giant knuckles. *Too clean.* "And good thing I found a chain too, or else his sinful blood would have been all over my hands." *But isn't it all over my hands? If I hadn't wrecked that van, he might have lived and I might be away from here...*

Jerry said "Yeah, we were wonderin' how your hands weren't broken, and where Zeke is, but we'll have to figure that one out later." *So he's still out there? Probably still running and screaming for all I know.* The leader stood up from the table. Suddenly looking older than he had the day before, he had to push off of the table to stand up straight. "It was the Lord's will, surely, for you to kill Babbalan. But this is an evil, broken, filthy world, and its crooked police are going to try to arrest you. We already burned his body and threw his bones in the lake, but they're going to come after *you. We* didn't kill him." *I don't want to believe him, but he's never been a liar. Neither have I, but now I'm a murderer.* "So we need to go ahead and get you out of here so that if they do come looking, we don't have to lie about the real killer having escaped. Say your goodbyes. You're leaving tonight."

Tonight. I'm leaving tonight. Right now. I get to say goodbye to this camp, to the Dark Corner, to the men, to Jerry, to all this crazy shit masquerading as God's will. Amittai monotoned "We'll be outside at the van, making sure it'll work to get you out of here." *I have to say goodbye to Dad to, just when I was starting to like him.* The screen door thwapped, and the other men were a blur of smiles and extended handshakes wishing Judge well, hoping and praying that the bomb kills millions of people, promising that they'll see him returning with Jesus in a few days. He mumbled a few words in reply to each man before moving closer to the waiting car outside.

Jerry was in the driver seat. Amittai was standing by the backdoors. "You're not coming with us?" Judge asked. He had never wanted to speak to his father more. He was hoping his Dad would drive him to the drop-off point, a mockery of the going-away-to-college moment he knew he'd never have. Maybe in those spare moments away from Jerry, his Dad would divulge secrets to him and act like the true, more lovable Amittai that Judge had never met but was sure existed.

There was no emotion in his voice. "No. Jerry wanted to talk to you, and I've got to start looking for Zeke." *I know he and I fought over who was more worthless earlier today, but I thought it was just talk. Does my Dad love him more than he loves me? No...can't be...that's why he's doing this – because he loves me and wants me to get out, right?* "But I'll be praying for you. That bomb is the most important thing I've ever made." *Ouch, says the biological son.* "Now go do the Lord's work with it."

His eye did the same single twitch that it had done earlier in the day. *Another wink.* Judge took it in, grateful that his Dad gave one last reassurance before he had to leave. *Ok. I need to calm down. That wink said everything I need to know – that he loves me, that he needs me to escape, that the bomb isn't real, that he wants me to live a real life.* Amittai's eye began the real twitching in earnest a few seconds later, slamming up and down like hands clapping in ravenous applause. *And that's probably the cover up just in case Jerry is watching.*

Judge smiled, extended his hand and shook his father's. *Be strong, old man. I'll find you somehow when this all blows over. I love you, and I wish you could say the same to me, but I understand why you can't.* The eye twitched on furiously as Amittai let go of his son's hand, handed him the ratty backpack holding the activator, and headed back inside.

A bang came from the van, and Judge turned around to see Jerry rapping his hand on the driver-side door. It was hard to hear him over the roar of the engine. It sounded more guttural than before, as if Judge's wreck had given it a tracheotomy. "Come on! We've got to get a move on, son!"

I'm not your son.

Good Riddance

Judge set the bag under his feet and watched Jerry switch gears. The car labored up to 45 miles per hour but didn't make any audible complaints about it. *I don't understand how he does it.* The van was in surprisingly good shape after Judge wrecked it. The side door was smashed in and the lone headlight that still worked winked to the world, but otherwise the car was fine.

"Judge, I want to talk to you." *Surprise, surprise.* "I feel the need to…to warn you. I know you spent 12 years out in the world, but now you're a man and everything is probably going to look a lot different to you."

Maybe I can shut him up. "Are you questioning my devotion to setting the bomb off?"

Jerry's eyes widened in panic. *This might work…* "No, no," he answered. "It's not that at all. It's just that there are some temptations out there you didn't have back in camp. At least that I hope you didn't have back in camp. That's why we were going to wait until the day of to send you to Brookland, but now you're going to have some time in between, and with how hard the Devil is going to be working against you, who knows what'll come up against you?" *Or what I'll bring up against myself.*

Although...he's right that I haven't really experienced the world in seven years. It's gotta be different. "Like what?"

Jerry gathered his thoughts and said "It's just that, everyone else in the world is ok with living in such filth, know what I mean? How can they stand it? 'As a dog returneth to his vomit' isn't just a proverb. It's why we don't keep any animals at the camp, and why we keep away from the world. These people out here..." Jerry motioned to a church they were driving by. "...even if they know what they are doing is a sin, they keep on doing it, pretending it's a good thing. I just...there have been good men sent to do good work that were turned by the world."

Is he saying I'm not the first? The Leader continued. "We might be hard people, but we're good people, and we'll stand by you no matter what. These people out here are just...animals. They might say they love you, that they'll never betray you, but they'll end up eating you alive...they always return to their vomit, and pretend it's a fine steak. I have the ultimate faith in you and the Lord, but any of us can be tempted away. I just want you to know it's coming so you can resist it." *Or so that I can run to it. If it's the opposite of the Dark Corner, I'm all for it, whatever it is.*

Judge was feeling playful in his defiance. "Like what? What kind of temptations? Like...naked ladies and fornicating?"

Jerry looked at Judge like he was already chewing on a vomit sandwich. *I may have pushed it too far.* "I don't want to get into that, and you should know better than to even let the thought of thinking about it cross your mind. Your father named you, but the Lord gave him your name for a reason. But yes, there might be something like that out there, and I know from experience that you might want nothing more than to taste that forbidden fruit. I've seen the ways you looked at some of the women when we went protesting. That's your sinful nature trying to lead you astray, son. I've had it happen to me. I had a very active fantasy life before I crucified that part of myself." Judge accidentally pictured Jerry naked with his faux-mother from the university. *Ewww...if ever I was tempted, all I have to do is think of that. Actually Jerry, you should have taught that as a strategy. Much more effective than your method of flicking your erect penis until it goes down.*

They drove past a McDonald's and Judge's stomach growled. *I completely forgot about food. I'll finally get to eat real food.* Jerry continued. "I think the temptation I'm more worried about for you is that your family...your old family might be out there."

Family?

"I don't know if your father ever told you, but your mother's kin is from Brookland, and they even adopted your brother...your biological brother out to some family in

Brookland." *Seriously? Why did they pick this city? Why would my Dad even joke about killing his ex-wife and both of his sons? Unless he wants me to find them. That would be a decent enough plan, but I thought he was telling me to run far away so The Hand can't find me. Dad, I wish we could have spoken more honestly with each other. There's so much I don't know...*

"I guess what I need to know, son, is...if somehow you see your mother standing next door to where you're setting the bomb off, will you still be able to do it?" Jerry didn't pause before answering his own question. "I think you can." *I guess he didn't want to hear my answer.*

Doesn't matter anyways. "Of course I'll be able to do it," Judge said reassuringly. "If anything, it'll be more reason to do it for her being so evil. Sometimes at night I think about her and I imagine she's crucified and I'm holding the hammer. I get a spear and I start stabbing and stabbing and stabbing..." Jerry looked eager, like he wanted Judge to keep going. *I guess he has no limits. Good to know.*

"That's good, son. Real good. Exactly what I needed to hear." The leader looked a little too happy, his smile a little too broad, his eyes a little too bright after Judge's story about mutilating his mother. *I don't think he crucified all of his fantasy life. Maybe that's why we don't have any women left.* "I just don't want the Dark Corner to leave your mind for one second while you're out there. But I don't think I've got any reason to worry. And here we are. Pick up your bag."

Jerry pulled the van into a truck stop that they drove by every time they went to protest at St. Edward's Catholic Church. The fluorescent light was harsh in a way Judge hadn't seen since he'd first gone to the camp seven years ago. *Actually Jerry, you've got every reason to worry. If the rest of the world is as bright as this, the Dark Corner will be gone by the time I'm out of this van.*

He felt a hard push on his shoulder and turned to see Jerry pushing him towards the door. "No one can see me dropping you off. Get out!" he barked. Judge opened the door and hit the ground like a newborn – filthy, lost and alone except for the nuclear activator in his backpack. The van peeled away with a loud screech. *The Hand* had finally let Judge go.

Part Two: Born to Run

Pardon Me, Sailor

Coming in from the dark surrounding the truck stop, the harsh light inside the gas station hurt Judge's eyes. His coveralls were still filthy with sweat and Officer Babbalan's blood. He was astounded at all the food, aisles upon aisles of it, just waiting in front of him. Glancing around the store, he noticed some truck stop hookers, covered in wrinkles, but barely covered with the rags they were wearing. *I don't think Jerry needed to worry about me being tempted. It looks like whatever is waiting between their legs would dissolve a dead body.* One of them smiled and approached Judge, but she walked away when he only expressed interest in the endless variety of potato chips in front of him.

The world sure has changed. Buffalo wing flavored chips? What does that even mean? He picked up a bag of original flavored lays and went to open it. A bright red '$.99' on the front of it caught his attention, and he remembered that outside of the camp, you needed money to buy goods and services. Making sure no one was standing near, he peeked in his backpack and saw it was empty except for the shiny, deadly machine inside it. *I guess we didn't have time to think that through.* The chips on the shelves were driving him crazy. He hadn't eaten anything since early that morning, before he ran for his life, before his Dad taught him how to kill millions, before Zeke killed Officer Babbalan, before he left the only home he'd known for the last seven years. The thought of eating actual food drove Judge to begging.

He sat cross-legged next to the glass door to the gas station, like he'd remembered seeing homeless men and veterans in front of the bus station when he was young enough to be around normal people. A certain spindly hooker that reminded Judge of reanimated road kill saw him sitting on the ground and strolled up to him. The shortness of her skirt made her look ten feet tall. "Looking for a good time honey?"

"Do you have any money? I'm starving. I'll do anything for it." Judge hadn't realized what that meant.

The hooker looked at her trashy friends and laughed. "Well, that's new. Normally it's the other way around. But don't worry honey. A guy as pretty as you can make some money pretty easily."

I feel bad for judging this girl. Yeah, she looks like trash, but she's trying to help me out. "How?" he asked. The hooker quickly realized that Judge really had no idea what she was implying.

She smirked and said "I tell you what, if you're really hungry enough, go up to any of the truckers with a pink bandana hanging out of their windows and tell them you need some money. The pink bandanas mean they're the nice ones." She laughed and walked back over to her friends.

I don't know what's wrong with Jerry. Yeah, people out here might not know the Bible like we do, but they sure are nice. They even put out bandanas as invitations for when they want to be nice to someone! "Thanks, lady." Judge's stomach spoke to him as he walked over to the trucks all lined up in neat rows. *I wonder where they're all going? Maybe I can get one of them to give me a ride.* Judge paced the rows and saw that most trucks had blue bandanas hanging out of their windows, and a few of those windows were steamed up. *I wonder why truckers would put out a blue bandana. Wouldn't they all want to be one of the nice ones?*

He finally found a pink bandana hanging out of a big yellow truck. The front grill had been painted to look like fangs. *Neat.* Judge went around to the driver's side door and pounded on it. A big man in a red and black flannel shirt hung his head over the open window. His beard, long and graying, came halfway down to Judge's head. *Uh oh, Jerry. A man with a beard. Wonder what trouble we'll get into.* The thought made Judge smile. "Well, hello!" the trucker said eagerly. "Are you....?"

"They told me you were one of the nice truckers, and I was wondering if you could give me some help."

The trucker smiled broadly. *Like Zeke's smile, but different. I wonder how Zeke is doing. Is he at a truckstop in the opposite direction? I hope he finds someone as nice as this guy.* "I'll give you anything you need," said the suddenly sober trucker.

Judge smiled back and said "Great. I...don't ask for too much. Just food and a ride if you're...you're not heading for Brookland are you?"

"Nope. Heading west. You know what? Let's go inside, get you some food and then we'll get going."

The trucker got out of his rig, pulled the bandana out of his window and stuffed it in his back pocket. Judge followed. They passed the lot lizards, laughing. Judge waved at them and said "Thanks for your help, ladies."

The two walked back into the gas station. It looked less imposing to Judge now that he had a friend and means to get whatever he wanted. The other truckers inside went silent as they walked by, and Judge's nice trucker shot back dirty looks. "Get whatever you want, boy." The trucker stood guard as Judge picked up two bags of chips, a microwave burrito and a large coke.

"Is this all right?" Judge held up his haul.

"Yeah. You're a cheap one, aren't you? No funny business, right?"

Is that a good thing? Gotta remember to watch that funny business. Whatever that means. Judge didn't know what to think, so he grabbed two hot dogs, loaded them up with chili and headed for the register. He had already scarfed down one of the hot dogs by the time they got back to the truck. Judge shuffled his food around to try to open the door, and the trucker trotted around and opened his door for him. "Get on up in there and get comfortable, big fella." *What a nice guy.*

The truck roared to life. The trucker shifted the gears around and pulled some levers without looking. *How do they do it?* "You keep on eating. I'm a little late on my shipment, but we'll get to it later." *Get to what?* The thought escaped Judge as he stuffed his face full of food which, despite its terribleness, was the best thing he had ever eaten.

The trucker kept glancing over at Judge as he ate. "How can you eat that stuff and be so happy about it?"

He slowed down. "If you knew what I've been eating, you'd understand," Judge said with a mouth full of processed pork parts.

"Oh yeah? What's your story?"

Oh shit. Does he know? Did he notice the blood on my coveralls? Did he see Jerry push me out of the van? Has the news of Officer Babbalan hit the news yet? "My story?"

The trucker pulled a cigarette out of a pack and offered one to Judge. Judge refused, having bad memories of stinky bowling alleys before the Dark Corner. The trucker lit his up. "Yeah. Your story. Who are you?"

Who am I? I can be anyone I want. Judge thought for a moment and said "Well, I...wrestle bears for a living." *Sounds pretty damn impressive to me.* "Yeah, we had a ton of bears where I used to live out in the woods...chopping wood...yep, just us lumberjacks."

The trucker smiled and said "So you like bears?"

"I don't know if I'd say I like them per se, but I was so good at it, I couldn't help but be the one who took care of them. At least that's what all the other guys said."

The trucker flicked his ash out of an open window. "That's what I like to hear. A real man's man, right?"

"Yessir." Judge inhaled the rest of his food. The trucker turned on the radio, and a simple but strong acoustic number blared out of the speakers. A man in an oddly charming warbly voice sing-shouted over the top of it. It was the first non-hymn Judge had heard in seven years. It wasn't the Backstreet Boys he loved so much as a pre-teen, but he tapped his foot all the same.

The trucker smacked the dial and changed the station. "Kids today wouldn't know good music if it bit them in the ass." He glanced at Judge and said "Do you like that?"

"It sounded like a pretty good song to me."

The trucker turned the radio down. "I meant getting bit in the ass."

Judge started to feel queasy. *What? Why would...* The trucker put his hand on Judge's thigh. Having a strict no-touching-unless-it's-a-beatdown policy at the camp, it felt weird for someone to touch him in a non-aggressive manner. A sharp, nauseous feeling rose in his stomach. *Is this how people hug nowadays?* As the trucker's hand creeped higher up and inside Judge's thigh, he decided it wasn't how people hugged. *This is weird.*

As the trucker's hand finally reached the tip of Judge's penis, he vomited all over the trucker's hand. Little flecks of hot dogs and potato chip covered Judge's coveralls. The trucker pulled his hand away slowly, but seemed otherwise fine. Judge moaned until he recovered his voice. "I'm so sorry. It must be the food. I haven't eaten anything like this in years."

Judge jumped when the trucker put his hand back on his thigh, vomit and all. "It's all right. I'm into some weird shit." The trucker's hand got more aggressive and dove into the puddle of vomit pooled in Judge's crotch.

"Whoa. What are you doing?!"

"What do you think I'm doing?"

"I don't know. That's why I asked."

The trucker pulled his truck off the road and into the parking lot of a Holiday Inn. His face changed from coy to something more worried. "So you're not going to fuck me?"

"What?" *Is that physically possible?* "No. I...thanks for the food mister, but could you let me out here?"

Pulling his hand from Judge's vomity crotch, the trucker unlocked the door. "I'm sorry man. I thought...never mind what

I thought. I can take you wherever you need to go. No funny business."

If that wasn't funny business, what is? Despite being into the weirdest of shits, the trucker was being perfectly nice. Judge thought about taking him up on his offer, but decided against it. *I don't care how nice he is. I've seen too much. What kind of man likes reaching his hand into a pool of vomit?* "No thanks." Judge hopped out of the truck as it pulled away. *No one will pick me up looking like this.* He tried to knock all the vomit off with his hands, but it was already stained into his coveralls along with the officer's blood.

I guess I was wrong about people being nicer out here, but that doesn't make Jerry right. I just need to find a way to stay away from people for a while. A tour bus was parked over five parking spaces behind the hotel. Men were pulling suitcases out from a compartment underneath. *There's my chance.* When they weren't looking, Judge slid into the darkness underneath and hid in an empty corner. When they came back and shut the compartment, Judge laid his head down on his hard backpack and went to sleep.

Last Man Standing

He woke up intermittently throughout his time in the cargo hold of the tour bus. The darkness, the constant motion, and the hum of the road helped Judge sleep most of the day away. He had nothing to eat or drink, and when he had to, he peed through a crack where the cargo door had been dented so that a point of light came in from outside. Through it he spied that the world outside had gone from night to day, and back to night again.

Then the bus stopped. *Good. I'm about to starve to death. And I'm tired of being in the dark.* There were voices outside the compartment. Judge couldn't make out what they were saying. *Are they going to be nice people, or the sort of people who enjoy vomit and man sex?* He hid behind a giant speaker in case they were the latter. When it did open, a team of dirty looking men started pulling out the instrument cases that had been Judge's only company for the last day. They all walked away with armfuls of stuff, and Judge took his chance to escape.

What's that smell? After stretching his stiff legs, Judge looked where the men were walking and saw a young tattooed woman setting steaming trays of food out on a plastic folding table. A fruity, acidic odor wafted towards Judge and the rumbling noise coming from his stomach almost gave him away. *Oh God that smells good. What is it?*

As if he was on the same wavelength with the other men, one of them shouted at the woman "What we got tonight?"

"I whipped up some Spaghetti and meatballs," she said with a sense of glib pride. "Free-range, organic beef, locally sourced bread crumbs for the-"

A man porting multiple guitar cases interrupted her with a grunt of approval, and the rest of them walked off. *Spaghetti. That's what it's called. I need to eat.* Judge turned back to the bus, grabbed two guitar cases that he'd had his legs propped up on, and followed the other roadies. It took every ounce of effort he could spare to not dive into the spaghetti as he passed by, but he knew blending in needed to be his first priority.

The other men went through a door that said 'authorized personnel only', but when Judge got to it, it was locked. *Oh shit. I'm going to get caught, and they're going to think I'm stealing these.* The door swung open, and the team of men flowed out. One, whose red bandana covered a balding head, looked at Judge and wrinkled his nose. He said "God, I knew this tour was going down the shitter, but now they're hiring junkies to be the local crew?"

Two of the other men, who looked every bit as blood and vomit soaked as Judge, laughed. The fourth one held the door open. The extended arm coming out of his sleeveless shirt showed Judge the hairiest armpit in existence, as if a fully grown child was birthing headfirst out of his underarm. "Just through there, set'em on the stage."

It took a while for Judge to find the stage, but he did as they said and went back for another load before he saw the rest of the crew sitting at the table. They were shoveling the spaghetti into their mouths fiercely, and the cook looked like someone had painted over her masterpiece. *I've been following their lead so far...* Judge loaded up a mountain of food on his plate, but remembered his hot-dog blowout and put some back. He sat next to the man with a jungle under his arm and ate ravenously. When the food barrage slowed, they started chatting about something, but Judge was too enamored in his spaghetti to pay attention to what they were saying. *I think my Mom used to make this, but I don't really remember too well. I know I've had spaghetti before.*

The plate was getting emptier. *None of them have gotten seconds, but I bet I could sneak it.* Before he could get up, a short woman with horn-rimmed glasses walked out of the 'authorized' door, clutching a clipboard to her chest. She was wearing loose jeans and a plain black t-shirt. Her face was covered in freckles. With her hair pulled back and her clothes hiding either an adult definition or no definition at all, the woman could have been 12 or 30. Judge found her pretty, and had to fight Jerry's disapproving voice echoing in his head.

The bandanaed man saw her coming. He stabbed his fork into a pile of noodles so that it stood up straight. "Hot damn. Payday!"

The clipboard woman sighed. "Guys, it's no secret. This tour hasn't been doing well and…I hate to tell you this, but we're going to have to delay your paychecks again for another week." The men started to grumble indistinctly. The tattooed lunch lady stood up and removed her apron, revealing a shirt so low cut that Judge averted his eyes on instinct.

A crew member whose beard was as much spaghetti as it was hair slammed his fist on the table and said "Yolanda, that's a load of bullshit and you know it." He sounded like he had a mouth full of marbles and Judge had a quick memory of Pentecostal Jake worshipping when he had laryngitis. "We've seen how the talent lives. We all like to get high too, but aren't we a little more important than the mountain of blow Simmons is climbing right now?" The other guys agreed.

Band? Is this a rock tour? Jerry would be spinning in his grave. If he were dead. Wouldn't that be nice. Yolanda sat down between Judge and the bandanaed man. Her hair was wet and Judge got a whiff of her shampoo. *Like a tropical hideaway in this rumbling sea of B.O. and smoke.* She set her clipboard down and said "Y'all know this isn't coming from me. I'm not getting paid right now either, and at least you don't have to hang out with them. It's like I can see my money going right up their noses."

The tattooed woman threw her apron in front of Yolanda and bent over. She almost fell out of her bra and Judge had the sudden urge to flick his penis. "You know I can actually be making money elsewhere. Sorry Hunny Bunny, but I'm gone."

Yolanda looked at her pleadingly. "No, Clare. Come on, wait. You'll be getting paid next week. Davis said so!"

"That's what you said last week. No offense hun, but you should get off this sinking ship while you can." Judge watched her saunter away. *When did walking become so attractive?*

Shoving a large final bite into his mouth, the man with the bandana stood up. "Sounds like a good idea to me. Come on guys. No offense to you, Hunny Bunny, but we're gonna try to land somewhere that's actually making money."

Yolanda stood, but only came up to most of the crew's chest. "Guys, come on. Don't leave me like this! I need…" They were all already on the bus. Yolanda sat down and put her face in her palms. The crew came off the bus carrying duffel bags and walked off towards the street.

All that spaghetti, all for me. Judge loaded up another plate and sat down across from Yolanda. Stuffing his face, he watched her, and could almost see the gears grinding to a halt in her head. *A tour would be a great place for me to disappear. When we get to the west coast, I can just hop on another one and stay disappeared.* "Ummm...Yolanda, Hunny Bunny, whatever it is, I know I'm just a..." *What did he call me?* "...local crew, but I can come on full-time. Travel with you and do the job."

She glared at him. *I know the other guys were covered in vomit and spaghetti but she makes me wish I'd had time to take a shower.* "And you are?" she sneered.

"My name's Judge." *Shit. Should I have told her a fake name? Too late now.*

"Well, umm...do you have any experience in...we don't have time for this. You're hired." Yolanda wrote his name down on her clipboard, then crossed out five other names. "Do you know what you're doing?"

I better look useful. "I already carried in a few guitars and some other stuff. Did it pretty well, if I do say so myself. Set it right on the stage, didn't break anything."

"What a monumental feat." *Ah. Now that was definitely sarcasm. It hurt a bit, but at least I know what she's saying.* She shook her head as if she regretted her barb. "Can you restring a guitar?"

Before getting felt up by that trucker, I don't think I'd heard a guitar in at least seven years. "Sure."

"All right then. I don't think the sound team will be leaving...they at least get the c-team groupies, so you'll just have to do." She extended her tiny hand. "I'm Yolanda. Nice to meet you."

Judge shook it. *Man, that's soft.* He hadn't touched a woman since his mother left. Judge was in love. She looked back towards the bus and into the compartment where Judge had spent the previous day. "Looks like they've already gotten everything off the bus, and we're having to stretch the string budget, so we'll just wait on that a few more days. As if Jammer would notice anyways." She looked at her messy clipboard. "All right. I need you to take the guys their dinner. After that, just stand by during the show. Afterwards, you're going to be doing the work of four men." *Easy enough.*

Yolanda boxed up three spaghetti meals, wrote *Simmons, Jammer* and *Grenade* on them and handed them to Judge. *Is this code for something?* "Where am I taking these?"

She looked annoyed. "Dressing room A is just down that hallway." She pointed through the 'authorized' door and walked over to the food table. Judge walked off and heard her mumble "Guess I'm the cook now".

This is perfect. Free food, a pretty woman with good-smelling hair, and no way for Jerry to find me. I hope Zeke finds something this sweet if he is too scared to go back to the Camp. Walking down the hallway, Judge heard pounding footsteps. *I know that sound. I'm not getting taken this time.* Judge turned around towards the sound and took the stance that Jerry had taught him. *Low. Hands out. Eyes open. If he's running, I've already got the upper hand.*

A man dressed in all black and sporting a top hat turned a corner and ran straight at Judge. *I can take this guy*. His voice cracked as he shouted "Is that for me?!" He stopped on a dime right in front of Judge and fidgeted like a child that couldn't find a bathroom. *Please don't pee on me.*

"Are you…"

"Yeah. Jammer. Just…yeah…sorry man…you must be new…fine with me…I like your look…nice and…clean shaven face…I'm…sorry dude, too much speed." Judge handed him his dinner. He grabbed it greedily, opened it up and ran off in the opposite direction, eating it with his hands as he ran. "Fuck yeah, man! Fucking spaghetti…"

I wonder if he's on the drugs Jerry was always warning us about. I kinda thought he was making a lot of that stuff up. Judge found Dressing Room A and knocked on the door.

A gruff, drawling voice spoke from inside. "It's open." Judge walked in. One man in a pair of gray boxer briefs looked to be asleep on a couch. Another person was sitting in a chair facing a television tuned to a show about dogs. Long black hair hung from the head and went halfway down the chair. *That better be a woman. That hair is too pretty to be a man's.* The voice spoke again, and it was the person sitting in the chair. He didn't turn around. "Is that dinner, Ron? Just set it on that table." He pointed toward a counter on the wall. Tattoos covered his arms, thin as the twigs Judge had tried not to step on during his chase training.

The man on the couch looked dead. Judge walked past him and set both boxes of food on the counter. He turned around to look at the man in the chair and saw that he was naked. His eyes closed in ecstasy, a blond woman knelt in front of him. *What is she doing? Why is his penis...oh. Oh.* The man in the chair opened one eye and looked at Judge. "You're not Ron," he said.

Judge tried but couldn't take his eyes off the woman servicing the man in the chair. "No. Ron quit. My name's Judge."

"Oh, cool man. My name's Simmons." He reached out his skinny arm to shake Judge's hand. There were dark purple lines running up and down the crook of his elbow. The woman didn't stop moving her mouth up and down. *This is...Jerry was wrong about EVERYTHING.* They shook hands. Simmons pointed at the man on the couch and said "That's Grenade." Judge was able to break his gaze, and saw the man on the couch had changed positions so that he was sitting up. The box of spaghetti was open in his lap and he had a fork in his hand. However, he was every bit as motionless and dead-looking as he was a few seconds before. *How did he do that?*

"Nice...Nice to meet you both." Judge looked down at the blond woman, and then at Simmons, who had closed his eyes again. "Nice to meet you too, miss. I'm going to go." Judge looked at Grenade again. Same dead position, but the box of spaghetti was empty.

Judge shook his head as he walked out into the hallway and shut the door. *Of course I'm going to be surprised, having lived in the Dark Corner for most of my life, but Jerry was wrong. Simmons was really nice, no matter how sinful he was. And is whatever that lady was doing even sinful? It looked like it felt pretty good. I bet Jerry's never even done that before. If he did, he'd see the world isn't so bad.*

Yolanda came to the door just as Judge was walking away. She knocked and shouted "Five minutes!" She looked at Judge, but her shortness put her eyes at just under his chest. Craning her head up, she said "We'll need you on stage. Follow me." She hurried off up some stairs, her little legs pumping furiously, and Judge followed. *I wonder if she'd do to me what that girl was doing to Simmons. Maybe that's how ladies hug nowadays. Could the world be that beautiful?*

They stood at the side of the stage. A group of burly guys were coming off in a storm of applause. Judge looked out at the crowd and said "Wow. That is a lot of people."

"Yeah, and it won't be in a second. Just watch." Yolanda was right. As the peels of feedback from the last band was fading from the speakers, many in the crowd were getting out of their seats and heading for the exit. "I hope you don't mind not getting paid. I don't really see this getting any better. The new album is tanking."

Judge could only picture the tanks Jerry had told him about, the ones that would be pulled out in Armageddon. He said they'd roll over their enemies, crushing the rotten bones of anyone who stood in their way. *Why would people leave if an album is doing as well as a tank?* "I don't mind not getting paid as long as you're feeding me and getting me away from-"

"Are you in some kind of trouble? We can't have that-" Yolanda was interrupted when Jammer poked his shaking head between them.

"We on yet?"

"Just as soon as the sound crew moves the drums up and sets the levels," she said.

Jammer nodded vigorously and ran away from the stage in a full-on sprint. "Is he always like that?" Judge asked.

Yolanda checked on her clipboard. "Yep. That's where all the money's going. That, and out the door when Four Times Quiet drops off this tour after tonight. They were the only thing keeping any real money coming in."

As they pulled the drumhead that read 4XQ off the stage, Judge saw what she meant. The theater, which had been jammed full of people a minute ago was now just a fragment of the previous crowd. Regardless, Jammer ran onstage like he was on fire. Simmons walked up behind Judge carrying a guitar, patted him on the shoulder and said "Sorry about earlier, man." They shook hands and a few drops of blood dripped out of his nose. He wiped it on his sleeve and spoke as if bleeding from the nose was a normal bodily function. "I was a little busy strolling through pleasure town, if you know what I mean. Nice to meet you." Simmons strutted out onto the stage as if he was playing in front of a million adoring fans.

Somehow, Grenade, whom Judge had just seen wasted on the couch in the dressing room, appeared behind the drum kit perched on his stool like he'd just been hung from the gallows. *How does he do that?* Simmons grabbed onto his microphone like the girl had grabbed onto his dick earlier and said "Hello! We are Sherlock Bones!"

After a few consolation claps from the crowd, Judge was hit with a wall of sound. There were muddy guitars, loud drums, thumping bass, garbled vocals. Jammer seemed to have calmed down a bit. Grenade was stiff as a marionette, looking bored and moving just enough to hit the right beats. Simmons, Judge had to admit, looked pretty cool, even though the songs were so terrible. Halfway through the first number, the crowd grew smaller by half and the ones that were left looked disgusted. *I'd hate just standing in a room this empty. How does Simmons look so excited?*

After the first song, someone in the crowd shouted "I'll Fly Away! Play I'll Fly Away!"

I don't know the first thing about music, but anything has to be better than that last song. PLEASE play something else. Simmons sneered and said "We aren't playing any of our old shit anymore!" The band launched into another plodding tune.

As if in reply, Yolanda muttered "And that's why we're going broke."

Stay Cool, Hunny Bunny

It was easy enough for Judge to unload the stage after Sherlock Bones finished their set. It was just him and his thoughts, and every instrument had it's own place to slide into. *Just like Dad's fake activator.* Even carrying them all to the bus by himself was a simple task: living in the Dark Corner and doing everything for himself had prepared him to do well in a life of manual labor. The hard part was actually getting through the band's performance.

The few people that stuck around after the first song were trickling out like a busted colostomy bag. The band continued undeterred and played sludgy, sloppy song after sludgy, sloppy song. Watching Jammer and Grenade at the highs and lows of their physical activity actually grew kind of entertaining for Judge. But Simmons looked pitiful. He was likely the only one on stage who could actually see how bad things were going, and as hard as he tried to defiantly play the songs he wanted, he eventually caved into the dwindling crowd's constant demand to "Play the old stuff!"

The crowd was right. Judge loved the old stuff once Simmons finally caved and played it. It was simple, and quiet, and didn't feel like it was written by a bunch of drug addicts who just wanted to get through it so they could get their next fix. *Is this the song I heard in that pervert's truck earlier?* The lyrics reminded him of Psalm 43, a passage he liked even though Jerry had turned its promises into curses. He turned to Yolanda and said "I think I heard this song earlier today."

Yolanda smiled. *I like that.* "Yeah. This song was huge, but this new stuff..." Simmons grew frustrated and stopped the song, launching back into the same muddy crap that even Judge, who had been starved of any pop culture for the last seven years, grew tired of.

Once all the packing and loading was done after the show, Judge headed back to the bus. Yolanda was sitting on the steps clutching a cell-phone to her pretty head. *Since when are phones that small?* She screamed into her phone. "But we're in the middle of fucking nowhere!...fine!" She hung up and saw Judge standing by the food table, picking at the cold spaghetti. "Well, I hate to tell you this on your first night of this tour, but we're staying here. Next two shows have been cancelled due to lack of interest."

Good thing we're away from the Dark Corner. "How's the band going to take it?"

Yolanda stood up and dialed another number into her phone. "They'll probably be happy. They can go on a bender and not have to worry about call times. I, on the other hand, have to get us a hotel and find a way to pay for it."

Her smile disappeared. *I don't like seeing her sad.* Judge continued to eat the cold spaghetti as Yolanda made her phone calls, each one wearing on her voice. Eventually, Simmons walked out with two worn-in looking women on each arm, one of them sporting a dark purple black eye. Jammer followed with his head tilted up in the air, his top hat giving him the air of a fine British gentlemen who was really just a hobo that stole someone's hat. "Go ahead and go to the back, girls." Simmons smacked one of them on the butt as she walked up the stairs. "Hunny Bunny, what's going on?"

Yolanda's face grew even more annoyed. "We've been canceled in Atlanta and Nashville. We're going to camp out for the next two days in Ninety-Six."

Simmons breathed in for a long whine and said "But-"

Yolanda put her hand up and stopped him. *How can someone so small be so powerful?* "No complaints. We're running out of money and you know why. The hotels are cheaper out in the middle of nowhere. Get on the bus. Judge, pack up those leftovers somewhere other than your mouth and get'em on the bus. We need to get going."

Judge did as she said, then found an empty bunk and settled in. It smelled of old sweat and latex. *It's probably for the best that we're canceled for the next few days. I don't want to be exposed as a fraud so soon. But what'll I do once the tour starts back up?* Judge dozed off quickly out of the old survivalist habit to get as much sleep as you can, whenever you can.

He was jolted awake by the bus stopping, it's air brakes pumping as it parked. He heard voices whizz by, inches from his head. There was a whoosh of air. *Jammer.* Then two giggling women, followed by heavy footsteps. *Simmons and company.* Then the sound of nothing. *That's probably Grenade. I imagine he's half-ghost.*

Pulling back his curtain, Judge saw Yolanda walking down the corridor and started to follow her out. "Sorry, Judge. Us lowly crew are staying in the bus." *But it smells in here.* "Let me check them in and we'll talk about your pay." *Talking to you will be pay enough.* Judge sat by the front door and watched her follow the band into the hotel. The small-town desk clerk stared at them with wide-eyes, but the band didn't care. He'd seen the same aloof look on Zeke when they'd met resistance at protests. *I wish I could not care about things.*

Once the bus driver got out and stumbled towards a diner attached to the hotel, Judge returned to the dark compartment under the bus and got his ratty backpack out. After hauling cases and amplifiers all night, the bag seemed strangely light. *Jerry is dumb to think something so little could cause so much trouble. Still, I don't want to keep it around, even if it is a dud. I'm starting a new life, and this is a sign of my old life.* Judge looked out in the distance across the street and saw a small creek flowing in front of a cotton field. *Perfect. I can just watch it all float away. That'll be pretty darn symbolic.*

Yolanda's pretty voice floated over the air. "Hey, Judge. Want to get some waffles?" Clutching the backpack in his hands like a bunch of dirty laundry, Judge couldn't say no to that question. *I used to love waffles.* He slung it over his shoulder and followed Yolanda into the Denny's. *Can't pass up waffles. I'll get rid of the activator later.*

"I love waffles," he said blankly as he caught up to Yolanda, the backpack smacking his back and clanking along. *That was dumb. Why can't I think of anything more cool to say? I need to figure out what Simmons would say – he's seems to know what to do with girls.*

She smiled at him, amused by his awkward statement. *Awesome.* "Yeah. Good thing, cause you're getting paid in waffles tonight. And possibly for the next few nights. But you can get have as many waffles as you want."

"Fine with me. I won't waffle." *Just stop talking.* She smiled again. *Is that out of pity or did she really find that funny? Maybe I should just let the puns fly.*

The diner was as harshly lit as the truck stop and smelled almost as bad as the vomit Judge left in the trucker's cab. *Maybe I'm not remembering waffles right.* Yolanda ordered a coffee. Judge did the same. When it arrived, Judge sipped his and was astounded that coffee could be so thin and drinkable. "Wow. This coffee is amazing."

Yolanda drank hers and turned her nose up. "Whatever you say." *That was cute. I wonder how cute she'd be if she drank Beard's coffee.* "What's in the bag?" With the coffee mug in his hands, Judge was unable to stop her hands from reaching in and pulling the activator out.

"It's a...." *A what? A radio? A computer? A synthesizer?* "...it's part of a nuclear bomb." *Shit.*

Yolanda started laughing. She pointed at Judge with her tiny fingers. "You are funny." *Ok, so she likes nuclear bombs. Maybe I'm barking up the wrong tree.* She took a delicate sip of her coffee and said "So, where are you from?"

"The upstate. We...uh...lived out in the middle of nowhere."

She scanned her menu. "So you're used to this kind of place?"

This kind of place a diner? Or this kind of place filled with filthy stinky men who lord power over others? "Sure."

Yolanda ordered a grand slam. Judge ordered scrambled eggs and bacon. When the waitress asked if he wanted cheese on the eggs, he ecstatically said "You can put cheese on eggs?!" The waitress took that as a yes.

"God, you really are from out there. I wish I knew what that was like."

Judge slyly slid his bag under his chair. "It's not that great, really. Just a bunch of nothing and weirdos."

"Well, there's weirdos in the city too."

"So you're from a city?" he asked. *This whole talking to girls thing is getting easier every minute.*

"Yep. Brookland. I'd still be there if I hadn't signed up to manage this godforsaken tour." *See Jerry? Beautiful things can come from such a 'godless' place.*

The bell hanging over the door rang and Simmons stumbled in, the two women behind him in even more of a stupor than he was. The noise from their chairs was loud, but they were silent as they sat and stared at the menu with glazed eyes and bloody noses.

His stomach rumbling, Judge stared at the waitress. "This tour. Yeah." *I wonder if this slang still works.* "What up wit dat?"

Yolanda laughed again. Judge liked her laughter, but grew tired of his inability to decipher whether it was out of ridicule or not. Her laughter slowed to small wheezes. She said "What up wit dat, indeed. I mean, you know the story."

Smiling, Judge realized she wasn't just using a euphemism. "What story?"

"You know." She changed her voice from a southern accent to the host of Masterpiece Theatre. "The rise and fall of Sherlock Bones." Judge's face showed no recognition of the story, but only joy as the waitress delivered a plate full of non-powdered eggs and non-burnt bacon. "You really don't know?" she asked.

"I told you I lived…out in a dark corner. We didn't hear much from the outside world."

Yolanda delicately cut all her sausage into bite-sized bits before eating any of it. Judge shoved the food into his mouth. "Sounds nice. Out here, you couldn't escape *I'll Fly Away*. It was like *Nevermind* or *Thriller*. Sold millions of copies. Simmons was a superstar." *He sure does act like it.* "People thought he was a genius, but then it came out that he might not have written the album. The public didn't really care so much about that until their next album came out. I know I didn't. I actually was hired as the tour manager before I heard any of the new stuff. If I *had* known…"

Across the room, Simmons pounded on his table. The waitress waiting on him backed away and motioned for her manager. "I said I want a PBR, and I'm going to get a PBR!" he screamed.

The manager, a giant of a man who either played professional football or moonlighted as a substitute wrecking ball, walked over and stared Simmons down. "I'm sorry sir. We don't serve alcohol here."

The rockstar must have been so out of his mind that he didn't see the size the manager had on him. "What kind of a bumblefuck town is this don't have PBR?" He saw Yolanda sitting across the restaurant with Judge. "Hunny Bunny, come take care of this!"

The manager's accent grew heavier as if the South was rising again in his voice. He put a hearty paw on Simmons shoulder and squeezed. "I don't think you should talk to the lady that way, ya'hear me?"

That sobered Simmons up enough to keep him from getting lynched. Still pouting, he said "Whatever. I'll just have a black coffee, I guess."

Glad he calmed down. I don't want to have to make that manager look bad. "Hunny Bunny? I thought your name is Yolanda. What's that about?"

Yolanda's freckled face was flushed from the embarrassment with Simmons. "You know, Ringo and Hunny Bunny." Her voice grew deep and slow. "'And you will know my name is the Lord when I lay my vengeance upon thee.'"

I don't think that's actually in the Bible. "Doesn't ring a bell."

"Holy shit. I think you're my new favorite person." Judge blushed. She said "It's from *Pulp Fiction*. There's a character named Yolanda, and her boyfriend calls her Hunny Bunny, blah blah blah." She took a long sip of her coffee like she needed it. "It's funny, y'know? My parents named me Yolanda, not because they liked it, but because they were afraid of how my grandma would react if they didn't name me after her." *I know the pain of being cursed by expectations.* "And then, I guess it's not their fault, but they had no idea how big Pulp Fiction would be..." *I still have no idea how big Pulp Fiction is.* "...and that everyone would be calling me Hunny Bunny. It bothered me so much that in college I went on this crusade about how stupid Pulp Fiction is. I searched for every negative review I could find, and believe me, they were hard to find."

I guess I need to watch this movie. "And people still call you that, even though you don't like it?"

"Well...yeah. I wasn't always the prettiest or smartest or whatever..." *I'll believe that never.* "...I hate it, but I try to see it as nice to have something to set me apart."

Judge waved the waitress down like he remembered seeing his mother do. "Can I get a waffle?" He turned back to Yolanda and said "So why don't you just ask people to stop calling you that?"

"I guess...hating my name made me a tough woman, and that's not a bad thing to be. Once you've lived long enough and gotten an identity with something, it's not so easy to run away from it."

Judge's eyes widened at the hot waffle placed in front of him. He pulled his silverware out and said. "It's easier than you'd think." She smiled, set down a twenty dollar bill and left him with his waffle.

What's Cooler Than Being Cool?

Simmons called from the other side of the restaurant. "Are you gonna eat all that?" It started as a shout but turned into a whisper when he noticed that the burly manager was watching and shaking his head.

Judge said "Yes." It wasn't a question Judge was used to hearing. *Of course you eat all your food. You don't always know if the next meal is coming.* Jerry always made them clean their plates, no matter how inedible the food was. The rebuking for not eating all your food, which Judge only had to witness once, was being forced to eat to excess, then to vomit it up and eat it again. "Cause that's how sinners live," Jerry would always say.

Simmons slinked over, glancing at the manager, wary not to get his face caved in. He stared at Judge's waffle with bloodshot eyes and said "I'm hungry, man." Now that Yolanda was gone, he felt comfortable begging.

"Why don't you just order another one?"

Simmons leaned back and ripped open a few packets of saltines that he'd picked up from the waitress' station on the way over. "Don't have any money."

At least we have something in common. "Why?" Judge asked.

Sighing, Simmons said "It's in our contract. While we're on tour, our manager handles all our money. I guess they think I'll

O.D. or something. They're probably right." He shoved the saltines in his mouth as an older couple came in wearing matching Hawaiian shirts. The old man was wearing a khaki fishing cap that might as well have had 'Tourist' embroidered on it.

But it's easier to OD with no food in your system, right? Judge cut his waffle in half and slid it onto Yolanda's empty plate. The rockstar tore into it and swallowed it in two bites. Judge wondered if he'd be able to see a waffle-shaped imprint sticking out of Simmons' meager frame.

When he was done, he leaned back and watched the tourist couple from across the room. The old man pulled out a blood meter, a bottle of insulin and a syringe. He carefully checked his blood as the meter beeped. Then, in a motion Simmons seemed to be dancing to the rhythm of, the tourist man stuck the needle into the bottle, sucked up some brown liquid and flicked the air bubbles out of the plunger with his pointer finger.

The manager was not in the room, and Simmons took advantage. "Hey. Geezer!" The old man looked over. "Yeah you, gramps. I'll give you twenty bucks for that." The old man ignored him, lifted up the hem of his shirt to reveal a hairy stomach and stabbed the needle in. "What is that?"

The old woman put her hand over her chest. "Insulin. He's a diabetic."

"Yeah. Me too," Simmons said. "How much for the rest of that bottle? I've got my own needles in my room." *If he's really a diabetic, why doesn't he have his own insulin? I'm starting to think he might be lying about that.*

The tourist man's voice came out sturdy, like a former drill instructor. "Yeah. I bet those needles are for diabetes." He turned his back to Simmons and studied the menu.

"Old fuckers." He turned to Judge and said "I don't suppose you've got anything tasty on you, do you?"

"I already gave you half my waffle." *Unless that's some kind of double entendre. That trucker showed me that words mean different things out here.*

Simmons laughed a bit under his breath, then suddenly stopped. "No. I'm serious. I'm out. Got any-"

He was interrupted by a pounding on the front doors. They were glass, and everyone could see Jammer attacking the door with the bottom of his fists. He was looking over his shoulder as if something was chasing him. "Let me in! Fast!" came in muffled through the glass.

"Door's open!" the manager said. His booming voice made Simmons jump.

I hope he's ok. Judge looked at his tablemate. *How is Simmons so calm?* "What's wrong with him?" he asked.

Simmons leaned back in his chair and ran his finger over his leftover syrup. "Wrong with him? Looks to me like he's having the trip of his life." He stuck his sticky finger in his mouth and sucked on it. *That looks too much like the girl mouth-fornicating on him earlier. Look away.*

Jammer kept on pounding, and his blood-curdling voice said "Please! I can't be out here!" The waitress walked to the door warily, craning her head around Jammer to make sure he wasn't being chased by the Lizard Man. She opened the door. He jumped in as if he was in an action movie and an explosion was going off behind him, his movements in slow motion until gravity set in and the ground rose to meet him. From the dirty carpet, he looked up at the manager. "Oh fuck! It's just as hot in here!" Jammer stood up, his clothes soaked through with sweat, and ran down a hallway.

"Did he..." Simmons watched Jammer until the swinging door leading out of the diner came to a halt. "Did he take the rest of it? That bastard!" Simmons waved a new waitress over to their table. She was as puffy as a baby and had a little too much hair on her lips. "Babycakes, you don't happen to know if I can get any cactus around here, do you?"

Cactus? We're in the South. The waitress smiled at him and shook her messy head. "No," she said. If I did know, I wouldn't be here, would I?" She smiled again at him, wider this time and giggled as if she was suddenly under his grungy, dirty, godlike rockstar spell.

Simmons said "I think I know where you'd like to be, don't I?" *This won't work, even on an ugly girl like her.*

The waitress's reddening face was more splotchy than flushed. She said "My shift's over at ten, and then I know where I'll be."

Simmons slid a room key to her. She tucked it in her apron and walked off giddily. *Ew. But still, that's a good skill to have.* "How did you do that?"

After watching her bounce and jiggle off, Simmons said "What? C-level pussy? Easy. Even you could get it. Specially with your big hands. You don't play guitar do you?"

"No." *I can break a man's neck with my bare hands and set off a nuclear bomb, though. What'll that get me, other than being burnt to death?*

"Fine. C-level pussy," Simons said. "Still shouldn't be a problem the way you look." *I do know how to pick up pink-bandana truckers.* "Although, I must admit, my charms are starting to wear off a bit recently. I don't get it. I look every bit as fucked up as I did two years ago. Can you believe I used to date Paris Hilton? Horse-faced bitch."

Paris who? "Really? That's...great...that girl you had earlier looked...nice."

"You didn't see her face, did you?" *Not much of it.* "She had a hair lip, but I just made a point to not look at her face." *That's sad.* "Two years ago, before I did *Sexual Lives*, a girl like that would have been a cast-off. Would've ended up fucking a roadie like you. Now? Shit. I'm lucky she'd get with me."

Of all the gigantic rock band's tour buses for me to hop on, it had to be the one where they suddenly have a girl drop off. Judge's eyes widened when he realized what Simmons had meant. He said "She would've gotten with me?" His flabbergastgasm was interrupted by a scream from the kitchen.

Simmons didn't notice it and stared off towards the bus. "Maybe she would've gotten with you if I was sick or something. Used to be if they came around and I had the right drugs, I could handle hundreds a night." *Yeah right.* As out of it as Simmons seemed, he must've had enough of his faculties to see Judge's disbelief. "Yeah? How much pussy have you bagged?"

Judge didn't have time to fumble through an answer. The elephantine manager slapped his paw on Simmons' shoulder. The second scream from the kitchen didn't phase him, but the manager's hand nearly made him piss his pants. "Is that naked guy in the top hat a friend of yours?"

He wasn't naked five minutes ago. Simmons cowered and said "Probably. Yessir. Unless the Nudist Costume convention is in town this weekend. He has always been a fan of Abraham Lincoln..." Simmons gave an easy smile. The manager didn't find it amusing.

"Well. He crawled up in the ice machine and we can't get him out."

"That cunt did take the rest of it..." Simmons stared off in the distance wistfully.

If Jammer stays in that ice machine too long, he is going to lose those precious fingers. Judge remembered a rebuking in February where he spilled coffee on his shirt. Jerry declared that the Lord needed Judge to learn to appreciate what he had, and he ordered Judge had to wear his Summer clothes in Winter. Jerry called it off when the early stages of frostbite set in. He said it was the also the Lord's will that we should appreciate our fingers and toes.

Simmons cowered from the manager and said "Just...he does this all the time. It's just a bad trip. Wait it out and he'll come to his senses."

The manager grabbed the back of Simmons' t-shirt and pulled him to his feet. "No. No waiting it out. I should have known better than to let your kind into my restaurant. I don't give a fig how much your manager paid. Go get him out of my ice machine or I'm calling the cops."

Don't want that. "Want me to go get Yolanda?" Judge said.

Simmons got up and walked towards the kitchen, looking over his shoulder to make sure he was going at the speed the manager wanted. "No. Hunny Bunny's probably already there giving him a hard time."

Sure enough, she was. *I hope I get to know her that well.* The waitress with Simmons' room key was standing next to her with her porcine, hairy arms crossed. "Jammer, come on out! Now!" Yolanda said as her face grew steadily ruddier. She saw Simmons and Judge walk in. "Simmons, get him out! You know we don't get many more free passes from the label."

There was a humming coming from inside the ice machine. Judge recognized it as the song Sherlock Bones opened with at their concert the night before. Simmons stepped up and tapped on the little plastic door keeping the ice cold. "Jammer. Open this door for me. I don't want you to come out. I just...want to know what you did with my mesc."

The small door opened a crack. Jammer's eyes were the color of pale skin after a vicious scratch. "Simmons? Hunny Bunny? New roadie? Hurry up and get in before you burn to death. You're going to melt and the little girls are going to suck you up with a straw. I'm going to open the door quick so you can get in, but do it fast so they can't reach their straws in. One, two-"

Jammer swung the door open. He was sitting Indian style on a pile of ice. His lips had started to turn blue. As his only piece of clothing, the top hat was holding up remarkably well. Simmons smiled at the waitress and said to the manager "Look. This'll pass, but I need to get in there with him to make sure he makes it through." As he was lifting his skinny leg to crawl into the ice machine, the manager grabbed his shoulders and pulled him back.

Wagging his finger in Simmons face, he said "Like heck you will! If you don't get him out now, I'll do it." He reached into the ice machine and grabbed Jammer's naked leg.

"Too hot!" Jammer screamed as he kicked his leg around, to free himself from the manager's grasp.

The manager scraped Jammer's leg over the opening as he yanked and the ice turned pink with blood. "Stop!" Simmons said as he swung at the manager, but the big man caught Simmons' weak fist in his other hand. Yolanda started to yell something incomprehensible.

"That's it. I'm beating the shit out of you two, then I'm calling the cops," the Manager said. *Can't have that.* Holding 2/3rds of Sherlock Bones in his hands, the manager was almost too easy of a target. *And here I thought I was done asking myself 'What would Zeke do?'* Judge pushed Yolanda away and kicked straight at the Manager's knee. He collapsed exactly like Judge wanted. On his knees, he was no taller than Yolanda. Judge brought his fist hard on the bottom of his manager's jaw. *Just like Jerry taught me.* The manager fell to the ground unconscious. *Just like Jerry said he would.*

I don't want to do this, but I want to see the cops even less. Judge turned to the portly waitress, raised his hand and said "You're not going to call the cops, are you?"

Simmons and Yolanda were wigging out at their new roadie's combat skills. The waitress kept her cool. "I won't call the cops. I hate that guy."

Yolanda's face was as red as Jammer's eyes. Her voice grew solid. "We've got to go! Just...Jammer! Come out, now!" Her Mom-voice didn't work. He slammed the door shut. *He must've seen the little straw-girls.*

Judge looked into the dining room at the old couple sitting there, still waiting on their drinks. *We've got to get out of here. I don't want to hurt them. Does this thing have wheels?* He saw that it did and said "Yolanda, get everyone on the bus." He ripped the ice machine's power cord from the wall and rolled it out the door. Simmons followed as Yolanda ran down the hotel hallway, pounding buttons on her phone.

I wish he'd help me push this. Judge made it out to the parking lot. Simmons was bouncing around him ecstatically. "Holy shit, man! You saved my life. You laid him out! That was certified badass material, right there."

They made it to the bus. Huffing, Judge said "Simmons, shut up and help me lift this onto the bus!"

"I couldn't lift that if I was on hog, man." He ran on to the bus. *Great. I saved him, and he just leaves me here to...do what? I guess I have to drag Jammer out.* As Judge was about to crack the ice machine open, Simmons floated down to the ground on a retractable ramp protruding from the door of the bus. "After the last time this happened, the label had this installed. Pretty fucking sweet, right?" *The last time this happened?!*

Judge pushed the ice machine up the ramp by himself as Simmons hopped around. Yolanda and the driver came running up behind them. Grenade was already on the bus, his bag in his lap. *I hope I don't ever have to fight him. He's gotta be some kind of ninja or something.* The driver started the bus up with a roar and scraped out of the parking lot. Judge turned to Yolanda, ignored how profusely she was sweating and said "What do we do if the cops show up?"

"They won't." She pulled out her phone and dialed a number. "The label'll get us out of this one, but I think we might be…yes…" She walked off towards the back, talking into her phone. Judge took a breath and followed her.

Grenade and the ice machine had moved to the back room of the bus. No one had seen how it happen. *That Grenade is scary. Maybe he has terrorist training too.* Simmons came up behind Judge and smacked him on the shoulders. "Man, you're the-"

"Simmons, get back here!" Yolanda's voice was the screech of a hawk that just had its catch stolen.

"Uh-oh," Simmons said. "Hunny Bunny doesn't think this is funny." He stepped past Judge and trotted off into the back room. "What is it now?"

Judge couldn't tell if her face was wet with tears or sweat. "Well, Simmons, they'll fix it, but that was the last time. I spoke with Mr. Davis personally. He said they've bailed you out enough. If you fuck up one more time, it's your fault. It'll be your ass getting raped in jail. I hear the big guys like long hair."

Simmons put his arm around Judge's back. "I'm not worried. Not with Mr. Fix-It here. D'you see the way he laid out that fuck face?" *If I had known he was a fuck face, I might have punched him in the stomach instead.* Yolanda rolled her eyes as Simmons turned, looked at Judge and said "Fuck the label. You're my new life-saver, right brother?"

Judge smiled even though he had no idea what Simmons meant. He just liked how it sounded. *Brother? I could use one of those.*

The Old Shit

Yolanda was the sort of person who proved that miracle workers aren't all hocus-pocus and faith; they're just people who know how to make a gentle push the most powerful act in the world. Without any help from the label, she singlehandedly repaired Sherlock Bones' tour.

While everyone else was still waiting for Jammer to crawl out of that ice machine, she was on the phone with every club promoter she could find. Judge could hear the promoters for the bigger arenas laughing at her, but the smaller club promoters were practically salivating at the prospect of a band like Sherlock Bones playing in their spaces.

She had gone through a list of names, numbers and promotions three pages long. Judge loved the way she would look determined when they said no, and justified when they said yes. After a particularly quick phone conversation, she breathed a sigh of relief and said "All right guys, listen up. Judge, can you open up the ice machine? Jammer needs to hear this." Judge did as she said. Sitting in water that had turned pink from the cut on his leg, Jammer was asleep, curled up like a baby in the womb. "Wake him up for me."

"Jammer. Jammer!" Judge knocked the top of the ice machine.

Jammer's eyes opened slowly and he smiled. "Oh, hey guys. I was just dreaming that I was fucking some broad, and I got her pregnant, but it wasn't just my sperm. Her pussy sucked my whole body up, and I was the baby in her womb, and I was growing smaller. Being a baby is awesome."

"Damnit," Simmons said. He reached his hand in and pulled Jammer out. "You better find some powerful shit to replace whatever you took." Judge tossed him a blanket and Jammer proceeded to swaddle himself in it. *It would be nice to feel like a baby again.*

Yolanda cleared her throat and everyone turned to look at her. "So, I've got some news. I found fill-in dates for the arena dates that dropped us. Which is all of them." Simmons sighed loudly and crossed his arms. Yolanda ignored him like she had been practicing it for months. "While the promoters didn't want 4000 people in a 12,000 seat arena, club promoters would *kill* to have 4000 people trying to clamor into a 1500 seat place. So, we are playing clubs from now on."

4000 people? There weren't even that many at that arena the other day. Simmons moaned like a child about to throw a tantrum. Yolanda ignored him and said "And, in what is a genius move, if I may say so myself, we aren't doing opening bands anymore. Simmons, you can complain all you want, but people only want to hear *I'll Fly Away*, so you're going to play that-"

"What?!" he said in a wounded voice. "I worked hard on *Sexual Lives of Conjoined Twins!*"

"Don't start that shit again. You've come out numerous times, in the press even, and said that you didn't put much effort into the new album. Now you're saying you worked hard on it? Any idiot could tell you how much it sucks."

"But-"

She waved her hand in the air as if she was swatting a fly. It shut Simmons up. He sunk into his couch and she said "Don't act like it isn't your fault the crowds aren't showing up. And don't act like you can't fix it. Everyone loves *I'll Fly Away*. I love *I'll Fly Away*. You should play *I'll Fly Away*." Jammer sat wrapped in his blanket cocoon, tranquil and oblivious. Grenade stared straight ahead motionless. Simmons saw they weren't objecting, and got up to storm out. "Simmons, wait. I'm not cruel. You'll get to play the new album too, but only in the support slot." He sat down. "You can play the entirety of *Sexual Lives*, then take a break, then play *I'll Fly Away*. We won't have to split the take, the fans will come for *I'll Fly Away*, and you get to play the new stuff." She sighed as if she was about to swallow some bad medicine. "You might even make some new fans." *She's not a very good liar.*

Simmons looked at the door as he thought about it. He shook his head and said "Nope. I don't want to do that." He picked up the TV remote and started flipping channels. "We'll have to figure something else out."

"This is a win-win, Simmons. Everyone gets everything they want if you just give a little." Simmons kept shaking his head. Yolanda raised her voice. "Well, I don't really give a shit, Simmons. We're driving to Nashville. We're playing at Rockettown. You're playing both albums. It's going to happen. Think of it as getting back to your roots."

Under his breath, he said "I fucking hate my roots." *I concur, brother.* Yolanda walked out the door, leaving Judge sitting with the former biggest band in the world. Judge and Simmons watched her go. "I could so hate fuck her right now." He looked at Judge. "What do you think?"

What does hate fuck mean? "About what?"

"About all this," he said with a limp flourish of his hand. "Playing the old songs. I mean, I thought people were starting to get wet on the new stuff, but maybe I'm just being delusional..."

Jammer started to snore. It was soft and high pitched and Judge had to try not to laugh. "I really don't know. I haven't heard either of them."

Simmons reached over the sleeping Jammer and pulled a small grey box out of Grenade's jacket pocket. He didn't react in the least bit. "You must have been living under a fucking rock." *Something like that.* Simmons tossed it to Judge, and then pulled headphones out of a drawer and handed those over. "Listen to both of them. I'd like to hear what you have to say, as a new listener, unspoiled by my previous shit."

Judge looked at in his hands. *What is this*? He started poking it, but nothing happened. Simmons reached over and grabbed it. "Seriously? Where the fuck are you from?" He ran his fingers over it and it lit up. *It's the future already.* Simmons found the Sherlock Bones album.

"I hate my...my fucking roots, too," Judge said. Simmons nodded at him and showed him how the iPod worked. Judge put it in his ears and *Sexual Lives of Conjoined Twins* poured into his ears. It was sludgy and dull and stupid. Simmons stared at Judge listening and smiled broadly, waiting to be rained with compliments. *This is too weird*. Judge paused it and said "Can I listen to it on my own and let you know?"

Simmons' face dropped. "Oh. Ok. Yeah. Fine." Judge got up to walk out of the room.

"I...I like what I've heard so far." *Lying is getting too easy*. Simmons smiled at him and pulled a bottle of whiskey out of Grenade's pocket as Judge shut the door behind him.

As Judge shuffled towards his bunk, Yolanda saw him clutching the iPod and called to him. "Is he making you listen to it? Please, *please* be honest with him about it. He seems to really like you and I need all the help I can get."

He likes me? What do I do? I've never had the option to lie before, but if the rest of this album is anything like the first minute, this'll be a hard lie to tell. I need a new brother, but...Yolanda makes me feel something new. Life in the Dark Corner might have been hard, but at least I didn't have to deal with drama bullshit like this.

Judge crawled into his little coffin bed and felt something hard pushing into his back. *Oh yeah. The activator. I could get used to forgetting about it.* He rearranged it so he could lie down comfortably and stuck the ear buds in his ears. It was worse than Yolanda had made it sound. Every song was the same: a few sludgy chords blared over a meandering mid-tempo drumbeat. Simmons' warbling vocals sounded like he was in the middle of taking a gigantic dump. None of it was compelling.

Judge knew absolutely nothing about music. He had to sneak anything other than hymns past his dad before they moved to the Dark Corner, and while there, no one ever made any music because Jerry viewed it as a distraction from the Lord's true purpose. His ignorance with music made his indifference to *Sexual Lives of Conjoined Twins* all the more telling.

The only variance Judge could tell between the songs was in the lyrics, and even these were hard to tell apart. "Threesome With Only Two Bodies" extolled the virtues of hearing two moans at once and being able to 'stick your dick between their separate faces' because 'having sex with Siamese twins is aces.' "First Orgasm", Judge figured out, was a dialogue between the two heads sharing one climax. "Conjoined Twins at the Orgy" was full of words Judge didn't know, but really didn't care to learn. *Gross. No temptation here.* "Make Out with Myself", "Head From Two Heads" and "Siamese, Suck it Please" only shared six separate verses between them. "Two Ponytails to Pull, Two Necks to Choke, One Pussy to Fuck" actually had less words in the song than in the title. Judge hated it. *Do I really want Simmons as my new brother?*

After slogging through that audio atrocity, Judge had to force himself to put on *I'll Fly Away*, but he was reeled in immediately from the first note. *Simmons did this one too?* The songs were every bit as simple as the ones on *Sexual Lives*, but instead of just sounding sophomoric, it became elegant and creative. The melodies were creative without being flashy and made Simmons' ugly voice somehow more beautiful. Judge quickly recognized the Biblical influence in the lyrics, and all the hatred and cloudiness Jerry had put into his head started to disappear. *Is this what Holy Spirit actually feels like?* Judge almost wanted to start praying. Suddenly, Jesus wasn't so bad as long as people weren't telling you to detonate nuclear bombs in the middle of a crowded stadium for him.

Once it was done, Judge started it again. When he finished it the second time, he listened again and hummed along. *I think even I would sound good singing something this glorious.* He fell asleep smiling during his fourth journey through the album. He had good dreams. Zeke and Amittai were in them, and they were singing along and smiling.

The bus squealing and jerking to a halt woke Judge up. He pulled back the curtain and looked out to see Yolanda sitting in the same spot at the front of the bus, her phone to her ear, her voice making miracles out of nothing. Judge crawled out, stared out the window and saw that they were next to a warehouse in the middle of nowhere. Yolanda hung up her phone and said "Evening, Judge. Ready to earn your keep?"

"As if you could actually pay me." He laughed at his own joke and looked towards the back of the bus. The door was shut. Jammer's strange high-pitched snoring was coming through the door. "Do we need to wake them up or something?"

Yolanda said "No. Honestly, the less time Simmons has to brood over this, the better it'll be. The bottom compartment will be open. Unload everything and I'll rustle us up some dinner."

Judge did as she said, humming *I'll Fly Away* as he worked. The local sound technician started hooking up the instruments as Judge brought them in. Once it was all done, Judge saw that

Simmons had crawled out of the bus and was skulking around the door. He was trembling and looked like he hadn't slept at all. "What did you do with my bag?" he asked. "The red one."

"Put it in your dressing room. You ok?"

He stumbled towards the venue. "I'll be fine. Come with me." They arrived in a ramshackle room whose walls were mere corrugated siding. "Only one couch?!" Grenade was already camped out in a beat-up leather chair. Simmons dug through the bag, pulled out a velvet pouch and stepped into the bathroom.

Judge looked at Grenade. "So. Grenade. How's your day?"

There was no answer. *And I thought my Dad had no use for body language.* Simmons stepped out of the bathroom. His shaking had ceased and there was a light in his eyes that must have been waiting for him in the bathroom. He put an empty Ziploc baggie in his pocket and said "So how'd you like it?"

I gotta find an easy way to say this. I already drove Zeke away. I need Simmons to keep me on this tour, and I don't mind having friends. "Like what? The albums?"

Simmons sat down on the couch and said "Yeah. How'd you like *Sexual Lives?*"

Sounded like shit. "Sounded like shit." *I didn't mean to say that out loud. I've got to stop thinking in such coherent, believable sentences.*

Stretching his arms out, Simmons calmly said. "Yeah? Well, what do you know?"

I've got to fix this. "I...that came out wrong. It wasn't that bad...or...I can't lie to you. As a friend, the new album is terrible. Just...I don't know what you were thinking. *I'll Fly Away* is great and you're acting like it's some curse." For a brief second, Simmons showed his teeth and Judge thought he was going to have to fight him, but it was just the drugs kicking in. "We all make mistakes, you know? But you should be proud to have been a part of something as great as *I'll Fly Away*. I don't know the whole story and I'm no expert, but I say if something good is happening, you grab it and ride it as far as it takes you."

The rockstar remained calm. "You're right." *Is it going to be that easy?* "You're no expert, and neither is anyone else. People don't get it. It's supposed to be terrible, y'know? That's what makes it so good. It should've been a huge seller." *I'd think writing a good album would be a better seller than a bad one, but what do I know?* "But...fuck it, right? As long as it pays for my brown, I'll roll with it. Doesn't mean I have to be happy about it. Doesn't mean Hunny Bunny has to be a bitch about it, neither." He put a wireless headset microphone over his ear. "It's all just been a play from the beginning anyways." He started to apply black mascara. "Dinner ready yet?"

"I'll go check." *I hope he isn't angry at me. Not everyone gets someone as earnest as Zeke or Simmons in their life.* Yolanda was by the buses handing money to a delivery boy.

She started to hand the bags of food to Judge, but she looked at him and squinted. "Are you ok? You look...oh my God, did you tell Simmons the truth?"

"Yeah," he said. "He didn't take it too well. He's going to do what you say, but I think he hates me now."

"Give him five minutes. He'll forget every bad word you said. And I hope it was a lot of bad words. Colorful ones. Take these to the guys. Tell them soundcheck is in twenty."

Jammer must have smelled the food. Still cradled in his blanket, he jumped off the bus and ran towards the dressing room. "I'm fucking starving!" *So much for the big peaceful baby.* Judge followed Jammer and handed the food to Simmons.

He was his normal, cheerful, drugged-out self. "Thanks, brother. You're the fuckin' man!" *Yolanda was right.* "You want a hit of China White with your cheeseburger?"

Jerry said there would be a lot of temptation out here, but this doesn't interest me in the least bit. "No thanks. I'd like to stay on this side of the ice machine."

Simmons laughed easily. "Right fuckin' on, man."

During the sound check, groupies started to show up by the bus. Yolanda told them to hold on and got Judge's attention. "Judge, it's a Saturday, so Simmons will only want redheads.

Take the gingers to their dressing room." She pointed a finger at two Latina twins whose heels made it up to her knee. "The rest of you, boo-fucking-hoo."

I wonder if these are C-level, or if this new tour is raising the quality of the groupies. Will I get some? Would I want it? These girls look like wet dogs, and they're not Yolanda. Judge let them into the dressing room as Simmons moaned the old songs through the speakers in sound check. *Sounds good, but it would sound even better if he tried.*

They came back from the sound check. Judge finally got to see Grenade move. His plain walk was nothing special. Simmons slapped Judge on the back. "Do-the-carpets-match-the-drapes-day. Fuckin' A, man." Jammer started clapping and jumping up and down as Simmons shut the door. *I'd rather be with Yolanda anyways.*

As Judge made his way to the stage, he could hear Simmons moaning and giggling as if he was standing in the room with them. *Where is that coming from?* Yolanda caught Judge staring at the ceiling and said "He does this every day. Just get used to it."

"Yeah, ladies. Suck on that..." Simmons moaned over the speakers.

"The sound guy goes on break before the show starts, Simmons forgets to cut his headset mic off, and we get to hear his pre-show warm-up. I'm just glad that microphone doesn't transmit out smells." *What would it smell like?*

Judge tried to picture what was going on inside the dressing room. "Can't we just tell him to cut his microphone off?"

Simmons shouted "Stick it in my asshole!"

Yolanda laughed. "I always do remind him to cut it off. You learn to laugh at it." Yolanda's phone rang, and she took the call. Judge sat on the stage by himself, stared at the empty room and listened to Simmons' depraved yelps. *A brother who doesn't know how to cut himself off? Sounds familiar. At least with Simmons I can laugh it off and not have to worry about getting a concussion.*

Who Do You Pull For?

Yolanda tapped Judge on the shoulder and said "I don't think we want to be anywhere near the stage when he starts in with *Sexual Lives.*" *She must have read my mind.* "We can hang out in their dressing room until they're done." *Hot damn.*

Judge followed Yolanda into the dressing room. It was a mess of used condoms, empty baggies, powdery residue and hairspray smell. She sat down on the couch, cut the TV on and motioned for Judge to sit down next to her. *I hope she isn't reading my mind now.*

"Game's on. Who do you pull for?"

The game? Judge looked at the TV and saw a stadium rocking. *100,000 people, all with their own 100,000 voices. A couple million in the city around. I wonder if Jerry found a TV so he could watch to see if my bomb goes off. I hope he's watching this same thing right now and I pray that he feels crushingly disappointed...but what will he do to dad when it doesn't happen?*

Yolanda saw Judge frowning. "You ok?"

"Yeah. I'm fine. I just...don't watch football too often."

"Me neither. But, my parents are there and I need to know whether I should act disappointed or not when I go home for Thanksgiving." *The bomb would have killed her parents.* Judge could feel the creak in his back that sleeping on top of the activator had given him. *If dad gave me a decoy activator, why am I still worrying about this?* Yolanda broke his concentration and said "So how was Simmons after you told him how you liked *Sexual Lives*? Did he tell you it was supposed to be bad?"

"He did. I don't think I really understand rock music, so I guess I'll have to take his word for it."

Yolanda shifted in her seat. Her knee touched the side of Judge's leg and he instinctively backed away. "Well, it's a load of bullshit. This critic in *Rolling Stone* couldn't figure it out. The new album was so terrible, but *I'll Fly Away* is so good, and he couldn't reconcile the two. He said that Simmons must have done it on purpose. As if he's some genius postmodern performance artist playing a long joke on the public. I guess that argument might make sense until you actually meet Simmons and realize that he can hardly plan what drugs he's going to take in the next hour. The rumors that he didn't write *I'll Fly Away* have got to be true. There's no other way to explain it. Did you listen to *Fly*?"

The TV showed a blimp-shot of the stadium from high above. The height of it made Judge dizzy and he had to look away. "I did. It was...beautiful. Amazing. I've never heard anything like it." *I didn't really think about the writing of it before. It was so great I kind of just got the impression that it appeared out of air.* "It is hard to believe that Simmons wrote it, especially if he owns up to writing the second one. You'd figure he'd be proud of it, but he's just..."

"An asshole about it? I feel the same way. I signed up as tour manager cause I loved that first album, thought I could get in on the ground floor of the greatness that would be the second album, but then it came out and I couldn't get out of my contract. Before tonight, he refused to ever play any songs from it. And if he ever did play the old stuff, it was always a joke to him." She looked at her watch. "But...he might be the king of all assholes, but you can bet I'm going out there when he plays that second set."

I was kinda just hoping we could sit here all night. Me and her. She looks pretty good, and I know what this room can do to women and I wanted to finish watching the game and try to pinpoint the moment when Jerry is going to go insane. "Yeah, I was wondering how a girl like you got on tour with a guy like Simmons."

"A girl like me? What do you mean?" She sounded defensive. *Must be a reflex from being around Simmons so much.*

Judge's body tightened up like it did whenever Zeke was about to hit him. "I meant...an intelligent, nice person. You're nothing like any of the guys in the band or the girls that come running to them."

She turned her eyes back on the game. *Shit.* "I'll take that as a compliment, I guess," she said. *Score.* "It's just that, *I'll Fly*

Away opened so many doors for me. Spiritually, I mean. My parents were hardcore atheists." *Those aren't just boogeymen Jerry created to rile the men up?* "They said they wanted me to explore all religions so I could choose what I wanted when I grew up, but the only exposure I got was them causing a ruckus when we sang Christmas songs in elementary school. God, they could be embarrassing about it." *I bet my stories are more embarrassing.* She turned her pretty eyes at Judge. "And I was an asshole about religion, making fun of the Christian kids in school, but then in college this album was everywhere, and it made me feel...something I didn't know I could feel. It didn't make me start going to church or anything but..."

"It made you feel that God might really love us?"

"Exactly."

Judge's stomach turned when Yolanda gaze went deeper. It was an entirely different feeling from when he was listening to *I'll Fly Away* the night before, but it was every bit as beautiful. He almost spilt the beans. "Yeah. I was raised the same way, but different. My family were militant Christians." *Slow down.* "I mean...they were crazy about it, taking me to protest at abortion clinics and stuff. It was rammed down my throat so much that it made me hate all of it. That's why I ran away with you. But...I don't know how, but those songs almost made me...I don't know how to put it...it makes me think that there's something there. I think my family felt that feeling at some point too, and just took it the wrong way."

"That's crazy." *You don't know the half of it.* "The album was huge, and everyone had a copy, but I've never met anyone else who felt the same exact thing about it that I did." Yolanda turned her whole body towards Judge, and now it was like she was looking into him instead of at him. They stared at each other for a few seconds before she shut her eyes and leaned towards Judge, her lips coming together in a soft pucker.

Oh shit. What do I do? The door slammed open and the ginger groupies were giggling. *Oh thank God.* Yolanda leaned back as Simmons started laughing. "Oh shit! Hunny Bunny, were you about to try to fuck Judge?" Simmons said, stumbling. "You were! What a whore!" She stood up and shouldered her way past Jammer and out into the hallway. "Judge, if you wanted some pussy, all you had to do was ask me. You didn't have to go after Hunny Bunny's dirty old pussy." *How does he know if it's dirty*? Simmons pushed a girl forward. "Take her if you want to. B-level, on the motherfucking house."

Judge looked at her. Her skirt was practically non-existent and in some states the amount of makeup she was wearing would have qualified as a mask and disallowed her from entering banks. *No thanks. I guess I'm a fan of dirty old pussy.* Simmons saw the refusal on his grimacing face and said "No? Then get the fuck out! I've only got twenty minutes." Judge got up to leave as Grenade took his place on the couch. Jammer ran into the bathroom. As Judge shut the door behind him, he heard Simmons shout "All right, bitches! Let's see how many times y'all can make me cum in...18 minutes!" The girls giggled like a pack of hyenas chewing on carrion before the laughter was muffled to sound like children talking with their mouths full.

There might have been music over the loudspeakers in the auditorium, but in that hallway all Judge could hear was Simmons moaning in pleasure over his always-on headset microphone. It was like a cruel joke. *All the sounds I think I want to make with Yolanda are coming from him and ten girls who aren't half as amazing as she is.* Judge walked quickly to escape the hallway and its echoing love. He found Yolanda standing on the side of the stage staring out at the packed house.

"I was wrong," she said, not looking at Judge, her face still flush from the embarrassment. "Look at all these people. We can't be the only ones who feel that way about that first album." *Damnit Simmons. I can't get away from people who are just too damn earnest and out-loud about everything. And now Yolanda won't even look at me.* The sound guy came over the monitors and asked Judge to test the instruments. He reluctantly went, unable to think of anything to say back to Yolanda.

When the band came back out for their second set, Judge stood next to Yolanda again and watched. It was beautiful, like everyone in the crowd was Judge's brother and sister. It became like a massive church service, and Judge was surprised when had to hold back tears. Yolanda let hers flow freely. *Is this what Pentecostal Jake feels like when he speaks in tongues?* Occasionally, he'd think that Yolanda was looking at him and he'd try to glance back at her so they could stare into each other again. *It's ok. I'll kiss you this time and Simmons can't interrupt us. And if he talks to you like that again I'll beat the shit out of him.*

But it never happened. As soon as the set ended, she ran off to the bus. By the time Judge was done loading up, she was silent in her bunk, the curtain closed. *The woman I love is only inches away on the other side of a thin piece of molded plastic. It's going to be a long night.*

And You Will Know That I Am the Lord, When I Lay My Vengeance Upon Thee

Judge couldn't sleep. He tried thinking about what he'd do when the tour was over – disappear in the great redwood forest? Find a job as a sailor and travel the world? Make a costume and spend evenings fighting crime? – but the thoughts kept being interrupted by Yolanda's tiny, cute sleep breaths. *Like the wind whipping through a blooming dogwood.* He couldn't stop picturing how she looked when she made them. *Her mouth is probably slightly open. The worry wrinkles on her forehead will be gone. I wouldn't be able to see those pretty eyes, but.....* "Shit. I'm not sleeping anytime soon."

He crawled out of his bunk and looked at Yolanda's. *Simmons would probably just hop in there with her. What would she do if I just crawled in with her? Probably hate me forever.* Jammer's laughter flowed out from the back room. *Those guys are always up so late. What are they doing when there aren't groupies around?* He approached the door and knocked lightly.

Simmons' harsh whisper came through the door. "Sorry Hunny Bunny. We'll be more quiet." High-pitched giggling came from inside. "Shut up, man!"

"Simmons? It's me, Judge."

The door cracked open and Simmons poked his head out in a cloud of smoke. "Judge? Everything all right, man?"

"Yeah. Can't sleep." *Do I sound like a four year old?* "Can I hang out with you guys for a while?"

Simmons opened the door and motioned Judge in. Grenade was doing his usual corpse pose. Jammer was squeezing a forearm shaper and laughing maniacally. The singer plopped down on the couch and said "Can't sleep, right? I can tell from that throbber in your shorts." Judge put his hands over his crotch. *I didn't even notice.* "It's Hunny Bunny, right? Queen blue balls herself."

"No...it's...I just have to pee and-"

"This isn't a bathroom, Judge. And if you came in here to get your rocks off...I'm not in college anymore. I might be into some weird shit, but I told myself I'd never suck a dick again."

Ew. Judge's boner magically disappeared. *If that's all I had to do to make it go away, I could have avoided all those penis scabs back in the Dark Corner.* "All right...it is Yolanda," he conceded. "I just...I can't stop thinking about her. And what you saw earlier-"

"I'll tell you, man. You don't get where I am on top of Mount Pussy by just sitting around and waiting for it to come to you. You got to climb, brother." Simmons got up and opened the door. "Get up and crawl in bed with her. If she gets angry, see it as an invitation. A girl like her wants it that way."

What does he mean a girl like her? I don't think she'd fit in on Daddy Issues Sunday. Judge said "I thought about that, but...I don't know if that would work." He sat down next to Grenade. "I just want to go to sleep and forget about her. See how tomorrow works out."

"Well, which is it?" Simmons asked.

"What?"

"Do you want to go to sleep or do you want to forget about her?"

This isn't going to turn into some weird science fiction story, is it? "I don't...I don't think I understand what you mean."

Simmons turned around and started digging through a drawer. He pulled out two Ziploc bags. One had a couple dozen blue pills. The other held a roll of tape. "I got..." Simmons put the bags up to his face and squinted. "These will put you to sleep. These will help you forget about her for a while...I think."

Drugs. I've seen how these guys are when they're high. Grenade is a statue. Jammer is a lightning bolt. Simmons jumps through the entire spectrum of human emotion. But then again, they're kinda like that when they're not high. Unless they are just high 100% of the time. Could be possible. "Thanks, man, but I don't think so. I've always heard that-"

Jammer's laugh turned into a girlish titter. *Is he laughing at me?* Simmons ignored it and said "I've always heard that drugs were bad too. Heard it every day from my Mom and Dad and my teachers and my minister and my friends. But fuck them, right? Look where I am now. I learned to stop listening to people like that a long time ago."

And isn't that what I'm trying to do? Jerry talked about how drugs were weapons the government had unleashed on the populace to make them soft. But he also said that bananas were the most sinful fruit. *Fuck Jerry.* "Ok. Fine. As long as you say I'll be ok. I guess...the sleeping one."

Simmons reached into the bag with the roll of tape. As he brought it out, Judge saw that little pale yellow stickers dotted the tape. Simmons delicately peeled one of them off with a guitar pick and handed it over. He said "Put that on your tongue."

Judge held it between his thumb and forefinger. "Should I get in my bed before I take it?"

"It doesn't work that fast. You should hang out with us until then. You'll know when it kicks in."

Take this, Jerry. Judge slid the guitar pick over his tongue. The sticker turned into mush in his mouth. "Bleh."

Simmons held the bags up to his face again and squinted as if they had tiny words printed on them. "Shit."

"What?" Judge asked in a panic.

Simmons peeled off his own sticker and set it on his tongue. "Sorry man. I don't think you're going to be sleeping for a while. Just...roll with it, ok?"

Blood rushed to Judge's face. *Feels like the time Jerry hung me on the cross upside down because I got James the Brother and James the Lesser mixed up.* "Why? What did I take? What did you-"

He was silenced as the light in the room started to change into a color Judge had never seen before. *I wouldn't even know how to describe it. Would finding a new color make you rich? Then I could just buy my way out of jail. I'll call it 'Judgium'. Yolanda will have to love me when I give her a new Judgium colored pantsuit set. This is getting weird.*

The room around Judge started to wash away like watercolor paint in a rainstorm. The ceiling blended together into a muddy brown and washed down towards Simmons face, which dripped off into a pleasant blue. Soon the dirty carpet floor joined with all of it and disappeared outside the bottom of Judge's vision.

Behind it all, Judge was surprised to find out that the backroom of the bus was actually in the woods of the Dark Corner. Now that the room had washed away, Judge was alone in the woods. *Beautiful as ever. I don't miss being around Jerry and the Lord, but these pines smell much fresher than Simmons' constant sour haze of smoke and sex.*

Judge tried to walk and found that instead he was floating. *Neat.* The sun, high in the sky, started pulsing in a mad rhythm.

"Judge! It's me – God!" *God talking from the Sun. Makes perfect sense.*

"Damn right it makes sense." *Hang on...something is different. Oh yeah. I'm on drugs. I know this breeze and this smell and this air, but this is a hallucination.*

"No. No hallucination. This is really God. I am really God." *That's exactly what a hallucination would say.*

"No it isn't. Listen. I need to tell you something. Judge, no matter what you think, you *are* my chosen one." Jerry and Zeke and Amittai and the rest of *The Hand* appeared next to a giant tree. They howled in tongues and worshipped madly.

Wait. This is my hallucination. I don't have to see this if I don't want to. Judge thought hard. He closed his eyes and pictured them all somewhere else, pictured the wind carrying them away and putting them in the diner the band had escaped from. When he opened his eyes, *the Hand* was still in the woods, writhing in ecstasy.

The Sun pulsed in rhythm with his words. "That's not going to work, Judge. This isn't *your* hallucination. I'm really God, and I can only speak in truth. I want you to know that all of it, everything Jerry ever taught you is true." *Whatever.* "Don't sass me. Every face Zeke kicked in, that Officer he killed. I wanted it." *Shut up.* "The bomb your Dad made? It's real too, and I taught him how to make it. I want it to kill millions. And your name? I picked it from the stars and gave it to your father.

I want *you* to kill millions." *Please shut up.* "I won't shut up. I can't. I sing through the Earth, and I only sing the truth. You need to know this. You're going to die, Judge."

The Sun's pulsing started to burn Judge's eyes, and he turned to watch *The Hand*. Their tongues had silenced, and now, they were dancing. *I'm glad I never had to see this in real life.* "This is more real than you know, son." They danced in place until Jerry started to dance towards a distant hill. The others formed a line behind him and danced off into the distance. Judge watched them and saw Zeke bobbing up and down, Beard twirling his arms like a reed in a storm, his father pirouetting with a grace most ballerinas would have killed for. The look on their faces shined pure contentedness, and Judge started to grow envious as they disappeared over the other side of the hill.

The scene changed. Judge was on a hilltop overlooking a giant football stadium. *That's Brice stadium.* "Yes it is," the Sun said. "And now it isn't." A mushroom cloud bloomed over the stadium and everything disappeared into nothing. A shockwave came off of it and barreled toward Judge. "And then you won't be there." Everyone in Brookland became brothers and sisters of dust. The wave hit Judge and he joined the family. He felt his body tear apart and drift away on the air.

It was like he had no consciousness anymore, and was just a mere VHS tape playing back gritty images. He couldn't even think. He saw a man descending from the clouds with a sword. Jerry and *The Hand* stopped their dancing in the blinking of an eye. They grabbed their guns out of the air and stomped towards distant cities. With the cruel Sun pulsing down on them like a strobe light, they massacred everyone they saw. Blood flowed in the streets. Judge saw Zeke's famished smile as he dashed a baby's head against a brick wall. The head exploded exactly as you'd think it would. "This is what I want. And you're going to give it to me, Judge. I am God, and you know you can't ever run far enough."

Judge heard a sucking sound. It grew higher and more deafening in his ears until it hit a frequency too high for him to hear. He looked around. He was in the back room of the bus. Sunlight was peeking in from behind the shut blinds. Grenade was passed out, as was Simmons. Jammer was asleep and twitching. *That was...just a hallucination. But it was still terrible. Of course I'd hallucinate something like that with all the shit Jerry fed me for the last seven years.*

He stood up slowly to make sure the ground beneath him was real. *Real enough. I've never thought I'd be so happy to smell stale joints and body odor.* The door creaked open as he pulled it, but the band didn't stir. Yolanda was sitting at the table. She was on the phone taking notes on a clipboard. She hung up and looked at Judge. *Forgetting about her did work for a little bit, but...she's still there. She'll always still be there.* "Hey Judge. Good night?"

"Not really. I'm...I'll start unloading." He stepped outside.

The sun outside was a solid, blinding bright. *No pulsing. Good. I am never doing that again.* He pulled guitar cases and amplifiers out from the under the bus. He buried himself in his work to forget what he saw, to remind himself that it was all just some stupid hallucination from a stupid idea to do stupid drugs. But even as he worked, he couldn't shake the tearing, searing pain from the shockwave and how real the Sun's voice felt.

Prepare Your Anus

The next two weeks were exactly the same. They would sleep all day as they drove to the next venue. Judge made it as far as the Launchpad in Albuquerque before the route doubled back, further north this time. The activator became just another random lump in Judge's mattress that he had to adjust before he fell asleep. The Dark Corner and the hallucination were the same thing – something forgotten and hidden away in Judge's mind. Other than a few fleeting thoughts about his Dad's safety and the occasional sighting of someone that looked like Zeke in the crowd, Judge was a man without a past.

He spent most of his time growing his beard (*fuck you Jerry!*) and moving Sherlock Bones' heavy equipment (*fuck you gravity!*). Finding it hard to be around Yolanda for long periods of time before feeling a heavy ache in his chest, he followed the sound guys around and grew astute in setting up stages. *I could do this forever. Jerry would never find us. I could teach Dad and Zeke how to do it and we could just stay on the move together till our dying day.*

The disdain for the Lord that Jerry had inadvertently taught him slowly dissipated, and the hallucination became a silly dream. He felt the Spirit in the *I'll Fly Away* sets and Jesus in the clumsiness of young and awkward lovers making out in the crowd. *Why won't Yolanda do that with me?* Occasionally he'd catch himself praying silently, and it was always supplication for Simmons and Yolanda and his Dad and Zeke and sometimes even for Jerry.

After Judge would set up the stage, he would lead the groupies to the band's dressing room. Thanks to Yolanda's brilliant maneuvering, the tour was a rousing success. As Simmons had predicted, the women got prettier as the days went on. There were even enough to fully revitalize Simmons' surprisingly organized schedule of groupie days. There was Mixed Mondays where he only took bi-racial women. Titty Tuesdays, Thin Thursdays and Fat Fridays were self-explanatory. White Wednesday was easy, but Judge always had a confusing time sorting the girls out for Daddy-Issue Sundays. *Isn't every day Daddy-Issue day??*

Simmons always offered to let Judge "partake of the pussy", and Judge normally refused, afraid it would turn out as badly as his one attempt with drugs. One Sunday when Judge was particularly heartbroken about Yolanda, he took up Simmons' offer to try to make her jealous. *No way will it be as bad as the acid trip.* Judge sat on the couch. Simmons pointed at one girl with a pug-nose and said "Hey, you. Yeah, you. The ugly bitch. That tall guy with the fine beard over there? He's a friend of mine. Treat him right."

She seemed to have a hard time standing upright in her high heels. When she made it over to Judge, she plopped down into his lap. It did nothing for him. *She's warm I guess, and her hair is...well-done? Actually, upon closer inspection, burnt might be the better word for it.* Judge put his arm around her waist, but she started to cry. Her howls grew loud. Everyone in the room stopped their blowjobbing and blow-snorting and stared. Jammer seemed particularly agitated. He stopped spanking the girl bent over his lap and said "What did you do, man?"

The girl sobbed and said "My Daddy used to do this to me!" *That's enough of that.* Judge got up and walked out. Simmons followed him, naked and holding his junk in his hands.

"Come on man. This is the best day of the week. Easy pickings! A girl cries like that and says that shit? It's just her way of saying she's ready for you to fuck her. And the tears make sure everything stays nice and lubed." Simmons put his hands up in the air. "It'll certainly be easier than you getting with Hunny Bunny. She's wired up tighter than a monk's asshole."

I'd like to think that's just a euphemism, but I wouldn't be surprised if he actually knew how tight a monk's asshole really was. Judge said "Thanks man, but I just realized I forgot to tune Grenade's drumheads." Simmons shrugged his shoulders, ran back to the crying girl who had been in Judge's lap and shoved his penis in her mouth. *Is there something wrong with me that I don't want that? I used to think that if I wasn't thinking the opposite of what Jerry thought, I was doing something wrong, but Simmons' life just seems disgusting.*

He listened to Simmons' amorous exclamations over the speaker that day, and every day of the tour. "Stick it in my asshole!" "Suck on that like a lollipop!" "How much more can I fit in there?" "Piss on me!" "Squeeze the right one, as hard as you can!" Yolanda was right– they did become funny, at least until one of Simmons' exclamations of "Stick it in my asshole!" was followed by a hoarse, painful shout.

Yolanda looked at Judge. "That's new," she said. They ran together to the dressing room. *I hope I don't have to hit anybody.* The door flung open, and Yolanda immediately cracked up into proud laughter. *What is she laughing at...oh. Gross.* It was Titty Tuesday, and a woman so pale that blue veins mapped routes over her heavy breasts had a hand shoved up Simmons' anus, all the way to the middle of her palm. Her thumb was visible and wiggling around like she was trying to hitch a ride out of asshole-town.

"Judge!" Simmons was crying like a child who recently found out that vaccinations now had to be given inside the colon. "Come hit this bitch! She's raping me..." He trailed off into sobs.

Judge looked at Yolanda. She shook her head and said "Can't you just..." She did a karate chop motion with her hand. "...yank it out?"

The woman was trembling, and her breasts held onto the motion and jiggled. *Wow. Breasts are awesome. This would be my favorite day if all these girls weren't such massive sluts. And if they didn't shove hands up asses.* "No," she said. "He told me to do it. I-"

"It was just dirty talk! I don't...ooowwwww...I don't ever mean for you to do it! What kind of sick bitch are you?" Yolanda started laughing again. She took breaths in between the peals to try to calm down, but it only made her laugh louder. *She's so beautiful, even in a room where this is going on.* "What the fuck are you laughing at Hunny Bunny?! Get this woman's hand out of my ass!"

Wiping tears from her eyes, Yolanda looked at the naked woman. "You really can't get it out?" she asked as gentle as a woman teaching a class of preschoolers.

"No. It's...," she said as she tried to pull it out. Simmons yelped like a dog in a thunderstorm. "It's too tight."

Judge remembered the vivid rape dream that started this whole mess and felt a dry burning in his sphincter. *Is my life going to be defined by people sticking things up other people's asses without their consent?* "Simmons, you've got to relax, unclench it, or else..." said Yolanda. Her words were quickly overcome with wicked laughter. Grenade, who had been passed out on the couch, suddenly started to chuckle a little. *So he is human...* "I'm sorry Simmons. I can solve booking problems, but pulling slutty hands out of your ass is not in my contract." She laughed her way out of the room.

"Judge. Will you hand me that?" Simmons pointed to a joint and a lighter on a table. Judge did as he said. "Now get the fuck out of here if you aren't going to help!" Simmons lit up and Judge walked out of the room. He saw Yolanda and tried to work up some laughter to share with her, but he couldn't find it in him. *I know how that feels.*

Still, Simmons never stopped shouting out random sex commands over his microphone. Once Judge was again able to laugh at them, they became one of the few things he and Yolanda shared. They would talk together, stand and listen to *I'll Fly Away* together, sit and watch TV together during *Sexual Lives*, but it was never as deep or real as the moment where they realized that despite their opposite upbringings, they couldn't have been more similar. Judge wanted more, and he was pretty sure Yolanda wanted more as well, but he also enjoyed simply being in her presence, and didn't want to ruin that small good thing.

Simmons started to warm up to playing *I'll Fly Away* every night, most likely because it increased the quality of groupies it brought around and got Yolanda off his back. He still insisted on slogging through *Sexual Lives* every night, declaring to the captive audience it was his "true masterpiece", but even he seemed to find some meaning in singing the old songs, often closing his eyes and belting it out in a way that surprised everyone.

One night, as Judge was loading up the bus and Simmons was saying goodnight to the last of the Thin Thursday crowd, he came up behind his roadie and clapped him on the shoulder. "I just want you to know something, man. I know I might have given you a hard time when you told me how you felt about *Sexual Lives*, but you're the fuckin' man! You were right about *I'll Fly Away*, and…" He breathed out, his eyes got less wide and his voice lost its cartoony quality, resembling something sincere. "I just wanted to thank you for showing me that I should be proud of where I came from." Simmons hugged Judge, and it felt right. *Brother.*

Yolanda was standing on the bus steps, watching it all unfold. Once Simmons had let go of Judge, he ran up the bus steps and past Yolanda. She turned and watched him go. "You're not going to thank me?" she asked accusingly.

"Hunny Bunny?" Simmons said like a blind man just finding out he isn't alone in a room.

"Playing *I'll Fly Away* was my fuckin' idea, Simmons! God!" She stormed off the bus in a huff.

This might be my chance. Judge walked up the bus steps and caught Simmons. "Simmons, I think you should apologize to Yolanda."

"You mean Hunny Bunny."

"She doesn't like being called that, and this new tour was her idea. She's the reason Thin Thursday turned out so well."

The rockstar started to pull his shirt off, but quickly put it back on when he realized that it was the universal sign for starting a fistfight. *Good move.* "She likes being called Hunny Bunny, trust me. All women like being treated that way and...whatever, man. Don't get your panties in a twist. Tell her I said thank you. Maybe it'll help you get in her pants." He stepped into the back room as a haze of smoke poured out.

Maybe it will help. Judge stepped off the bus to find Yolanda sitting on a bench outside the venue. *Please don't be crying.* She wasn't crying, and Judge said a small prayer of thanks out of reflex. "Hey Yolanda, Simmons wanted me to tell you that he said thanks."

"Oh did he?" She looked up at the cloudy night sky. "I guess that's better than nothing."

Judge sat down next to her. "He also said you like being called Hunny Bunny. Said that all women like being treated that way. I don't want to seem like some dumb kid, but is that true?"

"No. I'm not playing hard to get. I guess some of his groupies like it that way, but not me," she said as she stared at the half moon peeking behind some gray clouds. "I just think he's angry that I won't let him sleep with me."

Oh. "Why would you think that?"

"Because before you came along, he used to beg me for it all the time, especially after I told him no groupies on the bus. I think I remind him of someone he used to know. She must have liked getting treated like shit."

Please don't hit me for saying this. "So why won't you? Sleep with him, I mean. I know you're not like all the other girls but isn't he, y'know, cool and stuff?"

"I used to think so," she said. "I probably would have a couple years ago. Who am I kidding? Of course I would have. I would have done whatever he wanted. I was enamored. He used to be the pinnacle, but then I got to know him and I figured out that he's no better than some horny teenager. Now...it's just kind of sad, don't you think?" The cloudy night sky stopped being as interesting and she looked at Judge. "I've seen how he really is and I've had to rethink the kind of man I'm interested in."

What does that mean? When Judge said nothing, Yolanda gave off an exasperated sigh and walked back towards the bus. *Did I do something wrong?* Judge heard bare feet slapping on the pavement. Jammer whizzed by and said "Way to strike out!" Judge followed him to the bus and climbed aboard.

Yolanda was sitting at a table across from Simmons. "Here he is!" Simmons said as he got up and hugged Judge. *Didn't we just do this a few minutes ago?* "Thanks to you, man...and Hunny Bunny, I've decided that on our day off tomorrow, we're going to hit the studio. I'm going to try to go back to my roots and write *I'll Fly Away* part two. I'm going to call it *Get the Fuck Out of the Way, Sky! I'm Still Flying!*"

Laughter bubbled out of Yolanda. *Shit. Is she going to fall in love with him all over again?* Simmons must have thought the same thing. He started humming a familiar melody from *I'll Fly Away*. She laughed all the way to her bunk. When she closed the curtain, Simmons looked at Judge and said "I bet she's beating it to me right now."

Judge had figured out what that meant. He reared back and punched Simmons hard on the shoulder. "Ow!!!! What the fuck was that for?"

"Don't talk about her that way." Simmons walked towards the back, rubbing his arm. Judge had to suppress the urge to keep punching until Simmons looked like raw hamburger. *Zeke may have always won the fights, but Simmons won't always get the girl.*

Electric Boogaloo

An acoustic guitar strumming simple chords woke Judge up earlier than he'd been awake so far on the tour. *How is it that I can get rid of all these violent habits from the Dark Corner but I can't seem to remember how to get up before mid-afternoon?* Judge rolled over, but the activator jabbed him in the back and he yelped. The guitar stopped.

Simmons whispered "Judge. Hey Judge, you awake?"

"I am now," Judge said from behind his curtain.

"Can you come out here?"

Naked, Judge sighed. *I hate getting dressed in here, but it's just Simmons. I see him naked all the time. Fuck it.* He pulled back the curtain and rolled out of bed in just his skivvies.

Everyone, Yolanda included, was sitting around the table, sipping coffee and writing on notepads. They stared. Simmons broke the silence. "Well, morning, Mr. Morning Wood." Judge looked down at his crotch. *Jerry used to rebuke Zeke for waking up erect, claiming it was a demon that hadn't been quick enough to escape completely before Zeke woke up. My Dad always just ignored mine. I wish Yolanda would ignore it too, but she won't stop staring. I don't know if that's good or bad.*

"Damn. I always saw you had big hands, but shit." Jammer nudged Simmons, pointed at Judge's dick and said "If he doesn't play any instruments, he can just stand naked on stage and no one will pay attention to how shitty your songs are."

Simmons pushed Jammer out of his chair. "Shut the fuck up man! As if your stuff is any better." Yolanda broke her gaze from Judge's dong and made sure that the two guitarists weren't about to cause real trouble. Judge took the opportunity to jump back into his bunk and get dressed. *Like dancing in a coffin.*

Judge heard the guitar strumming again from behind the curtain. Simmons hummed a few bars from *I'll Fly Away*. It was beautiful and pure. Judge just wanted to lie back down and let the song wash over him, but the music was interrupted by Jammer's jagged voice. "Ok, ok. How about this? Keep playing." Simmons started strumming. Jammer lowered his voice and sang "There's a hole in my heart, since we've been apart, oh baby, oh baby, let's not be apart." *That was terrible.*

Excited, Simmons said "Yeah! That's pretty good. Sounds a bit like 'Funeral Dance', right Hunny Bunny?"

No. That is nothing like 'Funeral Dance'. That song is beautiful, and makes astute points about the nature of death and moving into hope once you realize your own mortality. What Jammer just sang would have been worthy of chastisement if it came from a six-year old.

Yolanda agreed. "Well, they both have music and...words. Keep trying."

Judge poured a cup of coffee and sat down next to Yolanda. Simmons reached across the table and tried to grab her paper. "Well what the fuck are you writing then?" She snatched it away and hid it under her arm. "Oh. It's about how much you want to fuck Judge, right? Probably got even juicer once you saw his gigantic wang." He started strumming his guitar lustily. "Fuck me Judge, with your penis pudge, I want you inside me until you have to cum, then pull out and cum on my face yum."

He and Jammer laughed until they noticed Judge scowling at them. Simmons stopped and smiled at his roadie friend. Judge couldn't help but stop being angry. *Damnit. Why can't I stay mad at people?* Yolanda eased the tension and said "It wasn't about that." *Really? Shoot.* "I was more trying to think about what made *I'll Fly Away* so great. But it's hard to put your finger on, you know?"

Some ugly chords flew from the guitar. Simmons said "Yeah. I wish I could figure out how I wrote something so fucking awesome, but it's like, lightning never strikes twice, or something." *If it ever struck at all.* Yolanda's squinting eyes said that she and Judge were thinking the same thing, but before she could say anything the bus hissed and slowed to a halt.

She stood up and stuck the piece of paper in her pocket. *What did she write down?* "All right, guys. We've booked this studio for the rest of the day, but the label wants two good demos by the end of it, so don't just dick around like last time."

Simmons said "Don't worry, Hunny Bunny. I've got some sweet song ideas floating around my noggin. Half of them are about you." He smiled at Yolanda, picked up his bag and followed Jammer and Grenade out the door. Judge didn't get to see if she smiled back at him.

He grabbed her arm as she walked out the door. *Was she smiling or not?* "You know, if you want to take the day off, I can take care of them in there if...if Simmons is bothering you." *No reaction.* "How much trouble can they really be?"

"Thanks, but I am contractually obligated to be in that studio with them, as Davis Records Group's liaison. The order from on high, from Ahab Davis himself, is that if they don't write a hit soon, they're out of their contract and I'm out of a job." *And here I thought I was doing something nice.* "But it's kind of you to offer." She smiled, reached up and squeezed his arm. *That's got to be a good sign.* Stepping off the bus, she turned and looked at Judge. "And as good as you are at unloading equipment and beating the shit out of hotel managers..." *and having a giant dick?* "...these guys can be so unpredictable. They need me here."

Judge followed her into the dim studio. Grenade was parked on a couch like he always was. Jammer tore into a box of cheez-its. Simmons was thumbing his guitar. They were both laughing. Simmons said "Hunny Bunny, we don't care what you say, and it doesn't have to be about you, but Judge's Pants Pudge might be the breakthrough song for us." She scowled at them. "It isn't a joke. I think it's the best thing I've ever written."

"As the official label representative, I'm going to have to veto that." She walked over to the wall and hit the light switches. Jammer and Simmons whined as the room lit up bright. "This might not be the height of artistic integrity, but can you just try to copy what you did on *I'll Fly Away*?"

Simmons played the familiar opening chords to 'You are That Man'. "That's what I'm doing, Hunny Bunny." He hummed the melody to the song with his eyes closed. When he was done, he looked at Judge. "How was that?"

He didn't bring as many drugs as he normally does. I hope he's still high enough for me to be honest. "It sounded exactly like 'You are That Man'," Judge said.

"I know. Weren't you listening? That's what I was going for. I'm going to call it 'No You Aren't, That was Someone Else'."

Yolanda said "And it's going to be the same exact thing, just with different words?"

His head shaking like his Dad caught him with his hand up a girl's skirt, Simmons said "No, no. I'm uh…I've been thinking. *I'll Fly Away* is such a pussy album, you know? So I'm going to put in some loud guitars and I'm going to make the melodies simpler and start writing about shit that people actually care about."

Yolanda plopped on the couch next to Grenade. "Simmons, that's why *Sexual Lives* was so awful. You don't have anything else?"

Jammer had emptied the box of cheez-its and was digging around the bottom. The wrapper inside crinkled rhythmically as he grabbed for crumbs. He said "I read about this tambourine virtuoso on the internet the other day. Do you think we could get him? We'd have to fly him from Romania..." Simmons nodded his head as if Jammer had just invented a telephone that you can have sex through.

"No. That's it. You three-" Yolanda pointed at the band and used her Mom voice. Jammer looked excited. Simmons looked worried. Grenade looked like a corpse. "...get in that room right now. Take something if you have to, but I don't want you coming out until you write something good. No loud guitars, no penis jokes, no tambourine virtuosos. Just chords and words. Get the fuck out of here."

The band stood up, grabbed their bags and skulked into a side room. As if to fully complete his transformation into a spoiled teenager, Simmons glared at Yolanda and stuck his tongue out at her before slamming the door.

"Bastard." Yolanda reached into her bag and pulled out knitting needles and a ball of yarn. *I wonder if my Mom still knits.* She said "It's like since you've come around he's gotten even worse with me."

What do I say to that? "Sorry?"

"It's not your fault...I guess. I don't know. Simmons is just..."

Judge watched her move the needles effortlessly, her hands moving more intricately than Simmons' when he was playing his most complex part. He said "So what'll you do if he actually writes something good?"

"First, I'd probably shit my pants." *And here I was thinking she couldn't do anything to grow less attractive.* "Then I'd call the label and let them know."

"I meant...how would you feel about him?"

Yolanda kept her eyes on her needles as if looking at Judge would turn her blind. "I think I'd still hate him, but...honestly...*I'll Fly Away* was so beautiful and if this new stuff was half that good...I don't know. I'm just glad to know that he won't ever write anything that good again. I don't think he wrote anything that good in the first place. I think if he tried really hard, he could probably write something muscle heads might like, but I don't think I could love it. But..." *Or love him? But what?!* There was laughter from the side room and she suddenly snapped her voice into something loud and grating. "I don't hear any music!" The laughter ceased and a guitar started playing.

Did my Mom ever do that? "I didn't know you knit," Judge said to change the subject.

She finally broke her gaze from her needles and looked at Judge. "Yeah. I do it at night in my bunk when I can't sleep." *That would have been a much nicer option than hallucinating about a God that desires blood flowing in the streets.*

"You don't have much done there. You must sleep like a baby." She reached down into her bag and pulled out four scarves, three hats and a blanket. "Oh. Well, at least you have something constructive to do. You don't make sweaters do you?"

"I haven't done one in a while. I'm not exactly surrounded by the sweater-wearing element."

Judge looked down at the cheap work-pants he bought at a K-Mart and the Sherlock Bones shirt he stole from the merchandise stand. "I used to wear sweaters," he confessed. "It's faint, but I think I can remember that my mom used to try to knit them with little designs. Snowflakes and stuff, but they always turned out wrong. I remember one in particular got me in trouble at church because all the old people said I had scorpions all over my sweater." *Does Mom still go to that church? Does Mr. Whitaker still hand out candy to the little kids that can recite the week's Bible verse?*

She smiled and said "That sounds pretty bad-ass, actually. I think I will start a sweater. I might even put a scorpion on it for you, but you have to wear it."

I do love that smile. "Neat. How long will it take you?"

"Depending on how much sleep I get, maybe a few weeks." *Will I still be around then?*

Judge watched her fingers move like spiders building webs. "But the tour will be over by then, won't it?"

"Oh yeah. I didn't think about that. Maybe we can find a way to get on our next tour together."

*Swoon. Gotta capitalize...*Judge thought about pulling the old yawn-and-put-your-arm-around-her trick he saw on a movie when he was a kid, but the door to the side room swung open in a cloud of smoke. Jammer ran out, Simmons sauntered out and Grenade appeared out of nowhere on the couch between Yolanda and Judge.

Simmons spoke fast. "Hunny Bunny, get on the phone with Mr. Davis. We got the next big thing!" *Oh shit. What if it really is good? Would she still smile at me and try to get on the same tour as me and knit me scorpion sweaters?* Simmons stumbled a bit, but managed to sit on the floor in front of Yolanda cross-legged, his guitar sitting in his lap like a child. "We were thinking about what you said with *I'll Fly Away* part two, and I know you didn't like the part Jammer came up earlier on the bus, but we reworked it some and even found a way to fit in the tambourine virtuoso we're adding to the band." Yolanda frowned. Simmons patted her on the knee and said "Don't worry. I'm the rockstar genius, remember? Just listen."

Shit. There goes my chance. She's going to hear this and fall in love with him and his hand will creep up her knee and touch her demon mouth and that'll be it for me. At least I've learned enough to hop on another tour. Are all tour managers this beautiful? Simmons strummed softly and sang low. "If I could feel my way through a dark cave, and my life was lost on a canal, if I'm ever carried off by the cruel wave, I'll just remember when I came out the birth canal." He stopped singing and spoke while strumming frantically. "That was the chorus and this is the part with the tambourine solo."

Jammer pulled a tambourine off the wall and beat on it like he was trying to put a fire out. The rim firmly in his right hand, he beat the drum on his hands, knees, elbows, head. Once he even grabbed Yolanda's hand and beat it on that. *I wonder how he thinks that sounds in his head.* Simmons played his guitar in a rhythm disjointed from the tambourine and disconnected from any sense of musicality. Once he had stopped and Jammer rattled to a slow halt, Simmons smiled at Yolanda and touched her knee again, waiting for her admiration.

She simply said "No." *Yes!*

Setting his guitar on the ground, Simmons face grew pointed. "What? Were you not listening? Did you not see the sweet fuckin' action Jammer put on that tambo?" Jammer started beating on the tambourine again as if to prove his worth, but Simmons put his hand up and stopped him. He got to his feet and put his hands on his hips. "We worked hard on that shit!"

"Well, you've got to work harder." Yolanda kept her cool.

Simmons' breath grew heavy. "But it's exactly like *I'll Fly Away*. I don't...I don't know what you want." *Is this the first time a woman has confounded him this way?*

The needles in Yolanda's hands started back their quick clicking. "Get back in that room and write."

The singer said "If you're so smart, you fuckin' do it."

She kept her eyes on her needles and said "Isn't letting someone else write your songs what got you in trouble in the first place?"

Burn.

His sneer turned into a severe frown. *Is he about to cry?* Simmons picked up his guitar and skulked back into the side room. Grenade followed. Jammer lingered, watched Yolanda knit for a few seconds and said "Don't worry. We didn't really work that hard on that. I just kinda made it up so he'd stop bugging me to write his songs for him." He walked into the room, and as the door was shutting, Judge heard a deep humming sound that reminded him of his Dad's welding iron. *Are they building a nuclear activator in there?*

The two on the couch only shared the occasional small talk. Every once in a while Judge thought about putting his arm around her, but he knew that the moment had passed with Simmons' tantrum. *I can take my time. I waited seven years to escape from the Dark Corner, didn't I?*

It's a Hit

Hours passed. Judge sat on the couch and flipped the channels. Yolanda clicked her needles and quickly knitted the beginnings of a scorpion sweater. *At least, I think that's going to be a stinger...* Occasionally they would hear shouting or laughter or the sound of a wall being punched coming from Sherlock Bones' writing room, but the band never came out. An old Kung-Fu movie Judge was watching coincided strangely with the noises from the writing room. The sound of the Shaolin masters laughing lustily over bowls of noodles met peels of laughter from Jammer and Simmons. The standoff before the fight merged with Simmons hoarse shouts and the lightning-quick exchange of punches and kicks blended in with unknown thuds coming from inside the room. *Are they just watching TV in there?*

One particularly loud crash from the room happened when the Bruce Lee lookalike hero finally made an end of the bearded evil master with a dazzling array of nunchuck strikes. The movie ended, but the noise in the room kept bubbling up until there was a loud *SNAP!* followed by complete silence. Judge said "Should we go check in on them?" *If Grenade proved to be a ninja and killed one of them, I don't want to be around when the cops show up to do the questioning.*

"Fuck 'em." Yolanda stared at her needles as she spoke, and sounded as if Judge was merely questioning her on what kind of stitch she was doing. "If they die, I get severance pay. If they just get injured, the story garners press. And we get to laugh at their misfortune. Either way, I win." *Damn. Maybe she's the one that should be reminding me of Zeke.*

Judge was shocked at her disregard for their safety, but didn't want to get on her bad side, so he smiled sheepishly and changed the channel. The news was on. After not seeing it for so many years, he loved watching the news. It reminded him of the gigantic world he had been denied, and he liked to be reminded that Jerry was just as low as the murderers and rapists he saw being reported on.

A fat, ugly lady with an orange mole on her cheek and thin black hair said "Welcome to NBC news 11 at 5." Her lowest chin jiggled wildly when she talked. *I'm glad I don't live here.* "We've got some breaking news coming in to WBAL. Here with the report is John Ferelden."

"Thanks Carol," the mustachioed reporter said. "We've just received word that the Department of Homeland Security has raided the headquarters of a terrorist group known as *The Hand.*" *Oh shit.* The camera cut to the familiar camp in the Dark Corner that Judge knew all too well. He started sweating. Chills careened up his back as he saw men in blue ATF jackets wandering around his former home. *That's my cabin. My bed was through that window.* "DHS Secretary Napolitano has confirmed that, in conjunction with the FBI and the ATF, that they've been monitoring this group hailing from the upstate of South Carolina. While their suspicions have been of harboring illegal modified weapons..." They showed a man holding an AK-47 that Judge and Zeke had trained on. He knew it from the medical tape wrapped handle that had a jagged 'Z/J' written on it. *I hope Zeke never made it back there.*

Is Yolanda looking? Can she see me sweating? The man on the news continued. "...a search warrant was issued after a disgruntled member confessed to the murder of local police officer Matt Babbalan." Judge saw an agent leading Jerry away in handcuffs. *Good.* His face was covered in dirt and blood. *I wonder who he was rebuking when they caught him.* "This is a very recent development and DHS hasn't released much information, but a source is telling us that *The Hand* is a Christian Fundamentalist fringe group that has tried to acquire materials for making nuclear weapons in the past. We'll keep you up to date as this story plays out. For WBAL news, this is John Ferelden."

That's it? Was Jerry the only one they arrested? Maybe my Dad was the one that snitched, and they're out looking for me right now. He and I will go into witness protection. I'll tell them Zeke is my brainwashed brother and we can live somewhere together. We won't have to travel the country roadie-ing for crappy bands and...why is Yolanda staring at me?

She said "Are you ok? You're turning beet-red." It was the first time she'd stopped knitting since they'd sat down.

Judge reached up and wiped the sweat off his forehead with his hand. "It's...that story..." *Please don't have been listening...*

"I know. It's stupid shit like that that made my parents so crazy about religion."

"Mine too."

"I'm just glad they caught those sumbitches. If it's the same *Hand* I'm thinking of, then they're the same assholes that used to come to my college and protest." She set her needles down and reached into her bag. She pulled out a camera. "I even...I heard there was a riot last time they came. I wasn't there, but the time before, I took pictures for the school paper and..." The camera beeped and blipped as she scrolled through pictures and scenes that Judge remembered seeing with his own eyes. *Oh. Shit.* She handed the camera over to Judge. "Just look at these cunts, trying to tell us how to live our lives. It's shit like that..." Judge scrolled through the pictures. *Beard. Zeke. Dad. Pentecostal Jake with his hands in the air prophesying in gibberish. Haven't seen me yet, thank God.* "I got a pic of this one guy. I felt so bad for him because he didn't seem into it, but then again the stupid fucker was holding a picture of an aborted fetus and talking to my friend Becca. Later on she told me he was trying to pick her up. Fucking disgusting. Let me find it…"

She grabbed the camera from Judge and it almost slipped out of his soaked, sweaty hands. It blipped as she scrolled through and found the picture she was talking about. "I mean, look at this loser." *Does she really not recognize me? Maybe it's the beard.* She looked at it a second time, pulled it closer to her face and squinted her eyes. *Oh shit. Please don't…*

A loud CRACK came from the writing room. Jammer screamed "No! No! Don't!" The door swung open violently and Jammer walked out with his hands up. Urine soaked his pants and ran down to the floor in a stream. Simmons followed, clutching a silver gun pointed at his guitarist's back. He kicked Jammer in the butt and he collapsed on the ground in front of the couch. As Simmons pointed the gun at Yolanda, she dropped the camera to put her hands up. It fell to the ground and cracked open. *Never have I been so glad to have a gun pulled on me.*

The only sound was Simmons struggling to breathe through his teeth. The shiny gun trembled in his hand. *It's a shame he's so close. A hand shaking like that'll probably miss at ten yards or more. From here, though, Yolanda's brains will make a nice mural on the wall.*

Eventually, Yolanda broke the silence. She whispered, slowly and deliberately, as if Simmons wouldn't be able to understand anything at a normal rate of speed. "Jammer, what did he take?"

"He took some of Grenade's soy sauce. Or...all of his soy sauce."

Yolanda sighed and gently said "Simmons, lets put that thing down. You don't want to hurt anyone, do you?"

"Why would I have this gun pointed at you if I didn't want to hurt anyone?" He spoke through his teeth and sounded rabid. *If I can get up from this couch...* A growl bubbled up from Simmons' chest as if his heart had turned into a Tom Waits tribute band. "I have seen the future."

What? Jammer slowly scooted up on the couch between Judge and Yolanda. *Idiot. Spreading the gunman's attention is tactics 101.* Stinking of ammonia, Jammer said "This is...he should be out..."

Simmons finally opened his mouth. Every syllable was a violent, throat-shredding salvo. "I am out! Out of the correct timeline! This one is going to end with Hunny Bunny and me never fucking! But I can fix it."

Yolanda stayed calm. "Simmons, hey...look at me. Stay with me. We've been through this before. You can't see the future, and you don't have to shoot anybody. Just like last time, we can calm down and let this go."

"I'm going to write the most beautiful songs for you! Why won't you fuck me!?! Everyone else does! " *Maybe that's why. And if Yolanda doesn't want to sleep with him because he's been with thousands of women…hey, I haven't slept with anybody.*

"Why won't I fuck you?" she asked, practically spitting venom. "Probably because you're pointing a gun at me because I won't fuck you."

Simmons growled again. Jammer recoiled back into the couch. "That's not it! I saw the future! God hates us and we're in the wrong timeline! This one ends soon! I saw it! It's fiery and hot and we'll be gone and you and I never get to fuck! I can fix this! I have to fix it!" Simmons reached up and put both hands on the handle. "I don't want to live in a world where there are women who won't fuck me! A world this disgusting should end soon!" *Why does that sound familiar?* "And if you don't fuck me, that'll be the end! The terrorists win! There will be no fixing it!"

How is she so calm? How often does he pull a gun on them? She said "All right Simmons." *Please don't do this.* "How do you propose to make me fuck you?"

The gun grew steady in his hands and pointed straight out like a divining rod. Simmons snaked over to Yolanda. He lifted the gun slowly so it was kissing her forehead. He said "Hunny Bunny, I'm-" *Don't care.* Judge jerked his hands up and grabbed Simmons wrists, pushing the gun straight up in the air. The gunman growled out a gurgling "No!", but it was cut short. Judge hooked his leg around the back of Simmons' knee and drove him to the ground. He let go of the gun and it slid under a rack of guitars.

Judge positioned himself in front of the rack. Simmons stood up slowly. Growling through his teeth again, he slowly intoned "I have the power!" He reared back and punched Judge in the chest. Nothing happened. *I'm glad Zeke never pulled a gun on the girl I'm trying to woo.* This time, Simmons swung at Judge's face and connected weakly. When Judge didn't go down, Simmons' teeth started chattering and he wailed like Pentecostal Jake. *Sorry, brother.* Rearing back, Judge loosed his giant hand and hit Simmons under the chin. He collapsed.

Yolanda stood up coolly and said "Jammer, I don't know why you're so freaked out." She walked over to the guitar rack and picked up the gun. "You know it wasn't loaded last time, and-" She pulled the trigger, expecting to hear an empty click. A bullet shot out instead, narrowly missing Judge's right leg. The noise was dampened strangely inside that studio. "Holy shit!"

She held the gun daintily between her thumb and pointer finger. *Don't want her hurting anyone.* Judge grabbed it, popped the cylinder and let the bullets drop to the ground in one smooth motion. Jammer smiled and said "Damn, Judge. You're a pro at this." *How much of that picture of me did Yolanda see?*

He looked to see if she was scared, but instead of cowering, she was rifling through her bag.

Grabbing a syringe and small bottle, she filled the plunger with clear liquid. "Jammer, how much did he take? How long till the trip wears off?"

"Didn't you read *John Dies at the End?*" he asked. She shook her head, annoyed. "Give him just enough so it won't kill him. But no less than that."

Yolanda filled the syringe up, pulled down Simmons pants and stabbed the needle into his butt. *Why does she have that in her purse? Is she just better about hiding being a junkie?* "What is that?"

"Emergency sedative issued by the label. It's come in handy more times than I can count." *How often has Simmons done this?* "Can you carry him to the bus? I need to see if Grenade is ok." Judge nodded and slung Simmons over his shoulder like a bag of fertilizer. Blood dripped from his jaw to the floor. "Put him in his bunk. He should be out for at least...20 hours or so."

Judge did as she said. She and Jammer followed, propping Grenade up on their shoulders. Grenade whispered something in her ear and she laughed. "Yes. You two can have some of the sedative. You don't even have to pull a gun on me." After she shot them up and all of Sherlock Bones were tucked into their bunks, Judge and Yolanda had the bus all to themselves on the long ride to the next gig.

What do I do with this free time? All of his time on the tour had been spent either sleeping or schlepping around making sure Sherlock Bones was ready. Jerry never allowed any idle time at the camp, either. *No amps to carry. No wood to chop. No Bible verses to memorize. I think I'll do the exact opposite of what Jerry would like – I'll just waste the evening watching TV.*

The bus rolled on and Judge made his way to the back room. *No drugs this time.* With Sherlock Bones snoring in their bunks and Yolanda yapping on her phone, Judge had the room to himself. He cut on the TV and turned it to CNN. They were still talking about *the Hand* but had no new details. *I think I'm safe. After all I've done for them, would they give me up even if they knew who I was?*

Judge flipped the channels until he happened across two people sitting in a booth at a diner. They were babbling on about nothing. The man's British accent was hard to understand. The girl had Yolanda's mousy frame and frazzled red hair, but wasn't near as pretty. *If this lady can be in movies, why is Yolanda not the biggest star in the world?*

As if she heard him thinking, Yolanda stepped in the room, turned and plopped down on the couch. "Well, I got us shows for the next week. Booking this tour on the fly has been...what are you watching?"

Does she know how much prettier she is than this girl? "I think these people are about to rob everyone in this diner." They watched. Yolanda giggled at something the girl said. The man set a gun on the table. *Pea-shooter.* The two on the screen kissed and said they loved each other. *Did he just call her Hunny Bunny?*

"Have you seen this before?" Judge asked her.

The couple on the screen got up, shouting and brandishing their guns. "No, but it's pretty crazy."

"Do you want me to change it?"

She grabbed a pillow and clutched it to her lap. "No. It's fine." The screen cut to black and a frantic guitar faded in. Credits rolled and the words *Pulp Fiction* ascended from the bottom of the screen. "Shit," she muttered.

"What?"

She sighed. "Do you remember when I told you why I hated being called Hunny Bunny? About how it was because of a movie called Pulp Fiction?"

Judge picked up the remote. "Do you want me to change it?" *She just said she'd never seen it.* Before she could answer, Judge put the remote down. "Well, if you've never seen it, maybe you should give it a chance before you decide to hate it."

She squeezed the pillow tighter in her lap and scowled, but it soon faded as she became enthralled in the movie. Judge turned the lights off in the back room. When he put his arm around her shoulder, she didn't react. *Is that a good or bad sign?* He saw that she was in a trance staring at the screen. Occasionally, her pretty mouth would lift into a smile or open slightly in surprise. *I thought she hated this movie.* Eventually, Hunny Bunny and the British man came back into the picture and escaped with everyone's money. The screen cut to black once again.

Yolanda continued to stare at the screen, looking oddly shaken. She didn't say anything for a while. "You all right?" Judge asked.

She didn't break her gaze from the screen. "Yeah. I'm fine. I'm just…surprised. That was a really good movie. Why did I hate it for so long?" She turned and looked at Judge. *Way prettier than the real Hunny Bunny, and I don't think she'd have the heart to pull a gun on someone.* "Was I a bitch to everyone for no reason?"

"Well, if you told them not to call you Hunny Bunny and they wouldn't stop, you had a pretty good reason."

"Yeah, but I was blaming it on the movie. But it wasn't the movie at all, it was the people using the movie to act like assholes." She leaned back into the couch. "Are we hating things for all the wrong reasons?"

What does she mean we? Judge thought for a minute and said "I think it's ok to like something but hate the cult around it."

"I wish someone had told me that at 16. Would have made life a lot easier. I think we both needed to hear that." She paused in deep thought. "I'm going to get my knitting." She got up and left the room.

What did she mean we? Do I need to hear that too? She came back and knitted. Judge flipped the channels. They sat in silence and watched TV, comfortable and doing nothing on couches that had seen untold amounts of ass. *I think I could do nothing with her for the rest of my life.*

After watching a cartoon about a sponge that Yolanda insisted he stop flipping on, Judge crossed over the news channel again. The breaking news banner, black text on a yellow strip, immediately caught Judge's attention. The anchor was rambling on about something, but all Judge could read was the text on the bottom of the screen. It read 'DHS releases details on The Hand's plan to drop a nuclear bomb on Brookland, SC; Nationwide manhunt launched for missing members Ezekiel Booth and Judge Saxon.' *Zeke's free, and they know who I am.*

OH.

SHIT.

Keep That Bitch Cool!

Judge clicked the remote and cut the TV off. Yolanda kept knitting and said "What are you doing? I was listening to that. They were about to say who they were looking for."

So she didn't see that they were looking for me. That's good...I guess. Maybe I can just wait this out...but how long can I really keep it from her? What will she do if she finds out I've been lying to her this whole time....but I haven't been lying to her! I just didn't tell her everything. And I think she loves me. And if I'm wrong about that, at least I've proven myself useful, haven't I? I've proven that I'm not Jerry, I'm not Zeke, I'm not my Dad, haven't I?

Judge sighed and said "It's me."

She looked up from her knitting and giggled. "Shut the fuck up and turn the TV back on."

"No. Really. It's me they're looking for. I...I haven't told you everything."

She stopped and sat the needles on her lap. "What are you talking about?"

"My...family isn't just crazy Christian like I was telling you. They are...were *The Hand*, and..." He trailed off and hoped she would leap into his arms and tell him everything was ok. When she crossed her arms over her chest, he knew he had to keep going. Judge breathed out. "...the news was talking about me. I'm Judge Saxon. They sent me to nuke Brookland."

Judge kept his head down, afraid to look at Yolanda. He heard a thud and felt a sharp pain in his arm. "Ow!" He looked at the pain and saw that Yolanda had tried to stab him with one of her wooden knitting needles. *No cut, but that is going to be one hell of a bruise.* She started to scream incoherently. Judge squeezed her tight with one arm and covered her mouth with one of his giant hands. Her muffled screams grew more vicious as Judge sat down on the couch, clutching her to his lap. *Damn she's strong.*

She kicked and shook, successfully knocking over a sidetable and cracking the remote control in half, but she couldn't free herself from Judge's grasp. *Simmons, a guy she hates, pulls a gun on her and she is cooler than ice. Me, a guy that she likes, tells her he's been sent to set off a nuclear bomb in a major American city and she acts like she's about to get raped. Maybe I was wrong about her loving me...*

"Listen, Yolanda. I can explain, but you have to calm down." She calmed and he pulled his hand off her mouth. She screamed again. He silenced her again. "Look, I haven't set a bomb off, have I? Last time I checked, we were staying away from Brookland, weren't we? You have to listen to me. I'm going to let you go, but you have to be quiet." *One more lie, and then no more.* "If you don't...I'll have to show you how strong I can be."

He let her go slowly. She slid onto the couch and clutched one of her knitting needles like a sword. She said "As if you could hurt me." *She's got me there.* "What the fuck is going on?!"

Judge brought his hand down and whispered "Please. No one else can know about this."

"I think the entire world knows about this."

"No one else on the bus. Could you put the needle down?" She turned it in her hand so it faced down. *Stabbing position. Smart girl.* "Ok, fine. They sent me to set off the bomb, but I hitchhiked away and stowed away on your bus so I could get away. I don't believe like they do." He tried to smile at her. "Kinda like you and your Pulp Fiction. You can hate the people around it, but not the actual thing, right? I'm just like you..." She scowled. Judge gave up trying to gloss over it. "...and I only volunteered for the job so I could escape. They've had me trapped there since I was 12. I never believed any of it, but I didn't have any choice but to pretend to. They had a zero-tolerance policy for heresy."

She didn't seem convinced. Judge continued. "And the bomb wouldn't have worked anyway. My Dad built a fake bomb activator so he could convince Jerry to let me go. And I think my Dad was going to escape too and we could live together somewhere far away from the Dark Corner, but now it looks like he's in jail." The thought of his weak, frail father in jail finally hit him. *Dad's in jail?!* "You might think you're the only one having a hard time with this, but I could use some sympathy too."

"I don't have sympathy for liars," she claimed. Still, she set the needle down. "But I believe you. I know what it's like to..." She put her face in her hands, then ran them through her hair. "No fucking time for speeches. Let me think about this. Cut the news back on." Judge scrambled to the TV and did as she said. *Does she hate me*? They watched for a minute. "Who's Ezekiel Booth?"

Judge cringed when they put a picture of him and Zeke up on the news, taken from their most recent protest. *Right before the riot erupted. Zeke destroyed at least three of the people in the background of that picture.* Judge pointed at the picture of Zeke. He was smiling and clutching a sign that read 'Feminists created AIDS'. "That's him. He's kind of my brother. But not really. He got into *the Hand* stuff more than I did, but he had to run away when...when I left. I'm glad he-"

"So that *was* you in that picture from the protest! I thought the person looked familiar, but your beard threw me off." She looked at him and then at his picture on the TV. "Keep growing it. It'll probably be our only chance of passing you off as someone else while I try to figure out what we can do with you."

So she's not kicking me off? I love her. Judge absently whispered "I love you."

"What?"

"What?" Judge shot back.

"What did you just say?"

What did I say? Did I say anything? "What do you mean?"

She shook herself and tried to forget what she thought Judge might have said. "Whatever. Keeping you moving until this all dies down is probably the best thing."

"What do we tell Simmons?"

She said "About what? As if he ever watches the news." Judge leaned back into the couch and stared at the TV. Yolanda stood up. "I can't just sit here and watch TV with you. It's...weird. Let me sleep on this. Just...keep on growing that beard." She walked out of the room, rubbing her crossed arms to keep warm.

I guess it's a good thing she didn't just kick me off the bus, but... The TV kept talking about Judge's life, showing pictures of where Judge grew up, airing mug shots of all the men that taught Judge everything he knew he didn't want to believe. It all washed over him, and he soon realized that the news looped every twenty minutes. After the 10th time watching it, he fell asleep.

A jiggle of the door handle woke Judge up. It was the happy light of early afternoon outside. The TV was still broadcasting his visage, telling the whole world that he was out there trying to nuke your city. *Shit. Did she call the cops?* Judge heard Simmons wheeze out a "Why is this door locked?"

Judge cut the TV off and opened the door. *I'm glad he hasn't seen any of this.* "Mornin' Simmons. How...you feelin' ok?" Simmons had the meager look of someone failing to recover from major surgery.

"Groggy as all fuck, but..." He looked around the room and saw Yolanda's needles on the floor and the side-table laying on top of the cracked remote control. "Oh shit, did you finally bite into Yolanda's down-below taco?"

What? Simmons sat on the couch in the same spot that Yolanda had the night before. "Listen," he said. "I know yesterday was a little loaded..." *You don't know the half of it.* "...but I just wanted to apologize. It was just one of those rockstar moments. That gun wasn't loaded anyways." *I don't know if him thinking that makes me feel better or worse.* "If you want Yolanda to be your cunt, then fine. I don't think she'll ever be mine, and I'm ok with that. I can't think of a better fuck buddy for her to have than you."

Simmons picked up the table and said "Actually, it's probably for the best. I didn't get it before, but I think Yolanda being stupid and refusing to fuck me might be showing me a little bit of what *I'll Fly Away* is actually about. You know, pain and...stuff. All thanks to you." *Why is it brothers can pull guns*

on each other one day, and then make your heart melt the next?*
"And your punch? Damn, man! That fucker hurt, but I... think it woke something up in me. When I get tired of drugs, I might pay people to hit me or something." *I should introduce him and Zeke. We could all be brothers. Zeke could hit Simmons, Simmons would enjoy getting hit, and I could sit back and be the sane one.* The rockstar reached for a pad and paper. "That's pretty deep. I should write that down."

Yolanda poked her head in the door. Simmons stopped writing and said "Hunny Bunny! I hope you didn't use all the moose on me yesterday. That shit was balls."

She forced herself to smile, and looked at Judge. "We're here, Judge. Time to unload." He followed her off the bus. Jammer and Grenade were still snoring in their bunks. When they were outside in the cold, she handed him some band-aids and a pair of sunglasses. "Listen. This is the best I can do right now. Put your hood up, wear the glasses and stick some band-aids on your face. It's not perfect, but it should stop people from recognizing you. I'm going to make some phone calls and see what I can do."

It took Judge a few minutes to figure out how the band-aids worked, but he finally got them on his face. *If Jerry had let us use these, we would have had a lot less blood stains, but I guess he saw open wounds as a sign of solidarity with the bleeding Lord.* He unloaded the bus like every other day. The sound guy didn't act suspicious, and neither did the pizza delivery guy or the bronze-skinned groupies Judge let in for Mixed Monday. When he dropped the groupies off with the pizza, Simmons saw Judge's bandages and sunglasses. He said "Fuck man, if I had known Yolanda was into the hard shit, I might have tried a little harder." *How much harder can you try than pointing a gun in someone's face?*

The room smelled sweetly sour when Sherlock Bones and the groupies left for the sound check. Yolanda and Judge planted themselves on the couch and watched the news. There was no new info on Zeke or Judge, but they did put up a list of all the men that were arrested in the raid. Judge scanned it over, mouthing the names silently. *Everyone's there. Dad included. Shit. I'm going to have to find some way to get in touch with him without getting caught.* "Yolanda, how do you get in touch with someone if they're in prison?"

She was agitated. "Why would you want to do that?! You know you've got to make a clean break. They'll be watching all communications coming and going. They'll be gunning for you. Don't you dare try to get in touch with them." *Why does she sound like I'm trying to give her birthday presents to charity?*

They could hear Simmons coming, and Judge made sure to change the channel just in case Simmons thought it would be hot to watch the news during his orgy. Judge followed Yolanda out the door as Jammer ran in. One of the groupies, a beautiful woman who looked less like a mutt and more like the next stage in human evolution, glanced at Judge a little longer than he liked. *I think I'm Yolanda's now, lady. And I don't think you want to mess with her.*

Simmons started his usual sexclamations. As usual, Judge wasn't paying attention to them. Yolanda smacked him on the arm and said "Do you hear that?" Judge made a 'what?' face. "What Simmons just said?"

"Listen. I think I've heard more about sex in the last two weeks than most people would hear in a lifetime in Las Vegas. I used to think it was funny, but…now it's just gross and sad."

"No! Listen!" Yolanda pointed up at the ceiling.

Simmons was speaking quietly, a far cry from his usual bawdy shouts. "No I don't watch the fuckin' news. I had it on earlier on the bus but I was too hungover to pay attention…who, Judge?…What the fuck are you saying?…Fine, I'll cut it on." The gentle snap of a television cutting on could be heard faintly from Simmons' microphone, and then there was silence.

Suddenly indignant, Simmons said "Oh shit. No wonder that bastard laid me out. Jammer, you seeing this?" *He's my brother, right? Yolanda can be my wife, and Sherlock Bones can be the crazy uncles for when we have little Judge Jr.* "Fuck." More silence. *What is he thinking?* "Do you realize the publicity this'll get us?" He seemed to be responding to someone's complaint.

"So? I've gotta survive and…it's the right thing to do, right?" *The right thing to do?* "Someone read the phone number on the TV out to me." Judge couldn't move. "Hello? I think I've got Judge Saxon here with me." *Is this really happening?*

"Shit. We've got to run," Yolanda said, tugging on Judge's sleeve. *I'm ruined. And my 'brother' is the cause. Again.* Her voice bounced as she ran. "You need to…damnit, Simmons, why would you do that?" she shouted to the air. "We passed a truck stop two miles back. You'll have to stowaway in the back of a truck. No one can see you, so don't go asking truckers for rides." *Fine with me. Those people are freaks.*

The bus was in sight. Judge softly said "Do you want to come with me?"

She stopped and looked around to make sure the cops hadn't already descended upon them. "Why the fuck would I do that?" *Because you love me?* She must have seen the brokenness building on Judge's face. Her voice grew softer. "I don't like running around when I know where I'm going, let alone when I'm running for my life. Sorry, Judge." She reached up and rubbed his arm, then reached into her pocket and pulled out some cash. "Take this and get the fuck out of here."

Judge ran on the bus and Yolanda followed. *Is this going to be the big goodbye scene where she kisses me and confesses her love?* "What the fuck are you doing?" she screamed.

Guess not. "I have to get the activator."

"You had that on my bus!?" She followed him back to his bunk.

"Not anymore." He pulled up his mattress and picked up a ratty backpack. He shoved a few things from his cubby on top of the activator. "It's the only thing I have left of my Dad's, and besides, it's a fake." *Like Simmons' gun was supposed to be.* Judge stood up straight in that narrow bus hallway and stared at her. *This is awkward. Please make the move.* And she did, throwing her arms around him, pushing the side of her face into his chest. *No kiss? Still, it's better than nothing.*

"Thanks...for everything," she said. Judge could feel her warm breath through his shirt. "Now go. I'll figure out some way to slow the cops down." *Just don't beat them to death with a chain, please.*

She walked towards the back room. Judge watched her until she shut the door. *That's probably the last time I'll see her.* He made himself steel up and dashed towards the door of the bus. He stopped when he saw that Grenade had mysteriously appeared in a seat near the door. A newspaper was sitting in front of him. The headline read 'Potential Nuclear Terrorists on the Loose', and pictures of Judge and Zeke covered most of the top flap.

Oh shit. Is he finally going to ninja out on me? I could whoop most people, but I never could get Zeke. What's he going to do? They stared each other down for a minute, and Judge wondered whether he should brace himself for an attack or run for his life. Grenade simply waited a couple seconds and nodded. *At least I finally got to see him communicate, and it wasn't to break my face.*

Judge nodded back and ran into the night, alone again, towards the harsh yellow oasis of light of a distant truck stop.

Part III: Run to the Hills

Whale Belly

Huffing from a two-mile run to yet another truck stop, Judge climbed into a truck that had an advertisement for a grocery store painted on its side. *At least I can eat while I escape.* He had to jimmy a fat padlock to get in. *Nothing Jerry hasn't made me do a hundred times.* He ran so hard from the club and had hopped in so quickly that he didn't notice the intense, grinding cold flowing from inside the trailer. The truck growled to life before he was even able to shut the door. It started to roll away before he could figure out how to lock the door back, and he had to jam it shut so that he, along with the contents of the truck, didn't roll out the back door.

He turned around and tried to make his eyes adjust to the pitch-black truck. It didn't happen. He remembered a small keychain flashlight that a sound guy in Oklahoma City had given him. He found it hiding in the bottom of his backpack, buried underneath the activator. It bathed the inside of the truck in a tiny pool of grainy light. He had the distinct feeling that he was inside the belly of a shark. Looking around, he realized where that feeling was coming from. *Meat. I'm surrounded by meat. No wonder it's so damn cold in here.*

The small oasis of light searched the truck. *But these steaks look delicious.* Judge found the cold control on the end of the truck closest to the driver. The air blowing out of a grate nearby grew more frigid and fierce as he got closer. He had a memory of a rebuking Jerry gave to Ezra that started with frostbite and ended in nearly fatal hypothermia. *I have to stop the cold.* There was no switch or dial, so he had to cut the wires leading up to the refrigerator grate. It whirred to a stop and he suddenly noticed the absence of its humming. *I hate to ruin these steaks and this guy's shipment, but I have to stay alive.*

The trailer stayed unbearably cold for a few hours. *Am I going to get frostbit anyways?* He thought about running in place to stay warm but remembered Jerry's lesson about how dangerous it was to sweat in the cold. Instead, he moved all the steaks to the opposite end of the trailer and curled up close to the door. The vibration of the road lulled him to sleep.

The hissing of the air brakes woke him up and he thought he was on the tour bus. It was as dark and quiet as he had come to expect in his bunk when he had the curtain shut. When he found that he could stretch his body out to full height, he remembered that he wasn't with Yolanda anymore and that Simmons had betrayed him. *I just...*It made him too angry to think and he growled out loud. The sound absorbed into the steaks and Judge felt strangely better. He gathered his thoughts. *I'm on a meat truck, and...are we stopped? Time to run.*

He stood up and was pleasantly surprised to find that the trailer had warmed up to habitable levels. *I get to keep my fingers!* He pulled on the latch with those fingers and nothing happened. He pulled harder, and pushed and jiggled, but the doors wouldn't open. He tore a piece of metal off of one of the steak racks. *These are starting to smell.* The jagged piece of aluminum fit perfectly into the dark gap between the doors, but Judge couldn't pry it open. The truck started up again and rolled onto a bumpy road. Judge kicked at the doors, but they stayed shut.

I'm stuck. And he was stuck, on a truck full of rotting steaks, for a full day. While it had been cold in the weeks before the tour with Sherlock Bones, the current day grew warm and the inside of the truck became stagnant and hot. *He must be driving south. It's like an oven in here. I shouldn't have cut those wires.* Judge stripped down to his underwear, but was still dripping with sweat. Even through their plastic and foam packaging, the smell of the spoiling meat made Judge nauseous.

Through a tiny gap in the bottom of the left door, he could see that the day was turning into night again. *How long am I going to be in here? What if it's a cross-country trip and I die? I'd become just another piece of rotting meat.* Judge threw up, and his heaves were uncontrollable. He couldn't stop. *I don't know what's coming up.* Vomit covered the meatless end of the truck where he'd been sleeping. The smell got worse. It wasn't just rot and bile; Judge thought he could smell corruption and sulfur.

Like Hell.

Maybe I'm already dead.

Judge started to cry. Delirious, panicked words flowed out of him, thin and watery like his tears. "God, Lord…I know you can hear me. I mean, I believe you can hear me, even past all this stink and…" Judge threw up again. This time it was merely brown liquid that burned in his mouth and stuck in his teeth. "I know you aren't the God from my hallucination, but you really put me in some bad spots. A crazy dad, a mom who left me and a brother who could be anyone. And then it got even worse. Jerry, and The Hand…and Zeke is a pretty poor excuse for a brother, no matter how much I love him. And then I got a ray of hope, and my Dad was going to help me escape. He and I could have finally had a normal life together, but he's probably getting raped right now." Judge remembered his rape dream and stopped crying. Stunted breaths permeated his words every few sentences.

"And I met a beautiful girl and I love her, but now I'll never see her again, and someone I thought was my brother pulled a gun on me and tried to fuck her, and then he was just going to give me up to the cops. I feel like I'm drowning here." Judge looked around in the dark at the steaks. His eyes had adjusted somewhat, but everything was fuzzy, like the rot was polluting the air. "But, you know, being in this truck might actually be worse than prison. At least there, people beating the snot out of me would remind me of how much Zeke loves me." Judge looked at the metal ceiling. "Why do you hate me so much?"

He cut his flashlight on and tried to find somewhere to sit that wasn't covered in vomit or surrounded by rotting meat. There wasn't anywhere clean, so he laid his sweatshirt out in the smallest vomit puddle he could find and kneeled on it. "I don't know if there will ever be anything good ever again. I don't know if I'll ever get to stop and look at a sunset over the mountains or get to listen to *I'll Fly Away* or look at Yolanda again. Even if I didn't, it wouldn't be any good because I know how things always turn out. What did I do before I was born, or before I went to the Dark Corner, or, shit, while I was at the Dark Corner? Why do I get this? I only did what I had to do to survive, and you blame me for that?" Judge interlocked his fingers together, an instinct he hadn't felt since childhood.

"I tried to save Officer Babbalan, but you just kept running me through giant piles of shit." He looked at his hands. "And here I am, praying. I think you're the only one who can fix this. But, I thought I was doing it right, you know? *I'll Fly Away* and *Pulp Fiction* and Yolanda showed me that there's probably more to you than I thought. I thought life was good and getting better, but now…I don't feel like things can get any worse. I know they probably will because I *always* think that, and then I get raped in a dream or sent off to nuke a city or I vomit on a trucker and he tries to use it as lube or I find out my friend is dying to fuck the woman I love. Maybe you really are the God from the hallucination."

Growing angry, Judge stopped and took deep breaths to calm himself. He could taste the rot coming in with every breath. "But, I guess this is another chance I have right now, if I don't die here. I'm just...praying feels wrong, but what else can I do? Thank you for this chance. Just...help me get it right. Don't set me up with anymore religious gun nuts or pervert truckers or fading rockstars. Maybe it's taken me getting this low to realize that you *can* hear me and that you were just listening, waiting for me to come back. I know all this isn't my fault, and...I guess I don't necessarily think it's your fault anymore either."

Judge looked around at the decay and spoke like he was answering a question. "I should blame everyone I've been around. I could blame all this on Jerry, but...Simmons did betray me, just like Jerry said he would. He couldn't love anyone half as much as he loves himself. Why couldn't I see that? As soon as he sees a way he can use someone to get ahead, whether it's fucking 15 groupies or selling out a man who saved his life, he's going to do it. I kind of feel bad for him." The feeling of confession left Judge, and he suddenly had the open feeling of revelation.

"Jerry was right. He might have been an asshole, but he wasn't Simmons. He wasn't a liar and you knew where you stood with him. God, what else could Jerry have been right about? What if everyone, even Yolanda, even me, are really like Simmons deep down inside?" He felt for the activator to remind himself that he still had it. "This bomb...it almost makes sense. Who betrayed Jerry to turn him into who he is? Am I on the way to being him?"

The thought scared Judge. He brought his hands back together and squeezed his eyes shut. "Lord, what do I do? Please tell me. I've got no idea, and I know that...at least I read that deliverance comes from you and I'm so tired of running. And I might can run away from Jerry and Simmons and Zeke, but I can't run far away enough from you. Could you show me the way?" HE started crying again. He put his forehead to the floor. The sweatshirt he was on made a sick, squishing sound. "I give up. I'll do what you want. Everyone I loved has failed me, and Yolanda's gone and Jerry is starting to make sense...it scares me. You're the only hope I've got. I'm through running."

The truck jerked to a stop. Judge was knocked out of his kneeling position and into a puddle of his own vomit. *Son of a bitch.* While he was getting up, he heard someone pulling at the door. He hid behind a rack of gelatinous porterhouses. A husky voice said "Come on, stupid door." The voice's breathing grew heavy and the doors flew open. The light flooded in and blinded Judge. Whoever it was sniffed and said "Oh, fuck. My load!"

Judge could see the outline of the trucker, a tall, thin man that reminded him of a spider. He had covered his mouth and nose with a bandana, but his eyes told of great worry. *This is my chance.* Clutching his bag, Judge grabbed the biggest steak he saw and threw it hard at the trucker's face. It knocked him off his feet. In just his underwear, Judge jumped over the prostrate trucker and out the door.

It was warm outside, but still far cooler than inside the trailer. A breeze brought him the first fresh air he'd smelled in a day. *Is this because I prayed?* He looked up and around and saw city lights dotting the sky, but no stars. *This looks familiar.* He heard the trucker say "Who the fuck are you?" *I'm not answering that.* Judge took off, running away from the malodorous meat truck and past a series of warehouses. The clean evening air rushing over his naked body felt glorious. *Did God listen to me? Is this where I'm supposed to be*? As Judge ran, he saw a sign that read 'Stadium Farmer's Market'. Across the street, a giant stadium reached hundreds of feet into the sky. He felt the activator in the bag, weighing heavy in his hand and swaying in the breeze.

His smile of freedom turned over into a frown of incarceration. *Shit. I get away from Jerry and the Dark Corner, I get away from Simmons trying to sell me to the feds, I get away from a prison of rotting meat and I end up in the absolute last place I want to be.* Brice Stadium and Brookland stood towering in front of him. The wind whistled past the stadium and the skyscrapers, and he could have sworn it sounded like laughter.

The Finder of Lost Children

Fortunately, Judge had remembered to toss a few items of clothing in the activator bag as he was turning over his bunk on th tour bus.. He stopped running behind a ramshackle building called 'Philip's Pholiage' and put on a pair of blue work pants, a green Sherlock Bones hoodie with a silhouette of conjoined twins on the front and a black stocking cap. *No vomit, blood or rotting meat-stink. This is a nice outfit.* He spied a dumpster nearby and peeked through it for anything to eat. It stank, but was nothing compared to the inside of the meat truck. He found a mushy bag of apples. Sticking them in his bag, he walked away from the stadium and towards the city.

What am I doing? I could get on another truck and get far, far away, but...I did almost die on the last one. He'd been walking up a long, slow incline, and after vomiting all over the meat truck, praying his guts out and running from the trucker, he realized how exhausted he really was. *I said I'm not running anymore. Maybe God means for me to be here for some reason, like he's finally answering one of my prayers. Wonder what the reason could be? I hope it's something that would piss Jerry off, cause I'm certainly not setting off any bomb. Maybe I'm supposed to find Lawrence so he can let me know what they're doing with Dad or if Zeke's turned up or...Jerry did say my mom had family here.*

The thought of finding his mother made Judge smile wildly, and he had to wait for his mouth to return to normal to start eating one of his soft apples. *Do they still have phone booths out here?* Judge remembered, years ago, seeing fat yellow phone books hanging from phone booths, and there were fleeting memories of movies where people would tear out the page with the name they were looking for. The idea of ruining that phone book for everyone always bothered him. *I'll have to find some way to write down her address.*

Chewing his mealy fruit, Judge wandered the empty streets, but could find no phone booths. *Even if I did find one, I don't think she would have stayed April Saxon. It must be nice to start over with a new name, but what if your past needs to find you? Shit. What do I do now? The whole world is looking for me, and probably looking extra hard here in Brookland. I can't just wander the city till I find her. Where's my help going to come from?*

At the top of a hill, Judge passed a sign that read 'St. Edward the Confessor Roman Catholic Church. Confessional open from 7-9 every morning'. *They have to help, right? And, I can't think of something that would piss Jerry off more than walking into a Catholic Church.* Judge could recall long sermons where Jerry would perch on his rock and preach for hours on the evils of Catholics. According to him, the Pope was Satan's representative earth, a pimp selling out the whore of Babylon, a sheep in wolf's clothing pretending to be holy but doing their best to tear people from the bosom of Christ. The 'celibate' priesthood was a fostering ground for homosexuals, and Jerry spoke of rumors that Seminaries and Monasteries held secret nightly orgies to celebrate their 'celibacy'. The news of the pedophilic scandals took a while to reach the Dark Corner, but it only provided fuel to Jerry's fire. *Jerry was an idiot. The Catholics must actually be pretty decent for Jerry to hate them so much.*

    A sign on a nearby bank said it was 1:30AM. Judge walked down an alley next to the church, lay down on the ground, and bunched his few spare clothes into a pillow. The activator could still be felt poking through, but it was something he had grown used to. It didn't take long to fall asleep, and it felt like it had been only a few minutes when the traffic on the road grew loud enough to wake him. The dull brick exterior of the church was reflecting back a vivid orange sunrise. The LED sign said 6:45AM. *Just in time. Providence?* Judge ate two apples while he waited.

    7AM rolled around. Keeping his head down, Judge peered around the corner of the alley to make sure he was alone. He almost ran when he saw someone on the steps, but he figured out that it was just the priest unlocking the front door. *Jerry used to talk about their uniforms. He said the all-black suit was a sign of their refusal of the light of the Lord and that if you shined a black light on their small white collar, you'd see a small written pledge to touch as many little boy penises as possible. That probably isn't true, but I don't have a little-boy penis anymore, so I should be fine if it were one of those things Jerry was actually right about.*

The priest, a boring man with a close-cropped gray beard, walked into the church. Judge waited a few seconds and followed him in. *Wow.* He craned his neck around to take the sanctuary in. It was shaped like an upside down boat, with buttresses and columns and stained glass and intense, sweet smells. The priest's shoes made small clicking sounds that echoed throughout the church. Judge breathed heavy in awe. *I wonder if he can hear my breath echoing the same way I can hear his steps. The Dark Corner could be a beautiful place, but this is...* Judge was at a loss for the correct thoughts. The rising sun came in green and blue through a stained glass window depicting a man being spit from a whale. Judge found himself smiling. *This* IS *what the Holy Spirit must really feel like. I think I'm in the right place. Good thing I prayed in the meat truck.*

A loud creak interrupted Judge's awe. The priest had stepped into the confessional. Judge remembered a TV show he watched as he child where a priest and a repentant stepped into a similar box, and everything said remained anonymous. *This is perfect. I can get help finding my Mom and he won't even know who I am.* Judge walked over to the booth and tried to open the door the priest had gone in. It was locked. The priest's voice came from inside. "Other door, please."

Oh. Right. "Sorry," Judge said. He stepped in through the other door. It smelled of old sweat and he could see the silhouette of the Priest through a little translucent grill between the two rooms. Judge sat on the bench and waited for the priest to say something. He was silent. *I guess I'm supposed to get started.* "Umm...hello?"

"Yes, my son?" His voice was smooth. *A little too much like Jerry's.*

"This is my first time in here. I don't really know what to do."

"Do you belong to a Catholic Church?"

Should I lie? "No. I just really need some help."

The priest sighed and said "Well, this is a confessional booth, not a help desk." Judge heard another loud creak. "Normally people come here to confess their sins and receive absolution, and my duty right now is to the sacrament of penance." Judge remembered when Jerry made him and his father confess their sins out loud when they first arrived at the Dark Corner. *I wonder if Jerry knew how close to Catholic he actually was. Was his hatred of them really just a cover up for his own desire to touch little boy penises?* "But since you're the only one here, I can help you until other penitents show up."

Good enough. "I understand. What I really need help with is finding my Mom."

The priest laughed and said "You don't really sound like a lost little boy."

I might not sound like it, but I think that's what I really am. "Well...this is anonymous, right?"

The priest sounded like he was reciting a list he kept pinned on the refrigerator of his mind. "The sacrament of penance calls for absolute confidentiality for the confessor."

"Ok. Well, I'm wanted by the cops...and probably the FBI too. I think they're all over the city looking for me, but they've got it all wrong. They think I'm trying to set off a nuclear bomb in the city, but I don't want to." Judge paused and the priest said nothing. "I think God wants me to be here, in Brookland, and I think it's because my Mom is here, but I haven't seen her in years and I can't remember her name to find her."

The priest's voice sounded small, and lost its smoothness. "Are you...Judge Saxon?"

"Listen, I just want help finding my mother-"

"Is the bomb in that bag you were carrying?" *He was watching me?*

"Well, kind of. But it's not even a real activator. I-"

The priest interrupted again. "I think it would do us better to talk about this in my office. I can...help you better when we look for your Mom on my computer."

"Would it still be in absolute confidentiality?"

"For the confessor, yes."

This is getting a little strange, but didn't God lead me here? "Ok. What about other people who want to confess?" Judge asked.

The door creaked again, and Judge heard the priest's footsteps echoing in the church. He opened the door. The priest was standing there waiting. "No one ever really comes to confess anymore, except on holidays." The priest smiled, and light from a stained glass rendition of Saul on the road to Damascus lit his big teeth. "But I'm glad I can help you. Follow me." Judge picked up his bag and followed the priest through a series of doors that ended up in a brightly lit office. Although it was clean, the yellow fluorescent light reminded Judge of the truck stop where he first tasted freedom.

"There won't be anyone else in here, will there?" Judge asked, checking the corner for intruders. "I don't...I trust you, but I don't want anyone else seeing me."

The priest sat at a table and motioned Judge to a chair. He said "No. We'll be alone." *I wonder how many little boys he's said that to.* "This church isn't like it used to be. We've had to cut our staff back, and it's just me here on Fridays. It's sad how this world's going. I imagine pretty soon this church will be gone, and people won't even notice how much help they need in this filthy world." *Is this guy Jerry's brother?* "You've grown a beard since...the picture they have on the news." The priest smiled again. "I think I like you better without it."

Creepy. "So how can you help me find my mother?"

He pulled a cell phone out of his pocket. "I can look her up on this, just...sit tight and we'll figure this out." The priest started typing away on his little cell phone. Yolanda's phone had been the first cell-phone Judge had ever seen up close. The idea that you could talk to anyone, anywhere astounded him, but her phone was nothing like this priest's. It was like a little TV, and it lit the Priest's face in a gentle light. *I'm getting one of those as soon as I can.* Judge leaned over to look at the phone, but the priest leaned away and Judge saw nothing. *I don't blame him for being scared of me. I'm just glad this is all confidential.*

Realizing that things weren't adding up, Judge said "So how are you going to look her up if..." *If I can't even remember her maiden name?* Judge grabbed the phone out of the priest's soft hands. It read 'Text Message. Judge Saxon at St. Edward the Confessor. I'll keep him here. Please hurry.' The priest frowned and jumped out of his chair. He found a wall behind him and cowered. Judge was surprised at how loud and raw his voice grew. "I thought this was confidential!" he screamed.

The priest spoke as he covered his face with his arms. "You didn't confess anything! Please don't hurt me!" *Shit. I can't just leave him here, and...Lincoln! I had a Grandmother Lincoln.*

So, my mother is April Lincoln. That's it. Judge threw the phone against a file cabinet, and it cracked into pieces.

"You got a phone book?" The priest nodded. Judge said "Give it to me." While the priest was looking through a desk for the book, Judge fought with himself to decide what to do. *Jerry was right. These Catholics are slimy. He'll give me up as soon as I leave, and I can't take him with me. But I don't want to hurt anyone else. Unless I have a good reason. Goddamnit. Time to Zeke up.* "How many little boys have you touched?"

"What?!"

Judge knocked the phone book out of the priest's trembling hands and pushed him to the wall. "You heard me. How many little boys?"

"I've never…" Judge's giant hands fit easily around the priest's neck. The priest tried to gurgle out some words. Judge eased up. "I've never…I'm not a pedophile!"

Why is hurting him so easy? Goddamnit. "Liar." Judge reared his hand back and knocked the priest unconscious with one strike. His left eye started to swell and turn black. Judge let go of his neck, and the priest crumpled. Pulling the unconscious man to his feet, Judge hit him again. *What am I doing?* He picked up his foot and stomped hard on the outside of the priest's knee. There was a pop, and Judge thought it was a beautiful sound. *What's wrong with me?* Judge smiled, and his stomach rumbled. *The Dark Corner is inside me. I need an exorcism, not a confession.* He had to force himself to walk away.

Judge thumbed through the phone book and found an April Lincoln at 1251 Washington Road. *That's it. Maybe she can help. But how do I get there? They have to be watching her house.* He looked down at the ruined priest. *Those clothes do look a little baggy on him.* He stripped the priest down to his underwear. *Please don't have shit your pants...* He hadn't. Judge pulled on the clerical clothes. The pants stopped two inches above his shoes and the sleeves barely reached his forearm, but the neck fit surprisingly well. *Beating the priest up would have made Jerry happy. Dressing up like the priest will just have to balance it out.*

A hat and sunglasses Judge saw in a coat closet made him feel even safer. *I'll pretend to be blind. They might be looking for Judge Saxon, suicide bomber, but they won't be looking for Judge Saxon the blind, bearded priest.* He dragged the naked body to the closet and wedged a chair under the door handle. *He'll be fine until Sunday, if anyone even shows up. Time to find my mother.*

Stumbling around, trying his best to be blind, Judge walked through the sanctuary to begin his brief stint as a sightless sage. Preoccupied with being someone he wasn't, Judge didn't smell the old incense or hear his footsteps echoing in the eaves.

Tell Your Children Not To Walk My Way

For reasons he couldn't remember, Judge equated being blind with being a drunken hunchback. He angled his torso so that his left shoulder was up in the air. His right arm hung down at his side, and he bounced as he walked. Occasionally, if he saw a blue post-office box or a light pole, he would run into it and mumble a prayer. "Lord Jesus, forgive this...this...was it a car? A phone booth?...whatever thou hast for me to run into, Lord forgive it. Make my path clear. Amen." *This'll fool everybody.*

At the intersection of Washington and Leaphart, Judge saw that a small yellow dog had started following him. *I must still smell like spoiled meat.* Before *The Hand*, Judge's small family had never had a dog, and Jerry always made a point to shoot any dogs that wandered into the Dark Corner. Judge never liked the taste, and always saw himself with a canine companion when he was able to get away and live his own life. This small yellow dog, whose teeth seemed too big for its mouth, sniffed at Judge's ankles and followed him as he walked.

He looked around to see if he could pause without being in the way, then remembered that he wasn't supposed to be looking at anything. To make up for it, he ran into a brick wall he was standing near and bent down to pet the dog. It licked his hand with a long, rough tongue and Judge was smitten. "Hello, little friend. Don't worry. I won't shoot you." *Another way to stick it to Jerry.* Judge pretended to feel around a nearby bench, and sat down. The dog followed, sniffing.

"I think I'll call you..." *Yellow? Goldie? But then what if someone asks me his...her name and they realize I'm not blind then they call the cops and tell them I'm a liar and they figure out I'm not really a priest and then they make me shave my beard and find out who I really am?* "...Fido. Want an apple?" Judge looked into his bag. Pushing the activator aside, he felt around for the softest apple. *I might need the good ones for myself. No idea how far away my mom is.*

Fido tried to pull the apple from Judge's hand. "You can't eat the whole thing in one bite." Judge smiled through his words and the dog eventually figured out how to rip chunks from it. "That's a good boy...girl." Doing his best to pretend not to, Judge watched the dog eat the apple. It relaxed him. *This is nice. This is the life I should be living. I wonder what Yolanda is doing right now.* As he pictured her freckles and how the tip of her head only came to the top of his chest, a memory shot back at him like Fido's hungry bites.

Wait. Did I really tell her I loved her? When he first said it, he was still reeling from Simmons' betrayal and didn't know what he was saying. She only caught part of it, hearing his declaration of love like a ghost that can only be seen in the corner of people's vision. Now that he wasn't on the run, Judge could picture the moment perfectly. *I did say it. Shit. And she just seemed more confused than anything. Goddamnit. If I'd had more time, maybe I could've said it for real and she would have said it back and she would have finished the scorpion sweater and-*

"Ow!" Fido had mistaken part of Judge's finger for apple. *My hands have grown softer since I haven't been chopping wood with Zeke.* He held his big hand up to his face. The dog jumped up on to his knees. He batted it away as he pulled his sunglasses off and examined his hurt finger. The pink fang-shaped indentations looked like they would have broken the skin if Fido had bit a little harder. The dog jumped up on Judge's knees again. "Damnit, dog. Leave me alone!" Judge tossed the apple core across the street.

Fido started off after it. It made it halfway across the street when it stopped and put its tail between its legs. Judge watched as it convulsed and vomited up pink foam in the middle of the road. The apple core was in sight on the opposite sidewalk in front of a boarded up liquor store, but the dog stayed in the road and licked what it had just thrown up. *Damnit Jerry. Quit being so right about everything.* His finger throbbed, and Judge found himself wishing that a car would come along, not see Fido and run it over. *Why would that make me happy? What is wrong with me?*

Judge held his finger back up in front of his eye. The would-be stab wounds were getting darker. "You ok, father?" Judge turned and looked to see a cop standing next to him. His hands on his sizable hips, the gray-clad, portly officer looked like a whale that had learned to walk. *Shit. I'm supposed to be blind.* Judge crossed his eyes and glanced around wildly in imitation of what he thought a blind person would do.

Sliding his sunglasses back on his face, Judge smoothed his voice to sound like the priest whose clothes he was wearing. *He called me father. Am I supposed to call him son? I always hated it when Jerry did that to me.* "I'm fine," Judge said, trying to imitate how he thought a priest would speak. "That...that beast bit my finger whilst I was feeding it an apple. Tell me, fine fellow, did it break any skin?"

He pointed his finger at the dog, who had finished his vomit and made his way to the apple core. The cop said "No, father, but still, you might want to get it checked out for rabies or something. I can give you a ride if you'd-"

"No. No thank you, I mean." *Talking with this cop at all is dangerous.* "I've...I've got to go." Judge got up and walked down the street with his arms in front of him like Frankenstein's monster. *Please don't follow, please don't follow. Is he following me? I can't exactly turn around and look to see for him, can I? Not if I'm blind, I can't.*

The walk to his mother's house was one of the most terrifying times of his life, worse than any of Jerry's rebukings and on par with the time in the meat truck. Judge walked and was unable to look behind him. *He's got to be right behind me, playing games with me. Why won't he just come at me?* Judge picked up his pace and thought he heard steps behind him. *If I turn around, he'll know I'm not blind and he'll figure out who I am. Not only will I be arrested on charges of terrorism, but I'll have to deal with Jerry thinking that I've started desiring little boy penises.*

Judge walked faster and didn't bother hunching over or running into things. *What can I do? I guess I could turn around, take a stand and knock him out, maybe steal his clothes, but wasn't beating up a cop what got everything off track in the first place?* Judge's mind flashed back to Babbalan's house. Zeke's fist, wrapped in chain, swung down and split Officer Babbalan's face like a rotted log. *Destroying this cop might be fun, but that would just make it worse on me. I've just got to keep running.*

Remembering to pay attention to the street numbers, Judge found that he was getting closer and closer to his mother's house. *She'll help me. 1251 Washington Ave. That yellow house was...3459...3457. Not too far now. She'll tell the cop that I'm really a priest and not a terrorist and he'll leave and I won't have to hurt anyone else. Maybe she'll have some of those cinnamon rolls.* A truck roared behind Judge and he started broke into a full-on sprint. *3285...3279. Damnit, Mom. Hurry up.* Judge ran past a post office and a McDonalds. *Why can't we pass a donut shop?!*

He was starting to get sweaty under that woolen frock, but he knew not to stop running. *2395...2143...* The sidewalk started up a slow incline. Huffing, Judge tripped over his feet. *This is it. I'm as good as caught. Jail can't be that bad, can it?* Judge thought about it and remembered his rape dream. *Wrong. It will be that bad. I'm fighting my way out. Officer Whale won't be any trouble, but I'm tired. I've got to take him by surprise.* The cool ground felt good on his hands as he laid there. *First move he makes, I grab whatever he puts near me and break it.*

Something furry touched Judge's right arm. With lightning speed built from years of trying to stop Zeke from killing him, Judge grabbed something round before he opened his eyes. *This doesn't feel right. Officer Whale wasn't covered in hair.* Judge saw that he had Fido in his grip. The dog panted and licked his hand. There was no one else as far as Judge could see. *Seriously?* Fido's tongue was boring down into Judge's hand. *Ew. Gross. I know where that tongue's been.*

Judge pushed the dog away and looked around. *1381. And that house is 1369 and then that street and...that's it.* April Lincoln's house was tucked into a little pre-war bungalow neighborhood. Its white shutters stood out in a stark contrast against the faded dark blue of the siding. The grass was overgrown and the roof shingles were coming up in spots. *I can fix that if she'll let me.*

A white van was parked across the street. Two men in sunglasses were sitting in the front seats doing nothing. *I should have known they'd be watching for me.* Judge stepped down a side street and hid in an alley. Fido followed. *Hmmm...I guess if I had to I could just try to fight my way in, but I really don't want my Mom to have to see that.* Fido stuck its snout into Judge's bag. "Hey. Get out of there!" Judge kicked her away with the bottom of his boot. *I could watch and wait for their shift change and...then I'd have to fight off even more of them. Damnit, Jerry. You taught me a lot about destroying people, but nothing about subterfuge.*

Judge heard a rustling at his feet. It was Fido again, trying to get an apple. It had pulled the activator out in a fit of hunger. It shined in the sun. "Damnit, dog." Judge kicked the dog away and pulled an apple out of his bag. "Fetch this!" He chucked the apple without thinking. It sailed towards a busy intersection two blocks down. Fido ran after it. *Good. Now what can I-*

There was a loud SCREECH and a series of metallic thuds. Judge looked down towards the sound and saw Fido chewing the thrown apple in the middle of a semi-circle of twisted, smoking metal. *Oh shit. I hope those people are...* Judge heard the van's doors slam. The two sun-glassed men jumped out and ran towards the wreck. One of them said "Oh crap, Sam! Call an ambulance."

They ran. One of them whipped out a walkie talkie. He didn't hear what was said. *Fido, I take back my desire to see you get run over. Now's my chance.* He bolted towards his Mother's house. *No car in the driveway.* The front door was locked. *I'm going to have to break in.* He hopped off the porch and ran through thigh-high weeds to the back of the house.

The first few windows were locked, but the fourth one slid up easily. Judge pulled himself up and rolled into the house. He landed with a thud in a bathroom that smelled like it was losing its battle against the oncoming tide of time. The toilet emitted a sour smell of old rust water and the floor felt soft in spots. Once Judge found the parts of the floor that didn't creak under his weight, he became silent and listened. *No noise. She must be at work at the...what did Mom do for a living?*

Judge racked his brain in that sewer-smelling room. *I lived with her for twelve years and I can't remember where she would be working?* Once he was sure he was alone, Judge exited the bathroom and stepped into a hallway. The brown carpet and dark wooden paneling on the walls gave Judge the impression that he was walking through an underground tunnel. The cave-like kitchen he found fit in perfectly. Other than cleanliness, it wasn't much different from the kitchen in the old cabin at the Dark Corner. The light was poor. It smelled faintly of grease and didn't exactly make one hungry. *How does she make cinnamon rolls in a place like this?*

This is...not what I expected. Judge walked over to the refrigerator. The front was bare except for a magnet advertising a local pizza joint. He opened a cabinet and found only bare glasses and plates. He pulled a cup down, filled it with water from the sink and sat down at a small plasterboard table. *Ok. Great. I'll just sit here and wait on her to get home. I hope those people in that car accident are ok.*

The light outside had turned a few shades darker when Judge heard a car door slam. *That must be her.* A doorknob in the front of the house turned, and the sound of plastic grocery bags crinkling filled the hallway. *I guess I should stand up so she can hug me.* She walked in and didn't see Judge standing in the shadows in his dark priest suit with his dark beard.

She doesn't look anything like I remember. What exactly was I remembering, then? Judge knew that he thought the girl at the university looked like his mom, but this woman looked nothing like the girl at the university, and only vaguely looked like the mother Judge remembered from 9 years ago. She had the same curly hair, but it looked wet and flat instead of teased and large, and her body was more round than tall. *That's her all right, but...I must not have a very good memory for looks. I hope my mind doesn't do the same thing to Yolanda.* She set a bag of groceries on the counter and started putting items in the empty refrigerator. Judge cleared his throat.

She breathed in sharply, turned around and covered her whimpering mouth. "Who are…" She was scared until she saw that it was a priest. Her body relaxed, but her voice still held plenty of surprise. "Are you…what are you doing here?"

Judge tried to smile through the shock of finally seeing his mother and having her look completely different than he would have thought. "Don't you recognize me?" Judge asked, opening his arms up. *Time for that hug.*

"Oh shit." She covered her wrinkled mouth with a veiny hand. Her eyes moved to the doorway she had just come through. Her attempt to dart through the door was too slow for her son. Judge leapt in front of her and she recoiled. She tried the doorway leading into the dark hallway, but Judge beat her there as well. "Just let me go." Her voice grew labored, as if she was about to cry.

"Mom, just-"

"Don't call me that!" she screamed. She backed up from her son until she hit the table. It shook and Judge's cup of water toppled over. "Just…get out of here. Please. I don't want any trouble."

Judge stepped towards her. She braced up as he said "What are you saying? I just need your help." He tried to look deep into her eyes. *I always thought that I must have looked more like her, but I must have gotten my good looks from Dad.*

"I'm not helping some damn terrorist. I left your father cause this all scared me, and..." She looked at the doorway again.

Please don't. "But Mom, you don't understand! Jerry sent me to set off the bomb, but I just used it to escape and..." Judge tried to smile despite the slow realization that he knew nothing about his mother. "...to find you and live my own life."

She frowned. The lines on her forehead surprised Judge. *She can't be that old. I do have the right woman, don't I?* She said "Whatever. That's what someone like you would say."

"Someone like me?" Judge asked. He had to ignore the pit growing in his stomach. "Mom, what are you saying?"

Her fist slammed down on the table. *She does have large hands.* "Stop calling me that! I thought I was done with all this crap, with you and your Dad years ago, and then I saw you on the news and those g-men showed up and...I should just turn you in. I could scream, but you'd probably kill me before they could get in here to save me."

If you don't stop acting like that I might...wait. What? No. What's happening to me? "I wouldn't do that, Mom....I just really need some help. Somewhere to hide, maybe a way out of the city...you don't happen to know where my brother is, do you?"

She just stared at him. Her eyes had the same glassy vacancy that Yolanda had when Judge first told her who he really was. "I'm not giving you any help," she sneered. "I know who you are! I-"

"But you haven't seen me in years! You didn't even try to find me when Dad took me!" *I need to quiet down so those feds don't come in.* "You don't know what I've been through, what I've been doing. How do you think you know who I am?"

Anger was the last thing I thought I'd be feeling when I finally saw her again, but goddamn if I don't feel like punching a hole through this cheap house. She said "I know you cause I know who your Daddy was and…I know who I am."

"I'm not him!" *And I'm quickly realizing that I'm glad I'm not you, either.*

Her brown eyes slowly scanned the room. *I'm guessing she's looking for a weapon. Good thing I didn't inherit her terrible attempts at stealth.* "Well, the apple can't fall that far from the apple tree, can it? I can see it on your face right now. You're starting to think you know better than me, aren't you?" *Damn.* "Just like your Dad, always thinking he's holier than everyone else and then that damn Jerry told him that it was ok to think that because God needed him."

Judge said "Oh yeah? What did I get from you then?"

"Certainly not my common sense. I wouldn't ever steal some priest's clothes. I would know better than to walk into a house the feds are watching. I would know better than to set off a bomb in this city and if you really don't want to set it off, I would have known better than to show up in Brookland."

Is my face turning red? "I didn't come here on purpose," Judge said. He brought his voice low, afraid of how his mother might react to what he said next. "I...think God brought me here."

"I'd damn sure have more common sense than to believe that God claptrap. You sound just like your goddamn father."

This can't be my mom. "Whatever. Can't you at least give me a second chance? I mean...this is actually the first chance. At least give me that."

"I've been burned enough by men like you," she said, as she pointed a finger at Judge's chest. "Your father named you and claimed you, and I don't want anything to do with you. I didn't even want you in the first place. I convinced him to get rid of the first one, but he wouldn't have it for you. Said you were special. Don't want your kind of special."

Judge found himself clinching his fists up tight. *It would be so easy. She's just some old bitch. She'd deserve it too, for birthing me in a world where I've got nowhere to run.* Judge imagined hearing a snap as he made contact, the same sound he heard from Officer Babbalan and the manager of that hotel and Simmons' jaw and the priest and his footsteps echoing in that cavernous church. *It's a beautiful sound...but no.*

She must have read something sinister on his face. Her quickness surprised Judge. *There's my genetics*. She yanked open a drawer and pulled out a rusting butcher knife, thrusting it wildly towards Judge's midsection. He easily sidestepped it and disarmed her. The knife fell to the ground. He spun her around, squeezed both arms around her chest and clutched her back to his front. *I guess this is the only hug I'm going to get.*

Remain calm. Killing her might feel good for the moment, but I'll hate myself for it later, even if she did turn out to be a monumental bitch. "All right," Judge said in calm contrast to her frantic breathing. "You can't get away from me, and I don't think you want to know what happens if you try. I'm going to let go, and you're going to sit in that chair. I'm going to tie you to it and then I'm going to tape your mouth shut. Then I'm going to leave and prove that I'm a better man than my Dad. And a better person than you." Judge took a deep breath. "1, 2, 3."

He let go. She bent down to grab the knife. Judge kicked it away and said "Chair. Now."

She did as he said. "You know this isn't surprising at all," she said. "Why don't you kill me? You're a killer. Your Daddy wanted you to be one. I can see it in your eyes, son."

"I'm not your son." Judge tied her up with an orange extension cord he saw behind the microwave. He found a roll of grey duct tape and covered her mouth. "I don't need you going to the cops. You keep pushing at that tape with your tongue, you'll get free eventually. 18 hours or so, you'll be free and I'll be gone. That's all just so you know that I'm not my father, I'm not Jerry, I'm not a killer. I'm not you."

Judge walked down the dark hallway as her screams came muffled from the kitchen. *I always thought we'd be leaving together, maybe holding hands. I used to love holding her hand as a kid...I think. Did we ever actually do that? No, I guess we didn't.* He thought hard, and few actual memories of his childhood came flooding back. He remembered his public school teachers, and playing at playgrounds, how his room looked, scorpion sweaters, and cinnamon rolls. Amittai was always there, but he didn't remember seeing his mother in any of it. *Why do I remember so little about my mother? She must have never been there.*

No wonder Dad left. Would staying with her have been just as bad as the Dark Corner? The memories brought back pangs in Judge's chest, and he suddenly wanted to see his Dad more than anything else. *Life wasn't easy on me, but wasn't he just making the best of things?* He crawled through the bathroom window into a warm early evening. The light from the setting sun moved from bright orange to purple as the stars came out. He walked down the same street the feds had ran down earlier. The wreck had been cleared, but as he walked past the site he could smell spilt gasoline and blood.

The street was mostly empty. Some payphones stood stoically a block down, fat yellow phone books hanging beneath them. *There they are. That would have saved me some time. Then again, if I had found these phonebooks, I wouldn't have acquired these sweet priest clothes. What do I do now?* Down the street, a family was coming out of a restaurant. Judge watched as a little girl in a yellow dress stepped towards the street. The father grabbed her shoulders and held her back. The mother, a woman Yolanda's height, said something to the little girl and smiled.

Judge reached into his ratty bag and pushed the activator to the side. *There it is. I'm glad I didn't throw it away.* He pulled a yellowed slip of paper out, walked towards the payphones and dialed the handwritten number. *I hope I don't end up regretting this.* "Hello, Lawrence?" he said into the receiver. "It's Judge Saxon. I need help getting in touch with my Dad."

A Wee Little Man Was He

I wonder if Lawrence is aware that he lives 12 blocks from my mother's house. Probably not. Judge looked at the squat, brick apartment building that Lawrence said he lived at. *He wasn't lying about it not being much to look at. I really hated the Dark Corner. The cabins seemed to be older than the Declaration of Independence but the beauty of the area around it certainly made up for that. I'm glad I won't have to admit it to Jerry or Dad, but as much as I enjoy indoor plumbing, I think I'd rather live there than in this city. Actually, I think I'd rather be on the tour bus with Yolanda. She was more beautiful than the sunrise over the mountains. And we had indoor plumbing. I think eventually we could find a way to make a bunk big enough for the two of us.*

Judge slammed his knuckles on the door. A light cut on inside. *Why was he sitting in the dark?* There was a rusty, squeaking noise from inside, like the sound of the water pumps Jerry would make Judge and Zeke pump in the dry months. "Just a minute!" *He sounds just like I remember. At least I can get that memory right.* It had been two years since Lawrence left the Dark Corner. While he was there, he spent most of his time in the garage with Amittai. The only real memory Judge had of Lawrence was that he was exceedingly short and had a heavy southern accent that truly reared its redneck head during the worship services. Judge grew up in the South, but he still had a hard time understanding Lawrence's mushy mouth.

The locks slid out of place. "Go ahead on an' openit up!" Judge pushed the door open. He already had his gaze lowered so he could see Lawrence's face, but he had to look lower to see him in his wheelchair. "Well, Judge. You weren't but this tall last time I seen you." Lawrence had to stretch to put his arm high enough to shake Judge's hand. There were yellow bruises and red cuts snaking up and down his arms. "Come on in, fella."

It took some work for him to turn his wheelchair around. Judge grabbed the back to help, but Lawrence refused and did it himself, slowly. Judge said "Lawrence, what happened?"

"Call me Larry. None of this Lawrence business. I give that name up a long time ago," he said. His apartment was just as ratty on the inside. White cinder block walls loomed over a used-to-be-green shag carpet. "Set a spell." Larry pointed a few taped fingers to a cushion-less couch. "And here I didn't think you'd be coming round here." He spoke quietly and emphasized the wrong syllables.

Is that sarcasm? Maybe I'm just not deciphering his accent too well. Still, I don't want to blow my cover. "It took me a little longer to get here than I thought, but...you been watching the news?"

"I have. It's been some, uh...sad business, that's for sure." The sides of his mouth kept twitching up and down, as if he was struggling to fight a smile from appearing. "What's with the get-up? Turning penguin on me?"

"This?" Judge said. He glanced down at his priest outfit. *This oughtta get him on my side.* "I beat up a priest, stole his clothes. Figured it would help me get around the city undetected."

Larry rubbed under his chin. "Yeah, and that there chinstrap probably helps too."

Shit. My beard. I seem to remember that he sided with Jerry over the great beard schism. He even helped put Hank up on that cross. My beard is beautiful, but not beautiful enough to give me away. Judge's voice grew high as he made his excuses. "I know, it's sinful and ugly, but I haven't had a chance to cut it and-"

"No, no. I like it. Suits you well." *Really? What's going on?* He saw Judge's confusion. "I mean...it's an abomination unto the Lord!" He picked up his hand and pointed at Judge unconvincingly. He threw up his hands and said, in a less formal voice, "Aw, shit. Whatever. Y'all've already kicked me around enough. Ain't much else you can do to me, is there?" *What is he talking about? Is this some kind of test I've got to pass before he'll tell me where dad is?* "You know what Judge? I ain't scared of Jerry no more. Ain't scared of Zeke. Ain't scared of your daddy. I ain't scared of you. I ain't scared of God. He can't be any worse to me than Jerry was. So do what you will to me." He rolled his wheelchair towards Judge and rammed him repeatedly. Their knees touched over and over again. Larry winced with every hit. Judge had to hold back laughter. "Go on and do it. Beat me up. Tell me how I'm a traitor."

Calling Larry might have been the smartest thing I've done all week. Relieved, Judge smiled and said "I think I'm a traitor too."

Larry stopped his wheelchair assault. "Oh. Well, good. Always reckoned you had some sense in that head." *I still kinda feel like hugging. Wonder if he'd let me...* Larry turned around and wheeled towards his kitchen. *Guess not.* "Let me ask you. If you got in your right mind and decided not to do any of this Armageddon shit, why the fuck are you here?"

"I want to talk to my dad."

Judge followed Larry into the kitchen and watched him labor to pour two cups of coffee from his wheelchair. "Talking to your daddy is suicide, plain and simple. I know you're smarter'n that. I mean why are you here in Brookland? You do know they know the bomb is here, don't you? They're looking for you. That beard can't hide you forever."

"I know," Judge said. "I kind of...ended up here. As soon as you get me in touch with dad I'm going to disappear forever." Judge picked up his coffee and sipped. *Damn, that's a good cup of coffee. Why didn't you stick around the Dark Corner, Larry?*

Wheeling over to the table and motioning Judge to sit down, Larry said "Listen, Judge. I know he's your daddy and all, but you cannot talk to him. They'd get you in a second, and you'd be tossed in the stir forever. Do you even know what jail is like?" *The pain in my ass says I've got an idea.* "Besides, you don't seem to have Jerry's cock in your mouth anymore, so why do you want to get in touch with your dad? He might have been different, but he was every bit as evil." *Don't make me angry.* Judge squinted his eyes and Larry saw it. "Don't sass me, boy. I know we all get rose-colored glasses with our parents, but this whole bomb thing was Am's idear."

What?! Judge spoke through his teeth. "Larry, I know you and I have been through a lot of stuff trying to get over the Dark Corner, but you've got no right to slander my dad like that. I guess I can tell you this now, but the activator he gave me is a fake." Judge pulled it out of his bag. "He came up with this whole plot so I could escape."

He handed the activator to Larry. He examined it while Judge drank his coffee. After poking and prodding it for a few minutes, Larry set it down on the table. "Ain't no fake. That sucker's live and primed to ruin somebody's day." *I refuse to believe that.* "I hate to tell you this, but your daddy's where he belongs, in that jail. You and I were in the company of some evil men. I hate that you were raised in it. Shit, I was an evil man till I figured it out."

Was an evil man? "What happened?"

Larry sighed and rolled to his backdoor. The view of the city lights from that crappy apartment was surprisingly beautiful. "I got here the first day, and I hated it. I almost can't believe it now, but I missed *The Hand*, and Jerry and your dad and you and all of it. I weren't even that excited about blowing this city to shit – I just wanted to go back to where I belonged. And then I met someone," Larry said.

"Me too."

"Figured as much. Sometimes it takes someone loving you to show you the truth."

Am I going to get this wise? "Yeah. What was her name?" Judge asked.

Judge saw Larry look at him in the reflection of the window. *Why is he hesitating? And looking at me like I'm about to hit him?* "Steve," he said boldly, as if he was hoping it would make Judge mad. *That's a weird name for a girl.* "We worked together at the power plant. I was making the bomb, putting in late hours. He was the night janitor." *He? Oh. I get it.* "I just ignored him at first, and him talking to me just made me angry, and eventually I figured it all out...why I hated Steve talking to me, why I missed the Dark Corner, shit, why I went to the Dark Corner in the first place." Larry looked at Judge again with tears in his eyes. "I figured out that I'm about as queer as it gets. I just love being around dicks, Judge."

You know, a few weeks ago this would have made me angry. I would have ran out the door. But now after living with Simmons, it's hard to be surprised about anything. I like Yolanda. Larry likes dicks. Makes sense. "So that made you stop making the bomb?"

Larry wheeled around and glared at Judge. "So you aren't going to schiz out on me?"

"I've seen enough nasty, slutty vaginas in the last few weeks to understand why you might go the other way."

"Well...all right. I don't really know what to say to that." *I guess I wouldn't either. I need to work on this talking stuff.* "But to answer your question, no, that didn't stop me from working on the bomb. If anything, it made me work harder because of how sinful I thought I was. I just wanted to die, and the bomb seemed like the best way. I denied who I was long enough to finish, and one night I was at work, and I was going to end it. I thought I was alone. I put a gun in my mouth, and guess who was there?"

"Steve?"

Larry laughed and said "No. No one was there. No one telling me to stop. No God in the sky calling me home or cursing me to Hell. It was like standing in one of those freak downpours that just stops all of the sudden. The silence was goddamn deafening." It was quiet in the apartment for a few seconds until the air conditioner cut on and hummed the silence away. *I wonder what that means.* Larry continued. "And I realized all of it – that Jerry and your daddy had it wrong. There ain't no God up there calling for the end of it. There ain't no God telling me I can't suck Steve's dick if I want to. You might not want to hear this, but Jerry and your daddy are evil men. I'm thinking you never actually talked to your daddy. All he ever thought about was murdering millions of people. And they call gay people perverts? Your daddy was the sickest man I've ever met."

Larry might have been smart enough to figure things out away from the Dark Corner, but he doesn't know a thing about my dad. As cordial as he could, Judge said "I'm glad you figured out who you really were." *May you get to suck a million dicks.* "I've known for a while about Jerry being evil, but...I can't believe my dad actually wanted me to kill millions of people. He couldn't have. He was just doing the best he could have after he left my Mom."

Larry sighed and said "Zeke thought you might say that."

"Zeke?" Judge asked. "Zeke's here?"

"Yeah."

The thought of Zeke made Judge feel like someone had been whispering his name across a crowded room. *Simmons was the most disappointing brother anyone could have, but Zeke really does love me. Then again, he's a monster. Bu Larry changed, and I've learned so much since I've left. Maybe Zeke has* too. *Can someone really see the world and not realize the truth? Or maybe if he hasn't yet, I can show him that there are other ways to live. I've missed him. We can still try to find my dad, and if we can't get him out, he and I can still join a tour and find Yolanda and she can knit me that scorpion sweater. This is right.* "He's here in Brookland?"

"Not just in Brookland. In my goddamn apartment. Asshole comes by every other day or so asking after you, wondering whether you've come by or not and...Damnit. I didn't want to tell you this." He sighed again. "All right. He come by about two weeks ago and found out that I didn't believe Jerry's shit anymore and he rebuked me. Broke four of my toes. Beat me up. You probably recognize his handiwork."

Larry motioned at his face. *That's Zeke's all right. But he had no problem killing Babbalan.* "Why didn't he just kill you?" Judge asked.

"I wish the sumbitch had. But he tortured me. Kept stepping on my broken toes. I don't think I'll ever walk again. He wanted to know where the bomb was," Larry said. "I told him the truth. I had to. I told him where it was, but I also spilled that I'd sabotaged the bomb as soon as I broke it off with Jerry."

Was he the reason Jerry kept telling me about temptation? How did he know that Larry returned to his own vomit unless he had to vomit as well? What's Jerry's vice? "Why didn't you just go to the cops?"

"Because I stole plutonium and built a goddamn nuclear warhead next to a football stadium! They'd throw me in jail too! I figured if I break the bomb a little, Jerry wouldn't know any better and I could keep from getting prison raped like I hope he is getting prison raped right now."

The thought of Jerry getting prison raped does make me happy. But my dad's there too...maybe Zeke can help me find a way in? Larry said "And Zeke kept pushing, asking where I kept the bomb blueprints, what I done to ruin the bomb. I told him a lie and he disappeared for a few days. He came back angrier than ever and broke my legs. I couldn't help it. I told him the truth about what I did to the bomb. I thought he'd leave me alone, but he still comes back every few days. He cuts me and beats me and burns me. He said faggots deserve it, and that he'll keep doing it until I give you his message."

Judge looked hard at Larry. His speech about Zeke had gotten him huffing, and he leaned to his right side as he breathed. His left hand was over his ribs. The cuts and bruises on his arms were in precise rows and his nose was a shape no normal person's should be. "What message?"

Larry sat up straight and looked Judge in the eyes. "He said that the Lord would bring you here, and that the Lord was going to use me to send you to him, or else the Lord would use him to keep rebuking me until I turned back to the Lord." He reached over his counter and grabbed a piece of notebook paper, folded over. "And goddamnit, I'm tired of this. I thought I was done, and now I am." He slammed the paper on the table. "He's here, for fuck's sake. Go see him and end this." The paper unfolded to show an address. *Brother, I can fix you.* "You know it's a trap, right?"

"I know," Judge said. "But he's my brother." Judge drained the last of his coffee, stood up and shoved the address in his pocket. "I have to see him. He's all I got left."

"I figured you had a brain, but you're just as dumb as all of them. You people fuckin' deserve each other. I'm done. Now, get the hell out of my house." Larry whipped his wheelchair around and disappeared into another room. *I thought a person like him would understand, but he must not know what it's like to have a brother.* Judge let himself out of the cold cinderblock apartment, walked down to the phone he used earlier and ripped the map out of the phonebook. *This address is right next to the stadium. It'll take me all night to walk there, but that's good. It'll give me time to figure out what to tell Zeke to convince him to stop and disappear with his brother.*

Pilgrim's Progress

It took Judge all night and most of the morning to make it over to the stadium. He left Larry's apartment in the darkest part of the night and had to cross clear over the city to find Zeke. Judge found his body getting tired. *I've been running too long.* His feet aching, his legs burning, his back bending; it all reminded him that the last sleep he got was a few scant hours in the alley next to the Catholic Church.

A few times his flesh told him to stop, but he had become an expert on saying no to his flesh. *I've got to keep going. The sooner I find him and we work this out, the quicker we can get out of dodge and start our new life together. That sounded too much like Larry. Our new life together. Me with Yolanda, and Zeke tagging along. That's better.*

Along the way, he saw much of the city. The west end, where his Mom and Larry lived, was packed with baby boomer bungalows and sad apartment buildings, short and inconsequential. In the distance he could see silos and long pipes. *Is that the plant where Larry got the plutonium and met Steve? I wonder if I could get a job at a place like that. Just with less bomb-building.* As he got closer to downtown, the buildings grew larger and uglier. Most of them were nondescript warehouses built from tan corrugated metal. He crossed a giant bridge over a river into downtown.

At first he was accosted by a few ladies who didn't seem to be wearing enough clothes for the weather. From a distance, they seemed attractive. *That one girl, the redhead. She's pretty. Reminds me of Yolanda, but with more of a body. Maybe if I...* As he got closer, he realized that these were just the sort of girl that Simmons used every night. *Half of them have probably been with him. Her on Mixed Monday, her on Thin Thursday. I wonder if I could find anything beautiful about these women up close.* He looked and saw their wrinkles and flaps and moles and trackmarks. *No. Not at all.*

He kept on walking and glanced over his shoulder at them, as they disappeared into the distance. From afar, they transformed back into attractive women. *I wonder if we're all like that. From far away, when you can only get a vague picture, they can be beautiful and amazing and you can guess whatever you need to fill in the blanks, but when you get up close and really get to know a person you have to see what was fuzzy from far away. I know it ended up that way with the real world away from The Hand. And with my Mom. If I had known the truth, maybe seeing her up close would have been less of a surprise. Maybe I wouldn't have thought Simmons was my new brother. Have I really looked at Zeke that close before?* Judge decided that he had. *I know he loves me up close, and that he'd do anything for me. Maybe when you're that close to someone you* can't see how beautiful they are from the distance. Why can't I see both ways? Life's a scary thing.

The buildings grew taller and the streets grew absolutely empty except for a few bums on benches using newspapers for blankets. *I will not end up that way.* A large dome rose up in front of him, surrounded by green lawns dotted with statues. *The statehouse. I remember this place.* The Hand had protested there a few times early on in Judge's time in the Dark Corner. *We must have stopped when Jerry realized that we needed Lawrence to live here undetected. This building used to be a lot taller.*

Judge approached the familiar campus where Zeke had caused a riot a few weeks ago. *Was it really that recently that it happened? I feel like I've lived a lifetime since then. I used to love this place when it was always so far away. Is it still the same? I've got enough time for a short detour.* Judge took a turn and walked up the sidewalk to the quad that he'd been to a dozen times before. *It's weird to be here by myself, and at night.* In the daytime, it had been populated with smiling people carrying books and carrying on conversations. They would smile at each other and smile on the phone. They would sit together and eat and play Frisbee. Judge loved it, but he always felt like he was looking at it through a dirty window.

This is completely different from how I thought this would look. Instead of the studious heading off to their studies, the quad was populated more sparsely but more savagely. Packs of young men stumbled around after gaggles of young women. The men had hungry looks on their faces that Judge recognized from Zeke. The girls, all of them, attractive or not, dressed like hookers and had the same open, weak look Judge recognized from Simmons' groupies. *I used to picture myself here with some of these girls, but...this is a jungle. Did Yolanda walk around like that? Was she ever one of them?*

A murder of young men in backward hats and fraternity t-shirts pointed at Judge and laughed. One of them walked towards Judge and motioned for the others to follow. "Hey, father. Want to touch Stew's dick? It's as small as a little boy's!" They all laughed and came closer. *As tired as I am, I can take them. I even want to, like Zeke did. I'd love to quit running and take my stand. Why did Zeke feel so violent then when I didn't? Why do I feel violent now? Did he see them up close when I only saw them at a distance?*

I could hear that beautiful cracking sound, but I can't cause a scene. Judge ducked behind a building and ran from the frat boys until he was back on course. Soon, the cityscape gave way to pristine apartment buildings and closed stores. He stooped behind a dumpster at one point to poop. When he came out, the sun was beginning its climb. *This will be mine and Zeke's last sunrise in this city. Tomorrow, we'll be on our way to our new life somewhere else.*

The morning sun burned on as Judge got closer. He could feel the heat absorbing into his black priest's clothes. Quicker than he noticed, the way to the stadium began filling with people, all dressed in orange or purple or red or black. They parked along the street, in parking lots and on the grass, setting up tables and plates of food. *Is there a game today? It might make it harder for us to get out...unless the game's going on. Then no one will see us making our escape.*

Some of the same style frat-boys that tried to hassle Judge earlier yelled something out to him. Their music was too loud for him to decipher what they were yelling at him. Judge walked on, but slowed down when he heard the song. *I've heard this...it's "Two Ponytails to Pull, Two Necks to Choke, One Pussy to Fuck". Sorry Yolanda. It seems like some people are stupid enough to actually like Sexual Lives.* He thought about Simmons while he listened to him wailing over the speakers. *Why did I ever think he could be my new brother? Was I that desperate? Am I still that desperate?*

Judge's heart grew heavy when he thought about Simmons' betrayal, and listening to him scream about fucking a pair of conjoined twins just made it worse. He had to fight the urge to smash the stereo playing that song. *After experiencing I'll Fly Away, how can anyone listen to this? There's something wrong with this filthy world. Shit. Jerry's probably laughing in his prison cell right now, thinking about how I can't run away from the truth of what he taught me.*

The foot traffic grew heavier, sometimes near impenetrable, but Judge kept his head down and pushed on. It cleared out as he grew closer to the address where Zeke was shacking up with the bomb. The buildings around him turned back into sad warehouses and empty industrial offices. He found the one marked on the paper. It had the same decaying look of all the other buildings surrounding it. Judge stopped to listen for any sign of Zeke, but he could only hear the din of the crowds back by the stadium, like an ant pile crawling. *All right, God. You brought me here...I think. Help me come out with Zeke. I'm taking a stand now. No more running.* Judge pulled open a creaky metal door and stepped into the silent darkness.

Brothers (Reprise)

Judge found Zeke after navigating a series of dark hallways. He was in an upstairs room that used to overlook some sort of factory floor. A window looking at the football stadium was letting blinding white light into the room. It hurt Judge's eyes. Zeke's thin silhouette blocked half of it. It took Judge a moment to realize it, but Zeke was looking out the window at the people streaming into the stadium. *What's he thinking?*

A large barrel covered in sheet metal was in the corner of the room. *That must be it. It isn't even half as big as I am. How can something so small have held such a wide promise of destruction?* He looked at Zeke's wiry, muscular back and thought the same thing. Still, he was very happy to see his brother and didn't fight the smile that creeped over his face. "Hey Zeke."

Zeke turned around. The light behind him from outside kept his face in the shadows, but Judge saw that he was smudged with grease and sweat, his hands dotted with scrapes and cuts. His face was scrunched and rat-like as ever, and he was surprisingly clean-shaven. *Must be why he has those cuts on his face. Still trying to be Jerry's favorite, even when Jerry is probably someone's favorite shower-buddy in prison.* "Judge! Great to see you!" His ugly smile threatening to swallow his face, Zeke approached Judge and shook his hand. "I knew you'd come!" *No hugging?*

"How did you know I'd come?" Judge asked. *I imagine he figured that I was going to run far away from here.* As Judge's eyes adjusted, he got a better look at his brother. *He must have lost 20 pounds. He didn't have that much to lose before.* His clothes hung from his body like Spanish moss. His clean-shaven cheeks were sunk in, and his once muscular arms had grown past the point of lean and into the territory of holocaust victims. *It's like a stick grew hands and a face.* He couldn't help but see Simmons' body with Zeke's face, and was almost surprised at the lack of track marks in the crooks of Zeke's elbows. *Are my two faux-brothers becoming one person?*

"I knew the Lord would bring you here. You know good and well you can't run away from the Lord's will." *Of course. Must be some faith if he thought enough to hedge his bets against the astronomical odds that I'd be coming this way. Still, I am here, aren't I? Faith like that might be the most logical thing.* "I knew the Lord had special plans for you and me, and that's why I came here. Took you a little longer than I thought it would, though."

Not long enough. "Yeah. It's been a long strange trip. I've got a lot to tell you."

"I bet you do." The sound of a group cheering came from outside. Zeke walked towards the window and frowned, saying "Did you walk here? Did you see all these people?"

Judge followed him over. People were starting the mass exodus from their tailgate spots to the stadium. *Are Yolanda's parents out there?* "Yeah. I saw a lot of them on my way here. They're-"

"Sickening?"

"I was going to say busy, but-"

"Busy in sin," Zeke said. *Here we go.* "I don't know what you were doing these last few weeks, but I saw more need for the wrath of God than I ever thought was possible." Zeke squinted at the light and took them all in. "I knew Jerry was right while we were in the Dark Corner, and I thought I had faith in the Lord's plan, but now I know how weak I actually was. I had to see it to truly *believe* it. It was painful, having the scales pulled from my eyes but now I can see it all so clearly."

He's turned into Super-Jerry. Great. I've got to take this delicately. Judge said "I saw a lot while I was out there too, Zeke. It's a lot different from the Dark Corner, that's for sure."

"Don't worry." Zeke clapped Judge on the shoulder with strong, calloused hands. He could see every muscle tense in Zeke's forearm. "Pretty soon the Lord will bring the kingdom here. We might have thought our lives were perfect before, but even the Dark Corner will be bathed in the Lord's light after today." *Perfect?* He looked down at the ratty bag in Judge's hands. Judge looked down to see what he was looking at. *I forgot I was carrying this.* "Well, the sooner we're with the Lord, the better. Hand the activator on over and let's show these heathens how much the Lord loves them."

Zeke walked to the metal barrel in the corner of the room and slid open a slot in the bottom. He said "This stuff is complicated. It took me a while to figure out how to fix it, and that faggot traitor Lawrence didn't always cooperate, but after enough prayer and hard work, I found your dad's instructions and the Lord showed me how to fix it." He tapped it lightly with a knuckle, and it resounded as if it was hollow inside. Zeke smiled again at his brother, and it was the same hungry smile he'd worn at the protest riot when he was laying waste to people. "Come on, I'm ready to walk those streets of gold," Zeke said. "Give me the activator."

Judge's hesitation to hand it over turned Zeke's smile from something brotherly to something feral. *I don't like where this is going.* "Zeke, I don't want this to disappoint you too much, but...the activator doesn't work." Zeke continued to stare. "At least, it doesn't work like you want it, but it's going to work like my dad wanted it to. I hate that you went to all this trouble..." He motioned to the bomb, but was thinking more of Lawrence's beaten body. "...but dad made this a fake so he could fool Jerry into letting me leave, so I could escape and live a real life somewhere. And now, we can both do that. We can go and live wherever we want, however we want, Zeke." *This'll clinch it.* "We can even tell people we're real brothers."

Zeke said "Sorry, but I think you've got it wrong. Your dad-"

"My dad did this so I could see that the world outside isn't what Jerry said it was, and my dad was right. I know you aren't used to what you've seen out here, but the world can be a beautiful place." *The Yolanda part, at least.* "And it's not all evil. You can love the Lord and still be out here, living a life like everyone else does." *At least, I think you can.* Judge had a sharp memory of his hallucination and the nightmare God that claimed to be real. He tried his best to ignore it.

Judge saw Zeke's hand clench into a fist, and clenched his in response. Zeke said "I was worried you'd say that. I should have known when you walked in here with that unregenerate beard, dressed up like one of those pederast Catholics. You're just like my dad. And you know what we had to do to him."

Don't threaten me. "But you've been locked up in here working on this bomb. You've only seen the world from a distance and..." *Doesn't everything look uglier up close? Bad analogy.* "...there's beauty out there too. I think Jerry got God all wrong. I think God's more about wanting you to find your own way, not raining death and hate from above. Even if the activator did work, murdering all these people is not the right thing to do. Let's just forget about it. Disappear with me. We can be whoever we want."

"I am who I need to be, and I'm not running. I'm the Lord's, to the end, and you are too, brother," Zeke said. *This isn't working...* "And if you think the activator's a fake, why are you still carrying it around?"

He's going to try to take it. Judge slung the bag over his shoulder and said "Because...now that dad's in jail, it's probably the only thing I'll ever have to remind me of how much he loved me, even though he couldn't ever show it."

"You really are living in the mud. You didn't know your father at all. Not like I knew him." *That's only because he couldn't show me his true self.* "You know this whole bomb thing was his idea, right? Or at least, he's the one who got the vision from the Lord."

So? "Yeah, he thought it all up just to get me out."

"Believe whatever you want Judge, but it still won't be right. You're just as bad as all those sinners out there, making up lies so they don't have to see the Lord's truth. You know there's real plutonium in there, right?" Zeke pulled back a sleeve to show a festering clump of blisters on his right forearm. "Radiation burns. Why would your dad put real plutonium in a fake bomb?"

Judge pursed his head like a little girl whose friends just told her that Santa Claus isn't real. "He was just being thorough."

"Was he being thorough when he killed Officer Babbalan?" *What?* "I saw it, after the pepper spray wore off. I hid in the woods and saw them carry Babbalan out to the rock. He was still breathing, wheezing out, begging them to let him live. It was your dad's boot on his neck that killed him. Amittai squashed him like a ant."

"You're making shit up," Judge said in disbelief.

Zeke stepped forward. Judge stepped back in sync like they were dancing. "Fine. Believe what you want, but ask yourself this: have I ever lied to you?"

No. Not once. That's what so scary about you. Judge didn't answer. Instead, he squeezed the handles of the bag tighter. *He won't get this from me.*

Zeke said "The answer is no. I have never lied to you. I have no idea what you were doing out there for the last few weeks." Zeke looked out the window. "I could imagine it, but it would probably just make me angry. Answer me this: how many people out there lied to you? How many people out there betrayed you, treated you wrong? How many times did the world show you what a filthy cesspool it really is? What was Jerry ever wrong about?"

The hookers at the truck stop tried to sell me to a trucker. That trucker tried to have sex with me while I was covered in vomit. Simmons disowned his beautiful music and traded it for something vile and stupid. Simmons pulled a gun on me and Yolanda. I thought he was my new brother, but he tried to feed me to the cops. A priest did the same thing. My own mother told me she never wanted me. Damnit, Zeke, stop being so honest with me. Judge pulled the bag off his back and held it in his hands. He opened it up and peered in. Next to the apples and the yellow pages map to the stadium, the activator sat, cold and dull. Judge's heart raced, and his head felt the sudden pulse of revelation. *Oh shit. This activator is real. There are about ten feet between me and the death of hundreds of thousands.*

Zeke saw the regret on Judge's long face. He took another step forward. Judge was too distracted to dance back. Zeke said "Tell me, world traveler, defender of this demonic world, did you meet one person out there worth selling your soul for? Give me one good reason not to blast this whole city to hell."

One reason? "Her name's Yolanda."

"Yolanda? So some whore led you away from the Lord."

"Don't call her that!"

Zeke ignored Judge's outburst and acted more disappointed than defensive. "Figures. You always were weak. You were lucky you were like a brother to me, because if you weren't, I'd have killed you a long time ago, like I had to with my dad." Zeke relaxed his body. *What's he doing? This better not be the calm before the storm.* "Did you ever even think about me while you were out there? Or were you too busy running from the Lord, being someone you're not?"

How can he think that? Does he really think being out here in the world makes you forget everything you love? I guess Larry gave him some solid proof. Judge said "I thought about you all the time. It isn't so easy to be someone else and forget about your past."

"I know," Zeke said. "Jonah couldn't run far enough from the Lord, and neither can you. You might have gotten...led astray, but you're still my brother, so I'm going to give you the chance to repent and die with me, as a martyr. You take your stand, the Lord will forgive your sins, and when he comes back, we can be at his right and left hands. Now, kneel and ask the Lord to forgive you."

Judge didn't kneel. Instead, he thought back to that day in the recording studio. Yolanda was at his side, knitting him a scorpion sweater. He remembered the Kung-Fu movie that was on the TV, strangely matching the sounds from Sherlock Bones' writing room. The young asian man on the TV was beaten down the whole movie. His girlfriend was kidnapped by the evil masters. It looked like all hope was lost. But somehow, with the power of being right on his side, he found his secret strength and was able to overcome previously insurmountable odds.

At the time, Judge thought it was just a fun movie. He didn't realize it was the story of his life. He had a quick flash of how Zeke would attack. *He'll kick at my knee to knock me down. When I dodge that, he'll bring a fist up under my left side. I'll dodge that and his throat will be open. One chop to that, then a stomp to the back of his knee. From there, I'll choke him out. I love Yolanda too much to fail. And besides, maybe I can finally take him now that he's wasted away into Simmons' shape.*

"I'm not kneeling. And I'm not giving you this activator." Judge clinched his fists. *Get ready.*

"But Judge, don't you understand who you are? Who your father is? You were meant for this. You can't say no to something like that. You can't run from the Lord. He'll get what he will get. Now give me the activator." Zeke put his hand out. *Should I make the first move? No. I can only win if I'm playing the defense, even though he looks like a bunch of animated twigs. Wait for it.*

"No."

Zeke calmly said "Fine." *This is it. Brace yourself. Get ready to dodge. Move quick like Jerry taught you, like the guys in the kung-fu movie. He can still get me, no matter how haggard he looks. Watch his eyes. They dart right, left. His right hand twitches and what's that hissing noise...OH SHIT!!!*

"Ahhhhhhhh! That burns! Ahhhh….." Judge let out an animalistic howl and brought his hands to his eyes, dropping his bag onto the concrete floor. His face was burning. He had suddenly gone blind.

Zeke shouted over Judge's cries. "Pepper Spray. Burns like Hell, doesn't it?"

Judge pulled his hands away and the world looked like it was underwater on Mars, all red and blurry. He couldn't think straight, and he couldn't make himself move. Underwater, he saw Zeke pull the activator out of the bag and stick it in the front of the bomb. Lights lit up in a reddish tint of green. Zeke pressed some buttons. Judge brought his hands to his face again and felt a river of snot flowing from his nose. The bomb beeped from the corner. He imagined Zeke was smiling, but when he went to look, Zeke's face was a swirl of red and harsh angles.

A woman's blank voice came from the bomb and said "Bomb warming up. Atom split in…25 minutes."

Zeke shouted in exultation. "Praise the Lord! 25 minutes until I meet the Lord and the scum of this Earth is wiped away. *The Hand* will make this world clean again!" Judge tried to speak, but it only came out in odd groans and disjointed syllables. "Now isn't the time for tongues, Judge. Now is the time for truth. You wouldn't repent, and the Lord is lost to you. You're just like one of the hell spawn out there." A loud cheer came from the stadium, as if in reply. "Listen to them! Crying out for anything when the one thing they needed was right under their nose. Now the Lord will get his vengeance!"

I've got to distract him long enough so I can see and pull the activator out. Judge found his voice, but it was wet and whiny. "Zeke! You're no better than them out there. You really think the Lord is going to want someone who kills their brother? You might die a martyr, but you're going to die a murderer too!" Judge had to shout to be heard over the crowd and the bleeping of the bomb. "You're no better than Cain, and you know what the Lord did to him. You're just like those liars out there!" His own ugly pepper-sprayed voice sounded familiar. *Gruff and warbling and whining and...I sound just like Simmons. And with Zeke looking like him, he might as well be a third person in the room. That would explain all the betrayal going on.* "They say they love you and then they turn on you as soon as they can. Those people out there only love themselves, and you're no better than them."

Zeke's voice had calmed, as if nothing in the world could bring him down. Judge imagined his face was beaming with pure contentedness. Zeke said "No. That's not true. I love you more than anything. You're my brother, and that's why I'm doing this." Judge heard another hissing noise. *More pepper spray.* The fire in his face blazed back up, and his shouts joined in with the crowd's in the stadium. *They don't know they're cheering for their own death.*

Judge felt Zeke's tight hands on his back pushing him. Unable to fight their strength, he went where they led. Zeke's disembodied voice said "I really do love you, and I hate that your last few minutes will be filled with that kind of pain. Watch out for the stairs." Judge stumbled blindly down some stairs, but Zeke held him aright. He kept going where he was pushed and soon felt a breeze cooling his face. His vision grew less dim. He heard Zeke shouting over the crowd and the pain. "I might love you, but you're no better than any of these sinners out here, and you'll die like one of them."

He felt one last push and fell to the ground. He could feel the tears and mucus pouring from his face. He heard the warehouse door slam shut. With what vision he had, he found the door handle and pulled as hard as he could. It wouldn't budge. "Zeke!" He pounded on the door. "Zeke! Open up!" *He's probably up there smiling that hungry smile.* Judge pounded and yelled some more, but all his complaints were drowned out by the shouts of the crowd.

Where Does My Help Come From?

I'm not getting back in there. I can't stop him. I'm going to die and become dust. So are all these people. We'll all just blow away together. Shit. The thought crushed Judge. Out of habit, he tried his best to stifle tears, but when they helped ease the burning in his eyes, he let it all go. Judge sat in the dirt outside of Zeke's door and cried. *I'll never see Yolanda again. My asshole dad and Jerry will get what they want.*

Although the noise of the oblivious crowd rumbled on, sounding like a multitude speaking in tongues, Judge's lamentation had a distinct wail to it. They sobs were loud and raw, and he knew his voice would probably be gone tomorrow. *If there was going to be a tomorrow, which I know there isn't. No chance of me starting a new life. No brothers, no fathers, no mothers. No chance to hear if Simmons ever writes anything as pure as I'll Fly Away. No chance to ever see Yolanda's face again. No chance to hear her chew some promoter out on the phone. No chance to wear her scorpion sweater. No chance to finally kiss her.*

Fireworks shot up from the stadium in rhythm with Judge's bellows. He saw the flashing lights, smelled the smoke, and prepared to die. *Well, this is it. Goodbye.* When he didn't evaporate, he came to his senses. *The pepper spray did feel like an eternity, but I've still got at least, what...20 minutes? I could run.* Judge stood up and pumped his legs, but a few seconds later he was back on the ground, the burning in his throat and lungs overwhelming him. *Damnit. I wouldn't have been able to outrun the blast radius anyways.* The noise in the crowd died down. It had grown easier to notice the crowd's silence than their constant noise. *Oh yeah, there's tens of thousands of people in there. I can save them.*

He spied a police officer sitting in a golf cart in the parking lot next to the stadium. *At least I don't have to worry about getting prison raped.* Judge walked as fast as he could without passing out and waved the cop down. He looked to be the same age as Judge. *Maybe he can live the life I wanted. Or he could give me a ride out of here. Then we can both live the life I wanted. But separate. I'm done with brothers.* "What's the problem, father?" the cop asked.

Judge remembered that he was still dressed like a priest and said "Listen, officer. You know how they're looking for Zeke Booth and how he wants to set off a bomb? He's in that building over there!" The officer's bored face looked like he'd been listening to lying drunks all day. "The nuke's going off in 20 minutes or so. I tried to get in, but he's locked that building up solid. You've got to evacuate!" The officer just crossed his arms. "Do something!"

"All right, buddy. How much have you had to drink?" He looked closer at Judge's sanguine eyes. "Or smoked?"

"I haven't smoked anything..." *He's not going to believe me. What can I do?* "Look at me!" Judge pounded his chest. "I'm Judge Saxon. They're looking for me too. I'm trying to help you out."

The officer's eyes grew wide when he recognized Judge. He pulled out his baton. "Ok. You're coming with me."

"Weren't you listening? Get on your radio! There's a nuclear bomb going off in 20 minutes! We've got to get these people out of the stadium!"

He seems in over his head. But then again, aren't we all? "Stay there." He pointed his baton at Judge and grabbed his radio. "Dispatch? We've got a code 99. I've got Judge Saxon, and he says a bomb is going off next to Brice Stadium in 20 minutes. We need to start the evacuation plan."

Oh good. They've got a plan. I might come out of this a hero. The crowd erupted again. Judge couldn't make out what came back over the radio, but the officer nodded and said "10-4." He set the radio down and pulled out some handcuffs. "All right. You're coming with me."

"Fine with me." Judge turned around and put his hands behind him. "As long as you get me out of here. This bomb has got a big radius, so we better get moving."

A siren whirred somewhere deep in the city, like a wounded animal. The crowd grew quiet. "Nope," the young cop said. He put a cold metal handcuff on Judge's right wrist and snapped the other end to a metal pole holding up the golf cart's roof. "You're just going to stay with me till we get all these people out of here." *Damnit. If I could just run...* Judge yanked on his chain. *That's pretty solid.* He stared at it and shook it to try to find a weak point. He heard a click and turned to see the officer pointing a gun at him. "Try it, asshole. You're with me now. Get in."

A gunshot would severely limit my chances of getting away. Judge hopped into the passenger seat of the golf cart and the young officer drove off, holding his gun in his lap. *Oh my god this thing is slow. I could probably walk faster.* Judge eyed the gun. *I could probably get it from him before he noticed it was gone. And then I could get his keys and –*

The ground started to shake. The noise from the stadium grew closer and more shrill. Faster than Judge could comprehend, people poured out of the stadium like ants escaping their hill after a rainstorm. They were running, some with their hands up in the air, some with their hands in their loved ones' hands, some using their hands as clubs to get away as fast as possible. In the distance, Judge could see people getting in their cars and trying to drive away, only to get caught in traffic. Soon, the multitudes reached the golf cart.

Judge could see their panic. The officer started to shout and beep his weak horn, but it made no difference. When he tried to drive through the crowd, the golf cart was quickly tipped over. Judge's head smashed into the officer's head, which in turn smashed into the asphalt. Looking at the blood pooling under the cop's head, Judge shouted "Get up! Let me go!" The officer wasn't conscious. *Shit.* Judge yanked on the handcuffs and found that the roof had ripped off the golf cart. *I'm free. So much for this cop living his life. Sorry, guy.*

He had to push back against the flowing crowd to stand up, but he did, and he ran with them. *I think the fall loosened my lungs back up.* Horns were honking and epithets were being yelled. People were running and shouting, and Judge was one of them. *I think we can make it! I saved all these people!*

Judge ran along the street for a few minutes. *Won't be long now. I just hope I can make it.* The street he was running on started to wind up a hill. He kept pumping his legs. The sound of horns and shouts grew louder. The traffic grew heavier, as did the weight of his body. The burning crept back into his chest. *Thanks Zeke.* After the labor of reaching the top of the hill, his body had to stop. *Just for a few seconds. I can still make it. Why does this hilltop look familiar?*

He bent over to catch his breath, but it felt like every breath was fire trying to escape his body. *I'm going to burst.* He found that standing up straight helped, but when he stood up, he looked around and got a view of the entire city. *Oh shit. Oh shit. Oh shit. All these cars are stopped. Completely stopped.*

They're not moving. Everyone leaving at the same time has turned Brookland into a parking lot. There is no way out.

The four-lane highway behind him had been switched into evacuation mode, and all lanes were pointed away from the city. It was the same way as far as Judge could see, but no cars were moving. *Zeke's going to win. I wander what will happen afterwards. Jerry was right. And Zeke. And my mom. I couldn't run far enough, and now nobody can escape this. My dad wanted me to be a prophet, a warrior, a Judge of the nations, and here I am, while all these people disintegrate. If I hadn't gone after Zeke, hell, if I hadn't forgotten that the activator was there on the tour and gotten rid of it when I should've, none of this would be happening. All these people would still be in that stadium, loving their lives. I could be...I don't know where I'd be, but at least I'd still be alive.*

Will I end up in Heaven or Hell? I guess Jerry would say I'd end up in Hell for betraying the Lord. And in the end, he ended up being right about most things. He's probably right about me deserving Hell after this. Maybe he was right about the Lord wanting me here, doing this, and this was the only way it could have ended. Maybe that hallucination I had really was God, and everyone's worst fears are coming true. I never could run far enough. Judge looked around at all the cars stalled around him. *Maybe these people do all deserve the Lord's wrath. Maybe the Lord will still want me to come back with him to wage war on the rest of the world. I don't want that, but have I had a choice about anything else?*

Judge sat down in the cool grass. The sun burned and pulsed on his face, waking up the remnants of Zeke's pepper spray. He saw a tree in the distance and decided to go sit in the shade. *You know what, Lord? You win. I still hate that Jerry was right about so many things, and I'm not repenting like Zeke wanted, but it's better that I die now. I'm tired of running, and it never does any good anyways. It's not like things ever went well for me when I left the Dark Corner. Yeah, I thought I could find some happiness with Yolanda, but that all ended in the worst possible way. It's not like I'd ever find anyone who loved me as much as Zeke does. It's not like I'd ever be able to trust anyone again after what Simmons did.* Judge found himself smiling. *At least Yolanda will get to live on. I hope her parents were able to get away.*

His eyes caught a redheaded young woman in a blue SUV a few hundred feet away. Her pretty head rested on a delicate hand. *Looks like Yolanda. I can't believe I never did get to kiss her. But then again, I didn't exactly know this was going to happen.* He looked again and saw the woman in the SUV staring at him, her eyes agape. *Holy shit, that is Yolanda!*

Any thoughts about his and her immediate death were put aside in that moment of jubilation. She got out of her car, and Judge trotted towards her. They met, hugged, and stood in the sun. Judge had to shout to be heard over the symphony of car horns. "What are you doing here?"

She looked frustrated, but not in fear of death. "My parents brought me to the game, and the sirens went off and now we're stuck in all this stupid traffic. I don't think they thought about how this evacuation plan would work if a game was going on." She punched Judge like a nervous middle schooler might when she can't bring herself to tell a boy that she likes him. "What are you doing here? Why are you dressed like a priest?"

Judge ignored her questions and remembered what was going on. "I mean, what are you doing in Brookland?" he asked. "I thought you'd be...isn't Sherlock Bones in New England this week?"

"Oh, yeah." She smiled at him. He almost melted. "After what Simmons did to you, he offered to make it up to me by letting me give him a blowjob. I shot him with enough moose to knock him out for days and got on the first plane I could and came home. I felt like I had to do it...for you." *For me?* "Why are your eyes all red?" she asked.

"My brother pepper sprayed me in the face."

"Oh." She held her tiny hands over her eyes to block out the sun. "Your brother? I thought..."

"It's a long story." *And I hope you don't know how it ends.* "So what do you think is going on here?" he asked to gauge her worry.

She sat down on the grass. Judge did the same, and he let his knee graze hers. "They didn't say. I'm going to be real angry if it's just a drill."

You should be angrier that it's not just a drill. Judge looked down at the stadium in the distance. He tried to pinpoint the building that Zeke was waiting in, but they all looked the same. *At least she doesn't know that she's going to die. That makes me happy. Let's keep it that way.* Judge said "Yeah. It's probably just a drill." *We can't have long now, but I wouldn't want to go any other way.* "So what are you going to do now?"

She held a finger up. "Hold that thought." She ran over to the car. Like every other car in the blast radius, it hadn't moved one inch. Judge watched her bend over and pull something blue out of a bag. He stood up as she came back over. *God, she's beautiful.* He was flooded with the memory of their conversation after *Pulp Fiction*, and their time together singing *I'll Fly Away*. *Jerry was right, but I bet he's getting raped in jail right now. And that nightmare God probably wasn't a hallucination, but this world is...* He watched Yolanda's uncontrollable smile. *...this world is beautiful. I can't escape being my father's son, but at least my world ends in beauty.*

"I finished this for you." She extended her hands and held out a blue sweater. The outline of a white scorpion covered the front of it. "It's your scorpion sweater."

She loves me. There are good people out here. Fuck you, nightmare God. "Oh my god! This is amazing!" He had to hold back tears as he pulled it over his priest outfit. It fit perfectly.

"You look like a real badass," she said, beaming. "Especially with that clerical collar poking up out of it."

Judge looked at her. He took in her freckles and her green eyes and her red hair and the way she smiled at him like there was nothing wrong. The stadium loomed behind her, and the sun bright in the sky framed her in light like an angel. *This is perfect.*

The light behind her pulsed and grew brighter. Judge realized it wasn't just the sun. *I've seen this before, and I know what's coming. Time's up. I'm done running. This is my stand.* A humming filled the skies around them, and a whooshing noise joined it in the distance, like a hundred tornados gaining form. Still smiling, Yolanda's started to turn around to see what was going on. A gray mushroom cloud, illuminated with unbearable yellow light from inside, started to rise from where Zeke was.

Please die happy. Judge grabbed her before she could see it. He clutched her to his chest and planted his lips on hers. Judge kissed her as deep and long as he could. *This is right.* He opened his eyes and saw that hers were open, staring at him.

She shut them again in ecstasy and Judge could feel her lips smiling. The whooshing sound grew unbearable and the mushroom cloud towered in the sky. Everything behind her turned to ash. Judge stood strong, kissed harder and didn't let go.

About the Author

S. P. Harris grew up in South Carolina. He has a couple of degrees in religion and has written for many music websites. He has lived among both militant fundamentalists and drug-addled rockstars, and is currently somewhere between the two. In his spare time he cooks and thinks about starting a ska band that only writes songs in minor keys and ¾ time. Follow him on Twitter @authorspharris and on facebook under S.P. Harris. E-mail death threats and love notes to him at authorspharris@yahoo.com. Ask him anything you want. *Anything.*

If you enjoyed *THE ACCIDENTAL TERRORIST*, please leave a review on whatever ebook distributor you purchased it from. Tell your family and friends, enter it into book club discussion, start your own Sherlock Bones tribute band (complete with groupie days).

Cover Art

The front cover was designed by the incredibly talented Lauren Todd. Visit her at www.thelaurentodd.com .

Printed in Great Britain
by Amazon.co.uk, Ltd.,
Marston Gate.